Also by Lewis Robinson

Officer Friendly and Other Stories

WATER DOGS

RANDOM HOUSE | NEW YORK

Water Dogs

A Novel

LEWIS ROBINSON

Water Dogs is a work of fiction. Names, characters, places, and incidents are the products of the author's imagination or are used fictitiously. Any resemblance to actual events, locales, or persons, living or dead, is entirely coincidental.

Published in the United States by Random House, an imprint of The Random House Publishing Group, a division of Random House, Inc., New York.

RANDOM HOUSE and colophon are registered trademarks of Random House, Inc.

LIBRARY OF CONGRESS CATALOGING-IN-PUBLICATION DATA
Robinson, Lewis.
Water dogs : a novel / Lewis Robinson.
p. cm.
ISBN 978-1-4000-6217-1 (acid-free paper)
1. Brothers—Fiction. 2. Adult children—Fiction. 3. Missing persons—Fiction.
4. Guilt—Fiction. 5. Maine—Fiction. 6. Psychological fiction. I. Title.
PS3618.O33W38 2009
813'.6—dc22 2008016564

Printed in the United States of America on acid-free paper

www.atrandom.com

9 8 7 6 5 4 3 2 1

FIRST EDITION

Book design by Dana Leigh Blanchette

For CC

It was evening all afternoon.
It was snowing
And it was going to snow.

—WALLACE STEVENS

WATER DOGS

1

Bennie didn't recognize the sound. There were squirrels who sometimes nested in the attic, and barred owls in the nearby woods, and, during the summer, cats in heat prowling the backyard, but the cries he heard were from a place closer to his bedroom. When he was perfectly still, not moving his head on the pillow, every few seconds he would hear the faint crying. He climbed out of bed and crossed the cold pine floor in his boxers. It was still dark out. Standing in the doorway, he listened. It seemed to be in the living room. He felt his way to the standing lamp in the corner and turned the switch, waited, then heard it distinctly, coming from the far wall. He walked closer to the fireplace. The sound was loudest just to the left of the hearth. He put his ear against the plaster. A gentle bump against the lath, and scratching. He imagined a new hole in the eaves—or an old hole Littlefield hadn't told him about—and now something trapped inside the wall, crying.

At the bottom of the basement stairs, Bennie grabbed a saber saw and a crowbar from Littlefield's pegboard, and a pair of canvas gloves and a flashlight from the tool apron. Littlefield would have suggested poison—and he wouldn't have allowed Bennie to use the saber saw—but Littlefield had gone out to the bar, which meant he was probably now sleeping in his Chevette. When Bennie returned to the living room, he knelt beside the baseboard, listened a final time, then cut a rough rectangle through the plaster. With the crowbar he pried back the lath. He aimed the flashlight into the hole. Eight or ten raccoon eyes looked up at him, little quivering noses pointed toward the light, black fur around the eyes, a stripe of white across the ears and snout. Tiny bandits with miniature claws. They didn't move much but they continued to chatter and cry. He steered the light around the space within the walls and saw only the babies—nothing larger—so he put on his brother's canvas gloves, reached through the hole, and pulled them out, one by one, putting them in the cardboard box used for kindling. They didn't resist, though he felt the light touch of their thin claws. When he'd gotten all five out, he took the box to the porch, set it down, then walked through the breezeway to the barn, where he found the galvanized live-catch trap their sister had once used for opossum in the basement. This plan felt very efficient to him, well conceived. To catch the mother, Bennie baited the trap with an entire tin of sardines. He knew she'd be back. He looked under the eaves and found a hole beside one of the porch's support columns. He placed the trap next to the cardboard kindling box, on the corner of the porch, beneath the hole.

After switching off all the lights, he got back under the covers. Except for the billowing wind in the spruce trees outside and, occasionally, the steel chime of the bell buoy near Esker Point, all was quiet. Bennie's skin was still cold from the winter night. He tried to relax. He thought about what a victory this had been—the decision to cut the hole, making it the right size, saving the baby raccoons. He'd find a better place for them. Littlefield would laugh, but he didn't care. He'd done the right thing.

But crying in that box on the porch until morning—it was the first week of March, still bitterly cold—the raccoons would surely freeze. He shook his covers off again, stood up, and walked outside to retrieve the box. He put it on the kitchen table; the raccoons stayed quiet.

Back in bed, Bennie could hear them crying again. He got up, walked to the kitchen, and put the box in the mop closet, then returned to his room. Done.

Thirty or forty minutes later, the phone rang. Bennie marched back to the kitchen, this time aware of how tired he was, and how few hours remained before sunrise. It was his twin sister, Gwen. She lived in New York.

"Littlefield said you didn't want me to come home. For a visit."

"Gwen?" he asked. "Do you know what time it is?"

"For a visit. You didn't want me around."

"Gwen, that's ridiculous. Come home. Of course I'd love to see you. What time is it? Are you drunk?"

"I didn't think you'd answer the phone."

"You shouldn't believe Littlefield when he says something like that. He's just messing with you."

"I guess I just wanted to make sure. Could I visit next week sometime?"

"It's your house, too. Of course you can visit. I'd love you to visit. I'm kind of asleep right now. Can I call you back?"

"Is Littlefield there?"

"He's out. Down at Julian's, I think."

"Julian's?"

"Eddie's, the bar. Now they call it Julian's. Julian is Eddie's son."

"Right. That tall guy. I remember him. Really, really tall. Like a freak."

"I'm asleep, Gwen. Call back tomorrow, okay?"

"Will you pick me up at the airport?"

"When?"

"Next week. When I come."

"Of course. Good night."

"I'll be there for our birthdays," she said.

Growing up, they'd always celebrated together—they were born only fifteen minutes apart, on either side of midnight. "That'd be nice," he said. "I'm going to sleep now."

"Wow. Somebody's grumpy. Next time, just don't answer the phone. We'll all be happier," she said, and hung up.

As he tried to sleep, he thought about their old family house—its leaky pipes, chipping paint, uneven floors, drafty windows. Baby raccoons in the walls. They called it "the Manse," which had been a family joke, because the house was not grand or impressive compared to others along the coast, but now that Bennie and Littlefield were in charge, and the porch seemed one or two strong storms away from crumbling into the ocean, and the old copper pipes were failing, rotting the ceilings and the walls, calling the place "the Manse" seemed sad. The last time Gwen had come to visit them—the previous summer—she and Bennie had been sitting on the porch, drinking beer, discussing Gwen's latest rationale for living in New York and continuing her quest to be an actress. Gwen said that pretending to be another person was invigorating. Bennie wanted to relate this to his own experience, so after he let his sister finish, he took a big sip of beer and said that paintball was a pretty good outlet for pretending, too.

He told her that paintball taught him to be careful, and patient, and that he and Littlefield and Julian went out together, competing against a group of sea urchin divers at a year-round course called the Flying Dutchman, sometimes going for a full session without taking more than two or three shots. Two or three gumballs, hopefully kill shots, full of bright-colored sludge. They played every Saturday.

When Bennie looked at her after describing this, he knew they were both having the same thought: there'd been a lot of promise, once. According to their mom at least. He'd done pretty well in high school. They were the grandchildren of an original member of the Stock Exchange. But while Gwen had decided at Vassar to be an actress (it took her a few years to get to New York, and she wasn't doing much acting, but she'd landed two small roles at the Brooklyn Family Theater in Park Slope and she had a gig as a temp at an accounting firm), Bennie hadn't finished college. He thought there might be a time when he'd start up again—when he would have good ideas about how to put a college degree to use in midcoast Maine—but for now he just wanted to keep the Manse from falling apart. Working at the vet's office, taking care of the house—that was plenty. He and Gwen were about to turn twenty-seven.

The front door banged shut, and from his bed Bennie heard Littlefield knocking his boots against the wall, depositing, Bennie was sure, lumps of snow on the kitchen floor. Bennie heard the sink faucet turn on, and the clink of a glass. Littlefield tromped into the living room. After a brief silence, he said, "My fucking saber saw. Don't use my saber saw."

"I'm asleep," said Bennie. When they'd moved back into the old house, Bennie had chosen the downstairs bedroom. Most of the time, it was convenient, but there were occasional disadvantages to sleeping near the front door.

"Whoa! Did you cut a hole in the wall?"

Bennie flipped his light on and came to the doorway. "Take off your boots when you come inside."

Littlefield was poking the ashes in the fire, trying to find the coals. He was wearing a black sweatshirt with the hood up. "Those are my sardines in the trap out there."

"Has it sprung yet?" asked Bennie.

"That's no way to catch an animal. Have a heart? Please. Have some balls, Bennie. That's a better motto when you're catching an animal. Have. Some. Balls. Some scrotal ballast. I should design a grow-a-pair trap and force you to use it. A giant glue trap—with a guillotine."

"Did you look closely? Maybe it's already sprung," Bennie said, walking to the kitchen. It felt satisfying to ignore his brother's late-night bluster. Bennie held open the door and they walked onto the porch.

In his underwear, Bennie shone the flashlight at the trap. The beam sparkled on the empty trap's galvanized metal. "Did you talk to Gwen?"

"No," said Littlefield.

"She called tonight. She said you said we didn't want her to visit."

They walked back inside, Bennie holding the door again. Littlefield said, "No. I told her *you* didn't want her to visit."

Bennie felt a familiar anger rise in his chest. "What? Why?"

Littlefield crumpled newspaper and laid it on the andirons. "Where's the kindling box?"

"We're out of kindling," said Bennie. He grabbed a wool blanket from the back of the couch, wrapped it around himself, and sat in the rocking chair.

"I'll go chop some," said Littlefield.

"Hold on," said Bennie. "There's some in the kitchen." He retrieved the cardboard box from the mop closet and brought it to the living room, set it down gently, and opened it. The raccoon babies were clumped together, a mass of wriggling fur, squeaking quietly.

He waited for his brother's reaction.

Finally, Littlefield said, "Do you see those rats in that box?"

"They were in the wall," said Bennie. "They were keeping me up. They're not rats. They're raccoons."

"And you *put* them in that box?"

"I didn't want you to poison them."

"They'll give you roundworm. The grubs can get into your stomach. They eat your kidneys and your heart."

"The grubs can get in your stomach?"

"If you swallow them."

Bennie knew it was rarely worth arguing details with Littlefield. He handed him the kindling and said, "I'm just trying to catch the mom. Then I'll let them all go."

"Get them the hell out of here. They're wild animals. They shouldn't be in here."

"After I catch the mom I'll bring them all down to the ravine."

Littlefield shook his head. He arranged the kindling on top of the newspaper. Bennie closed the box and returned it to the kitchen closet and poured himself a glass of milk. When he got back to the living room, the fire was towering, yellow flames lapping the entrance to the flue. Littlefield was sprawled out on the purple couch, still wearing his boots.

Bennie asked, "Why'd you say that to Gwen?"

"Didn't you tell me you didn't want my friends coming around?"

"Just Skunk and those other guys living in his trailer." Skunk Gould and Littlefield had thrown an impromptu party at the Manse in January when Bennie was away for the night. They'd broken windows in the living room and someone had pissed on the rocking chair.

"And that you wanted to keep the place neater?" asked Littlefield.

"And this has *what* to do with Gwen?"

"I told her you were dating some girl from Bowdoin. And you didn't want the house to look too messy. In case you brought her back here."

"Admit you *do* want to see your sister."

"I'd be happy to see Gwen."

"Admit you're just being an asshole," said Bennie. "And for the record, Helen's not *from Bowdoin.* She went to Bowdoin College. And she lives in Musquacook. She's a cook. At Julian's."

"Impressive! That's some real fine cuisine they have down there. I just had their onion rings about an hour ago. Five stars."

"Screw you. She puts together their dinner menu. That kitchen is actually doing a much better job since she started there."

"I'm telling you—top-shelf onion rings." Littlefield kissed his fingertips. *"Magnifique."*

"I'm so glad you enjoyed yourself, retard, but that's the fry cook, not Helen."

"What a shame," said Littlefield, closing his eyes.

Bennie wrapped himself in the wool blanket again. He rocked back and forth in the chair, staring at the fire. Both brothers were quiet. Within minutes, Littlefield was snoring on the couch.

2

When Helen had moved to town in January, she'd started working at the restaurant, and Julian, her boss, passed along the following information to Bennie: she ate a PayDay before every shift, she listened to the Smiths, she liked watching zombie movies (*Night of the Living Dead* was among her favorites), and she'd grown up in Lewiston, the depressed French-Canadian mill town, where her mother still lived. Julian said she and Bennie would make a great couple. Bennie knew Julian was mercenary when it came to women; he suspected that Julian had already taken a crack at her himself and she'd been polite but clear in expressing her disinterest. She'd rejected him so tactfully, Bennie guessed, that Julian had convinced himself he'd never even flirted with her. Julian's only disclaimer was that she seemed weird. This, Bennie knew, was his way of protecting himself in the event that her rebuff of him ever surfaced. "She's a little odd," Julian had said while he wiped down the bar with a wet towel. "She's perfect for you, though. She went to Bowdoin, but she's not a jackass."

Bennie had asked about her after seeing her through the glass door to the kitchen, where she pulled orders off the wire. She was tall and had dark eyebrows and straight brown hair, and her skin glowed from the heat of the stoves. His first idea was to catch her on break and ask her to the porch for a smoke, but he knew if he got her onto the porch there might be too much pressure on the conversation; it'd be too quiet and intense, and she'd probably end up asking him how he spent his time and he'd be cavalier, he'd let something slip about hunting, or paintball, or living in his mom's old house with his brother, who also enjoyed hunting and paintball. He'd learned that the first conversation was especially important—you plotted a course that was difficult to recalibrate—so he knew he had to be careful. He could open with news of his part-time job at the Esker Cove Animal Hospital and Shelter, allowing her to perceive him as a kindly guy with a soft spot for wayward cats and dogs, but follow-up questions about the animals might lead to a description of the crematorium, and perhaps even the specifics of the pentobarbital injections, which, actually, were a large part of his job. He didn't want to talk about the injections.

He was occasionally struck by how the details of his life didn't show well. His paychecks from Esker Cove covered his bills, but his bills were small; he lived in his family's old house, which was falling apart. Guiltily, he liked war games; he'd dropped out of college. He didn't have a trust fund, but his mother was ready and willing to give him money (to get him "out of a hole") whenever necessary. She was a therapist. She complained about not having any money but he knew it was there. He never took her up on her offer. He hadn't felt desperate enough yet.

Helen probably drank wheatgrass and would hate that he smoked. He didn't smoke, not really—he just smoked out on the porch at Julian's. In the summer, he liked to smoke and watch the bats on the creek. Just when you thought you'd seen one, it was gone, but then three more would appear, and vanish. After a while, the flecks of brown blurring along the surface of the water seemed to be everywhere. Now, though, the water was frozen and the bats were asleep underground.

Julian and Bennie had only recently become friends. They'd been high school classmates, but Julian had spent most of his time working at the restaurant. The pub drew people down from Brunswick and up from Portland because of its views of the river, the tidal surge, the proximity to the ocean, its adequate food and comfortable atmosphere.

After first seeing her, on his way home from work Bennie stopped regularly at the restaurant, where he thought about approaching her but instead stayed quiet at the bar. One unseasonably warm afternoon in late January, though, Julian placed a pair of sunglasses beside Bennie's beer. "These are hers," he said.

"Why are you giving them to me?" asked Bennie.

"It's perfect. Just give them back to her. Say you found them outside. She dropped them."

Bennie looked at the black plastic frames. "You took these out of her bag?"

"Look, it doesn't matter," he said. "It's a great opening."

"No," said Bennie. "I'm not doing that."

"Bring them over to her. It's a built-in conversation starter. The glare off the creek, how tough it can be when the sun's shining. The angle of the sun. January thaw. You got it?"

"Give them back to her."

"I'm leaving them with you," said Julian, suddenly stern.

Bennie folded Helen's sunglasses inside a section of the newspaper and turned toward the kitchen to see if Helen had witnessed any of this. Julian was pulling back the Stella Artois tap, filling a pint glass, his hair hanging down in front of his face. Julian liked his place in the spotlight behind the bar, and at six-foot-seven, 230 pounds, with a booming voice, he was difficult to miss.

Bennie slid the newspaper across the bar.

Without looking up from the beer taps, Julian said, "You're a wuss."

When Julian got closer, Bennie leaned toward him. "What time does she get here in the morning?" he asked.

"Perfect idea," Julian said, pointing at Bennie and smiling. "I love it. Come by in the morning. You're the man!"

Bennie glanced back toward the kitchen, but his view was obscured. "What time."

"She gets here around ten," said Julian, leaning over the bar. "And she comes through the back alley. Bring the sunglasses. They could help."

"No. I'm leaving them here."

"Yeah you are, baby!" said Julian, swinging his fists like a prize-fighter. "You don't need nothing. You're a killer!"

So far the winter had been mild, though they'd weathered a few storms. Most of the snow had melted, as it sometimes did at the end of January, before the winter picked up speed again and kept everyone cold and snowbound until early May. For the past five years the January thaw had arrived predictably about a month after Christmas—rivers of snowmelt running along the shoulders of every road, everyone driving around in T-shirts, confused moose and deer trotting out of the woods to lick salt off the roads, causing accidents.

When he arrived at Julian's the next morning, Bennie didn't go inside; he sat on one of the dented trash cans beside a storage shed, near the restaurant's back entrance.

There would be no way around the awkwardness with Helen. He'd just muscle through, skip the bullshit, flip past the usual channels. With Helen, he would be ready to put forward his best self. With

Helen, he would make only occasional mistakes, and only mistakes that could be construed as charming and guileless.

He arrived at nine-forty, giving himself some extra time to relax and acclimate. The time passed slowly, though when she finally turned down the alley, her clogs clapping the pavement, the hood of her sweatshirt bouncing around her neck, her approach was rushed—he hadn't thought about giving her some kind of warning. He stayed quiet until she was just a few yards from the door, when he said, "Excuse me." She slowed her stride but she didn't look up.

"Excuse me?" he said again, this time a little louder.

"Oh, I'm sorry," she said, looking at the ground as though she had dropped something.

"Let's go sailing." Bennie was wearing his favorite windbreaker, with the stripe down the sleeve, army green pants, and running shoes.

Helen removed her sunglasses—the ones Julian had stolen from her—and looked plainly at him. The muscles in her face relaxed. "What do you mean?" She wasn't being cruel; it was a sincere question.

"Well, the ocean is right over there," he said, pointing east. "And it'll still be warm tomorrow. And windy."

"Do I know you?" The sweatshirt was zipped all the way up, and she wore a calf-length jean skirt.

"No," he said, without elaboration. He'd planned for this; he assumed she wouldn't like a defensive stance. He stood by his answer.

She folded the sunglasses and slipped them into her pocket. "Do you have a boat?"

"No," he said, and it felt even better this time. "My name's Bennie. I eat here a lot. I'm a friend of his."

"I've seen you."

"You have?"

"I think so." Again, she maintained an even tone and didn't smile. He had no reason to believe she was being coy. "Were you the one who returned my sunglasses? Julian told me. I must have left them on the bar."

During this first exchange he got a good look at her eyes, up close—they were, as he'd thought, brown, and big, and the whites of them were shockingly clear. Under her dark eyebrows, they were identical in color and shape and glossiness and brightness, but then you could see that her left one was pointed gently inward. Was this called a wandering eye? She told him her name, her full name: Helen Coretti.

She'd never been sailing before. He picked her up on his motorcycle at one the next day, when it was so freakishly warm that it felt like early summer. He knew there was a good place to rent boats near Meadow Island, Sagona's Marine, and he was surprised they were closed. He hadn't expected they'd have boats to rent in January, but he'd assumed someone would be around to loan him one. The owner had been a friend of Bennie's father.

The big doors to the back of the boathouse were wide open, though, and Bennie spotted a few small fiberglass boats tucked in the corner. He asked Helen to help him drag one down to the shore.

"Are you sure this is okay?" she asked.

"He's a nice guy, Mr. Sagona," said Bennie.

"Have you sailed this kind of boat before?"

"This kind? I think so. What is it, do you think?"

"I have no idea. It says 'Sunfish' here on the side," she said.

"Oh, yeah," he said. "Sunfish." He'd grown up on Meadow Island; he'd been around boats all his life. He didn't know much about sailing, but it didn't take him long to figure out how to let out the sail and drop the centerboard.

Out in the channel, even though they nearly capsized five or six times, it only happened once and they were able to climb back into the boat quickly enough. The air felt like June but the water reminded Bennie it was still January. Helen didn't seem to mind. She reminded him of bookworms he'd gone to middle school with—those girls who seemed to know so much more about the world than he did. Helen was surprisingly strong for a skinny person. He loved how her face looked with her brown hair slicked back as she came out of the waves, her thick green sweatshirt heavy with seawater. Helen easily scissor-kicked herself aboard, but Bennie was flustered and weak from the cold, so Helen helped him back into the boat, and even though the physical aspects of the moment were awkward, he had the presence of mind to breathe deeply and forget himself for a moment and simply be in awe of how pretty she was with the water shiny on her face, a drip rolling down her nose. He gripped the slippery fiberglass and she grabbed both of his cold wrists and pulled him up as he kicked in the water. When he was aboard he said, “You’re like a nymph.”

She waited a moment before responding, which made him nervous.

“Like in the myths, or the bug kind?” she asked. She made little pinching gestures with her hands.

“Yeah,” he said.

“Which one?” she asked.

“Maybe both,” he said. She seemed to like this answer.

Bennie had stopped thinking about how embarrassed he should have been for not knowing how to sail. Helen was shivering, and she looked out at the surrounding islands like she was flying through the clouds in a dream. When the wind gusted on their last tack across the channel, instead of flipping over they picked up speed. The wind died and they drifted in to shore, the bow pushing gently up onto the rocks. He still didn’t know Helen, but what he read from her eyes, and the way she huddled close to him in the boat, asking him for the names of the spruce-tufted islands they passed, was that she was glad to have involved herself in such a plan.

The drive home on the motorcycle made them colder than the capsizing. Bennie usually drained the oil from his motorcycle by Labor Day. But after asking her to go sailing he thought a motorcycle ride would be perfect, so he charged its battery and checked its tires. He’d been riding it off and on for a few years—he’d bought it two years earlier from his boss at the animal hospital, Dr. Handelmann—but it was more of an amusement than a mode of transportation, something to be used during a few weekend afternoons in July and August. It was mid-day and warm when they'd arrived at Sagona's, but when they drove home the sun was nearly gone and the wind was still blowing hard off the water. Their cotton clothes were sopped in seawater. Helen made it bearable, though. She latched on to him, pressing herself against his back. He tried not to make more of this than what it was; he knew she was cold. Still, ripping along those back roads, banking turns with Helen hugging him—it felt miraculous.

He gave her a lift to her house, less than a mile from the restaurant. When they arrived she was shivering, and she looked startled as she took off her helmet. Her lips were blue and her shoulders were raised, as though she was trying to keep her neck warm.

"Thank you, Bennie," she said.

He was too cold to speak, so he moved to kiss her, which happened at the same moment she handed him the helmet. This was a smoother exchange than he anticipated; he just took the helmet, instead of Helen, into his arms. He didn't go through with trying to kiss her; even then he figured they had a future, and he could wait. But then she said, "I've got to get out of these wet clothes," and she smiled brightly one more time and started walking up the sidewalk toward her house.

He followed her. When they got to the porch, Bennie could tell she didn't know he was right behind her because she opened the screen door and spun around. It looked like she was planning on waving to him as he drove away. But there he was, two steps back. The way she jumped—a tiny flinch—was almost imperceptible.

She said, "Oh!"

"Hi. Sorry."

"Do you need something?" she asked. Her eyebrows were arched and she seemed genuinely interested.

"I guess not," he said. "I thought you'd invited me inside." All of a sudden he was aware that because he hadn't been wearing a helmet (she'd worn his), his hair had dried like a stiff flag, flying straight back.

"You thought that I'd invited you inside?" she asked.

"No," he said, shaking his head.

"Wait, I don't understand. Why did you think that?" She couldn't tell that he was dying inside. She was trying to be precise. She was still holding the screen door partway open.

"Well, didn't you say . . . that you needed to take off your clothes?" he asked.

"Yeah," she said. Her hair had been matted down by the helmet. Her bangs stuck to her forehead.

"Never mind," he said.

As he turned back toward his motorcycle, she asked, "Well, did you need to take off *your* clothes?" and she opened the screen door a little further.

"Yes," he said. "I do."

"But you don't have other clothes to change into," she said. "Do you?"

"No, I don't," he said, deflated.

"Then I guess you need to go home."

"Yeah," he said. "See you later."

"Thanks again," she said, and she winked her good eye.

Later, when he got home, after lying in the tub for an hour, his brain thawed. He thought more about that wink. He remembered thinking how smart she seemed, how aware of everything she was. There was no way she could have been oblivious about her reference to taking her clothes off, even if she was planning to take them off on her own. But then again, aside from the fact she was a good cook, he didn't know much about her yet; in her line of work, put the linguini on the plate meant put the linguini on the plate, and maybe she'd simply been telling him she was cold—just sharing this information.

He wondered if it had really been a wink, after all. Maybe it was just a muscle spasm brought on by hypothermia, or a way to distract attention from her wandering eye.

They saw each other a week after borrowing the Sunfish from Sagona's. It was their second date and they went to the Musquacook Public Library, where they were showing *Babe,* the movie with the talking pig. Afterward, Bennie declared the movie stupid. "Talking animals—doesn't it seem silly?"

"I thought it was pretty cool," she said. His Skylark was in the shop and it was too cold for the motorcycle, so she'd picked him up, and was now dropping him off. They were parked outside the Manse in Helen's old Jetta, which she rarely used. If she had a shift at the restaurant, she walked.

"I mean, everyone hopes a pig or a dog or a horse will talk. Of course we do. But the whole point is . . . the thing about animals is . . . well, that we want them to talk and we think they might be able to talk, but they *can't.* They just can't."

She was staring out at the darkness through the windshield. She paused a beat before saying, "What?"

"It's too easy. It's like a person being able to fly, and making a movie about it."

"Like Superman?" she asked.

"I guess," he said. He was feeling grouchy. He wanted her to understand his annoyance.

He knew they were working their slow way toward an awkward goodbye, a silence in the car, the gearshift and emergency brake sentinel between them, so he told her they should do something like this again, smiled defensively, climbed out, then bent down and waved to her through the window, walked to the house, opened the door, and shut it without looking back toward her car. Of course he had wanted to kiss her. The logistics had seemed untenable, but now he suffered searing regret. After drinking half a beer and brushing his teeth, he climbed into bed. He hadn't even thanked her for driving. An hour later there was a knock at his window. She was wearing sneakers and a dark blue tracksuit. Bennie opened the window. It made sense to him that she was standing there, out of breath. He wanted to reach his arms out the window and give her a hug, but instead he said, "Do you need something?" She didn't get the joke. She just hitched an ankle over the sill and started climbing in.

"I can go open the front door," he said, but she ignored him. She didn't speak at all. She had a fistful of condoms. He didn't have a chance to turn on the light; she kicked off her shoes, crouched on the bed, and unzipped her tracksuit. He couldn't see her face very well, but he could see nervousness in her smile. She reached her hand into his and relinquished the rubbers. All but one fell like playing cards to the floor; there must have been six or seven. "How long are you planning on being here?" he asked. When she lay down on top of him, her breasts and her stomach were soft and warm. They kissed and it felt almost argumentative, and he liked the feeling. He put his hands on her small breasts but she grabbed his wrists and pinned his arms to the bed. He tried to move but he couldn't; she pressed him more firmly against the mattress. She released him momentarily to take off her tracksuit pants. Then she pinned him again, but only one of his arms, so he reached out and put his hand on her ass, which was cooler than the front of her body. He imagined her at the restaurant, dominating the kitchen, which Julian didn't dare enter. Her physical strength was a secret: the people who ate her food didn't know how heroic she'd been when the Sunfish had capsized. Soon she was squeezing him so fiercely, he couldn't see straight, and usually this would have made him want to escape, but somehow he recognized that being trapped beneath Helen was an almost perfect place to be.

3

Bennie loaded the raccoons into his car, including the mother, who had eaten the sardines and was sleeping in the trap when Bennie came onto the porch at dawn. He wanted to take them down to the ravine before Littlefield woke up, but as Bennie was backing out of the driveway, Littlefield emerged from the house and climbed into the passenger seat. "This is a stupid idea," he said.

They parked on the high shoulder near Esker Cove, and when they got to the bottom of the ravine, Bennie put the babies, first, on a flat spot in shallow snow beneath a gnarled spruce tree. When he released the mother, she darted away. Bennie and Littlefield waited beneath the crooked tree to see if she would come back for the babies, but after a few minutes she was still gone.

"It's because we're sitting here," said Littlefield. "As soon as we leave, she'll come back."

"You're probably right," said Bennie. They walked out of the ravine and returned to his warm car. Bennie was certain that in the cold the babies would die within the hour.

"They're rodents, man," said Littlefield. "They can survive anything. They'll be fine."

Later in the morning, Bennie and Helen ate cheese omelets at her house, listening to NPR, a report from California about the rise in the price of pine nuts, and a story about the beginning of Clinton's second term. Bennie wasn't paying close attention; he knew his brother would be picking him up soon to take him to the Flying Dutchman. Bennie hadn't yet told Helen about his involvement in the paintball league—the dynamics of competition, the protective masks, the highly pressurized plastic semiautomatic paint markers, what it felt like to run around in the snow at the Dutchman, playing on the same team as his brother—because they hadn't been dating for very long. He guessed she would have some kind of ethical resistance to the whole idea. He also suspected that she would enjoy it if she tried it; she'd revel in the irony. It would make her uneasy, like the zombie movies she loved to watch, but she would get caught up in the competition. She would be pleased to find how safe the game was, and that what they did in the woods was closer to cops and robbers or hide-and-go-seek than it was to war. It would surprise her. Maybe he'd take her to the Flying Dutchman for her birthday.

For now, though, he didn't say anything. Despite his rationalizations he felt immature about playing paintball so often and didn't think he could easily convince her that he was not. Just after they finished their omelets, they heard a car horn outside; it was Littlefield. The game started at noon. He gave her a kiss and told her he'd check in with her at the restaurant later in the day.

Littlefield and Bennie drove across Musquacook to pick up Julian, who was slouching on the front steps of his house with a cigarette tucked behind his ear. Julian climbed in the backseat of Littlefield's Chevette, then reached between the seats and popped *Back in Black* into the cassette deck. Bennie could see his own distorted reflection in Julian's silver mirror sunglasses. "Gentlemen, no more tears," said Julian. "I'm feeling it. We'll win today."

Julian and Bennie always rented guns from the Dutchman, but Littlefield brought his own. With one hand on the wheel, Littlefield lowered the volume as they sped down Masungun Road, and took a cigarette from a pack on the dashboard. Littlefield was skinny, like Bennie, but his eyes were brown, the angles of his face more distinct, and he rarely shaved. The Chevette's heater was broken, so Littlefield grabbed a wool hat from the dashboard and with one hand pulled it onto his head, covering most of his close-cropped brown hair, which—though he was only twenty-nine—was getting gray at the temples. He gently pressed in the lighter, rolled the window down an inch, brought the lighter to the end of his cigarette, placed the pack in his coveralls, and finally returned his hands to the steering wheel. Proud of this maneuver, he glanced over at Bennie. In the cemetery they passed, the snow was so deep that only a few of the headstones were showing. More snow was on its way that evening. Littlefield exhaled smoke over the top of the window.

The Chevette was a new acquisition of Littlefield's—Bennie had no idea where it had come from, and he didn't ask because he knew Littlefield wasn't happy to be driving it. His previous car, a Ford F-150, was rusty and temperamental but it had fit with his work as a builder.

Julian was usually good for some pre-contest banter, but instead he was focused on Littlefield's oversize paint gun resting in the backseat.

"Why'd you spend money on this?"

"You like it?" said Littlefield.

"It's not bad," he said, turning it over in his hands. "But I don't need it. The rented guns kill just as well."

"They charge you eight bucks every time you rent from them. We go every week. My gun cost one-twenty. It won't be long before I've earned it back."

"Nice work, math whiz." Julian put the gun back down on the seat. Bennie was embarrassed that his brother was earnest in his defense of this purchase. *Laugh at yourself, once in a while,* Bennie thought. *It's paintball. The gun's a toy.*

The guns the Dutchman rented were low end, but for battles with the urchiners, precision often wasn't essential. They tried to outfox their opponents and shoot at point-blank range. Bennie agreed with Julian: a poorly gauged sight wouldn't cost you a win.

Still, when they passed Rubin's Small Engine Repair, Julian rolled his window down. He picked up Littlefield's gun again and rested its muzzle on the car door and squinted his eye, lining up his sight. When he fired—missing a diamond road sign with a large black arrow—Littlefield shouted back at him, "Idiot!"

Julian fired another one, and again the paintball sailed off into the woods. Then he brought the gun back to his lap and rolled up the window. "I can't shoot for shit with that thing," he said.

"You think that moving along at fifty miles an hour has anything to do with it, douchebag?"

As they pulled into the Dutchman's parking lot, Littlefield opened his door and flicked the end of his cigarette to the snow. Littlefield pulled his Camel Lights from the front pocket of his coveralls, shook another one out, and lit it. Bennie tightened the cuffs of his gloves. Most of the time he found ways to get excited about paintball, but his brother's foul mood made the whole charade cringeworthy.

It was at some point late in high school when Littlefield completed the transformation from rich kid to local—from a boy who'd trained hard for their father's ski team, earning all-state honors in ninth and tenth grade, to a kid who sold an ounce of weed every week at the private school where their mother worked part-time as a counselor. When Littlefield finished school, he started learning how to build houses and started caring less about what the family thought of him. The change happened not long after their father died. Bennie and their sister, Gwen, helped their mother run the house, but Littlefield had always battled with Eleanor, so he moved in with Pete and Skunk Gould, sleeping on the couch in their trailer until she moved up to a place in Clover Lake. When she moved, she left the family's house to the kids. That was when Gwen packed up, too, and started her life in Brooklyn.

They zipped up their tan coveralls as they walked over to the office. Usually, Bennie liked watching Littlefield pull the headgear down over his face, the rigid mask with built-in goggles, and he admired Littlefield for his toughness, his stubbornness, his fierce approach to the game. He'd always been in awe of this, actually—Littlefield's ability to stay focused, to take the game seriously, to want to win, always, to never let the thought of losing distract him. Watching Littlefield check his gun this time, though—making sure the reloading action was working, lining up the sight, pumping a few gumballs at a nearby spruce stump—reminded Bennie of how pigheaded his brother was in general, how he took himself so seriously. Littlefield had isolated himself after their father's death—he'd become much more stubborn and smug—and while there were times when Bennie was envious of Littlefield's confidence, this was not one of them. *We're playing a game. Take it easy.*

Through the scratched, fogging plastic of his own mask, Bennie saw the urchiners. Their masks were down, too, and they wore belted white snowsuits. They held their guns tight against their stomachs, each in the same way. They were rugged, but with their new matching snowsuits, they looked like happy snowmen.

"Here's the thing," Julian whispered. "They've got a new guy. I don't even know his name."

"LaBrecque," said Littlefield. "Ray LaBrecque. The one in the middle."

Boak and Shaw were the veterans of the urchiner team—they were squat and muscular—and LaBrecque, the tallest of the snowmen, towered between them like an older brother.

"Yeah, okay. Well, he's their weakness," whispered Julian.

The game was better in summertime because more shots were fired and you sprinted around the course like a spooked dog; the anxiety about getting shot was heightened because you wore fewer layers and the paintballs left bigger welts. This was something the rookie paintballers didn't consider: the incentive to avoid your opponents' fire went far beyond just wanting to stay in the game. Getting shot was not like getting tagged in touch football. Getting shot hurt, like getting snagged on a barbed-wire fence. With paintball, you were always just one stupid move away from the shockingly sharp sting of humiliation and loss.

In wintertime, this fear was lessened because of heavier clothes and snow bunkers, but the starkness of the weather added to the drama. The margin for error was small. There was no greenery, and the drifts were difficult to run through.

Bennie and Littlefield's understanding of each other was best in evidence at the Flying Dutchman. Their father had been a marine, which made running around with guns especially appealing to Littlefield. (It didn't seem to matter to him that their father hadn't gone to Vietnam but had instead served stateside as a "logistical specialist," driving trucks.) Bennie, on the other hand, didn't care for paintball itself, but he liked the camaraderie—most of the time, he liked being on his brother's team. Julian competed for different reasons. He was both a pacifist and a hedonist, a guy whose idea of the perfect afternoon was getting stoned and reworking dessert recipes at his restaurant, thinking about pasta specials and new keg beers for the bar. Most people who knew him would never have guessed he was a top-shelf paintballer—not exactly an instinctual marksman, but a sneaky, ruthless, no-conscience killer. He played because he hated to lose.

The urchiners didn't wait around to shake hands. When they saw their opponents arrive, they started walking to the west side of the field. Julian and Bennie still needed to pick up their rented guns. Gendron Knight, the overweight ex-con who ran the Dutchman, knew they were coming, and he lumbered out of his shack and handed them two semi-automatic markers without a word. They hadn't been to other paintball courses, but they knew the Dutchman was a no-frills enterprise. It had banged-up rental guns and a wire-mesh fence containing an un-manicured thirty-five-acre plot of land with just about every possible New England geological variation: thick woods, fields, sand pit, low scrub, stream, pond, boulders, swamp, though the snow flattened everything out a bit. Even the man-made obstacles, plywood bunkers tall enough to stand behind in summertime, were half buried.

The rivalry with the urchiners was the worst kind, because the urchiners didn't consider Bennie and Littlefield and Julian much of a challenge. Once the game began, Bennie and his teammates moved around the course, sweating, squinting their eyes, searching the woods for any suspicious movement, wondering whether or not they'd get shot in the back. Bennie felt the urchiners' presence behind every tree, every bunker, but catching sight of them was rare. On a small paintball course, games lasted five or ten minutes, but on the big open course at the Dutchman, with practiced, paranoid soldiers, games lasted much longer. For the first hour, Julian and Littlefield and Bennie stuck together, and they didn't once glimpse the urchiners. They suspected the urchiners had taken hold of the interior, so they trudged their way along the fence. Littlefield didn't make any sprinting forays. He was usually a good one for the kamikaze mission, swooping through enemy territory at full speed, making kills or flushing meat out into open ground for Julian and Bennie, but everyone was more tentative that afternoon. Because of the urchiners' new guy, LaBrecque, Littlefield said they had a real chance to win.

Boak and Shaw, the mainstays of the urchiner team, were glass-eating gorillas, burly and tough and unpredictable. They were cousins, and both of them had military training, which helped with the game, but what made them better than most teams was that they didn't mind sitting in a snow hole for hours. They'd keep a man out front—in this case, LaBrecque, the rookie—and Shaw and Boak would bunker in the deep snow or camp out in the big plastic tunnel at the center of the course: "the snake." They'd had a few matches with the urchiners in which Littlefield had gotten shot by both Boak and Shaw, from either end of the snake, the barrels of their guns pointing up through the snow. What these gorillas did for a living (maneuvering a small boat in shallow waters during the wintertime; diving with two tanks on their backs in the surge around the shoals in a dry suit that kept you just warm enough to stay alive, gathering sea urchins) got them accustomed to being patient and weathering pain. The best strategy with the urchiners was to do whatever possible to spring them from their little rat tunnels.

The paintballer's credo is to kick ass. To blast hard and fast and to kill indiscriminately, to model yourself after soldiers or Indians or gangbangers acting fiercely in battles you haven't had to fight. Bennie tried to be fully compliant with the paintballer's credo whenever he was at the Dutchman. It was guys like Shaw and Boak who had originally established the credo, actual vets—they'd been in Saudi during the Gulf War. They had a good handle on how to set the tone at the Dutchman.

During the second hour, Littlefield ventured about twenty yards ahead—Julian and Bennie hung back in a snarl of spruce trees—but nothing came of it. As usual, the urchiners were perfectly happy just holing up, waiting for their opponents to make the wrong move. Just before the whistle blew, Bennie found LaBrecque. He was set up behind them, prone, most of his body hidden by a plywood bunker, but Bennie had a clear bead on his head. Because it was so late in the match, a hit would seal the win. Bennie locked him in. He had him fully FedExed (Julian's term), but just before Bennie squeezed his trigger, LaBrecque must have felt his gaze. His head popped down, out of view. Gendron Knight blew his whistle.

Ultimately, an uneventful match.

When the whistle blew, Bennie's fingers were stiff in his gloves, his back ached from crouching, and all he'd been thinking about (before he'd had the chance to aim his gun at LaBrecque's head) was heating up some beef stew, filling the fireplace with wood, and sitting on the old purple couch with Helen.

They all knew the Dutchman closed at two-thirty in the wintertime and that Gendron got crabby when he had to shut down late, so when the whistle blew everyone came out from the trees. Bennie was relieved, ready to end the game despite the tie score, but the urchiners were clearly annoyed. They all gathered by the frozen duck pond near the north fence, masks still on, as Boak and Shaw approached.

Boak was their captain. It wasn't until all six men had gathered in a tight circle that he pulled off his hat and mask. His hairline was just a few inches above his eyebrows and his cheeks were badly scarred from acne and other aggressions. There weren't many guys in town that just by standing in front of you made you consider exactly how to defend yourself. Boak looked capable of considerable bare-handed violence. The same was true of Shaw. The game was over and no one on his team had been hit, but still Boak looked like someone had kidnapped his sister. He was flushed and ugly. Shaw and LaBrecque removed their hats and masks, too. Bennie hadn't seen LaBrecque before today—he was six or seven inches taller than Boak and Shaw, had wide shoulders, whiskers on his sturdy chin, and gray eyes. He was probably younger than he looked. He gazed out and nodded to Bennie, to Julian, and then to Littlefield.

Boak said it was a cracker way to end the battle. Littlefield said he couldn't agree more. Tying was not part of the paintballer's credo. But when Gendron Knight came out on his snowmobile to reiterate the time issue, there was no room for discussion. That's when the snow began to fly; the storm was starting, little light pellets landing on Bennie's eyelashes. They all put their hats and masks back on and trudged to Gendron's shack to return the guns.

Within the hour, Bennie and Littlefield and Julian were bullshitting at Julian's. Through the window near the end of the bar, they could see the snow falling—now a heavy sugar snow churning in the gusts of wind. The sun hadn't gone down yet, though the light outside was dark blue.

Julian was officially off duty, but he was keeping an eye on things and helping collect empty glasses for the bartender. Helen was finishing her lunch shift in the kitchen—they stopped serving at three, but Bennie knew she had to Saran-wrap food containers, wipe down the stove and counters, and prep for the dinner shift before leaving, when she would drive back to his place, where he'd heat up the beef stew.

The beer made Bennie feel warmer, but his fingers were still numb. They'd just ordered their second round when Boak and Shaw and LaBrecque entered the bar. They'd taken off their white snowsuits. Each had a thin layer of snow on his head.

"Good battle today," said Littlefield. With the stubble, dark eyes, and angular features, Littlefield sometimes looked vaguely canine—especially when he was about to start an argument. Bennie knew the pleasantries were fleeting.

Boak brushed the snow off his black wool jacket, hesitating before saying, "Yup."

"Three pints for these boys," said Littlefield.

They didn't seem to know how to respond to the gesture, but each stepped closer to the tap. They stared at the Bruins game above the liquor bottles. Once they had the pints in hand, Littlefield stood and motioned for Julian and Bennie to stand, too. "A toast," he said, looking at Boak and Shaw and LaBrecque. "To your good fortune."

Boak smiled tightly. "You're the lucky one, friend," he said. Everyone drank. Then Littlefield suggested they all go back to the snowfields to finish the game. Shaw and Boak were interested. Bennie stayed quiet, wanting someone, Julian perhaps, to offer resistance. LaBrecque was nodding, his eyes fixed on Littlefield, and it seemed they knew each other from another context. Fishing? Logging? Construction? Dealing pot? If they didn't like each other, Bennie didn't notice, but Littlefield had plenty of enemies. Littlefield told them they could easily break in to Gendron's woodshed, get the guns, play for an hour, and see who came out ahead.

Just as he said this, Helen walked through the kitchen doors, toward the bar. She was untying her apron, a slick of sweat on her forehead, a small stripe of tomato sauce on her temple, her hair pulled away from her face. At the sight of her, everyone seemed to take it easy.

She tossed the apron at Bennie and smiled. "I can't wait to fall asleep on your couch. I'm completely wiped."

"Can I meet you later? Littlefield and I are going for a walk," he said, glancing over at the others, who didn't seem to be listening. "Out in the woods."

She was quiet, and then she said, "You know it's snowing, right? I think that storm is coming over from the White Mountains."

"It'll be a short walk, then."

He wasn't sure if Helen had seen the mask atop Shaw's head and the bag of paintballs still tied to Littlefield's belt, but she shrugged and said, "Well, I'm headed back to my place, then. Try not to drive into a ditch, okay?" When she took the apron off his lap he tried to catch her eyes but didn't; she'd already turned and was on her way to the kitchen.

The men tipped back their glasses of beer and rezipped their coveralls. "We'll meet here after the game," said Littlefield. LaBrecque was the first out the door, and the rest followed.

They dropped Julian off at his house so he could get more clothes, and Bennie and Littlefield went back to the Manse and bundled up, too. They had less than an hour of light left, and the wind was picking up. The temperature was dropping.

Everyone met back at the Dutchman, where Littlefield climbed the fence and broke into Gendron's office. When he came back with an armful of guns, Bennie felt a new surge of energy. His hands had warmed up. Littlefield tossed the gear over the fence. They walked as a group to the quarry.

The air in the dark purple woods was thick with quiet snow. They labored through the drifts, barely able to see each other, the wind cold on Bennie's face. Even though Keep's Quarry and the forest surrounding it was less than a quarter-mile from the road, it took them a half hour. With snow covering the thicket, every few steps someone's feet would get tangled in brambles. The wind gusted in the trees and the shadows dulled as it got darker, and they had to pay close attention to the branches that hung down by their eyes. Everyone was winded and sweating. When they finally got to the woods, they stood in a circle and Littlefield said that he, Bennie, and Julian would take the far side. When the urchiners lined up on the near side, Bennie could see them, faintly, through the snow.

Littlefield signaled the restart by raising his arm. The urchiners jogged three abreast along the rim of the quarry, out of range. Littlefield turned to Julian and Bennie and said, "We only have an hour. Bennie and I will head up to the north edge, and we'll try to flush them out in your direction, Julian. You stay put—we'll get them out in view."

Bennie's legs felt weak. He said, "How about if Julian goes with you and I stay."

"But he's a better shot than you," said Littlefield.

Julian shrugged. "Whatever, man. Let's try it. Let's kill these fuckers."

Littlefield looked at Bennie, sternly, and asked, "What are you, tired?"

"I think . . . I'd just rather hole up right here," said Bennie.

Littlefield shook his head. "All right, Julian. Let's go. Just don't fall asleep on us, Ben. Quit being a pussy and make sure you blast away when the time comes."

Bennie wanted to respond, but his brother and Julian were already jogging to the north edge of the quarry, past the same spot where hippies jumped from the ledges on hot summer days. Bennie walked over to the spruce trees, hunkered in the deep snow, rested his back against the largest tree, and watched his steaming breath. There was still enough light to distinguish the sky from the canopy above.

It wasn't long before Bennie lost sight of Julian and Littlefield, which brought him some relief—he was fine letting Littlefield lead the charge. It was Littlefield's game, really, and Bennie was happy to let him win or lose on his own. Once the others disappeared, Bennie knew his only responsibility was to keep from getting shot. He did what he expected Boak and Shaw were doing: he dug a little trench and holed up and then pointed his gun out in the direction where he expected LaBrecque to be. He thought of Helen, briefly—the way her nose would have crinkled up if he told her about these war games, in the storm—but then his focus returned to the shadowy gray forest and his cold body in the snow, his back against the spruce tree.

He could have called it off then, could have yelled loud enough to bring everyone in. He could have surrendered. It's what he'd wanted to do, not only because he was getting cold again but because he was suddenly worried someone was going to fall down and get hurt. There was a brief window, before Littlefield and the urchiners got too far away, when he could have stopped the game. But he didn't want to disappoint his brother—chances were, everyone would be fine and it wouldn't be long before they were back at the bar, warming up and drinking beer—so he kept quiet.

After twenty minutes of silence Bennie saw from a distance through the billowing sugar snow two squat figures moving from one tree to the next, crouching, the black barrels of their guns raised and ready, pointing out from the trunks of each tree they hid behind. They were making a wide arc toward Bennie through the woods. The figures weren't running but they seemed to be moving steadily. With his eyes wide open in the dusk, through the blowing snow he could see their silhouettes blurring against the stands of spruce. He considered climbing the tree he was leaning against—they wouldn't guess that in the faint light of the snowstorm with a Kingdom semiautomatic marker in his hand he'd be above them, in a tree—but the gorillas were getting too close and he didn't have time. He tried to be a quiet rock beside the spruce tree. The urchiners continued to walk toward him in a nearly direct line, but they were still far enough away that through the snow he must have been invisible to them. Bennie kept his barrel raised, holding his breath.

He heard it first, then glanced quickly over his shoulder, behind the tree he was leaning against. A white blur, silent, sprinting across the top of the snowpack. A snowshoe hare.

He could see they were watching the hare, and the commotion gave Bennie enough time to lock in on Boak. For a split second he felt sorry, knowing how seriously Boak took the paintballer's credo. Bennie squeezed his trigger and sludged Boak in the shoulder. He fell to his knees. "Man down!" Boak screamed.

Shaw charged, and Bennie jumped out of his trench, turned, and ran. Shaw was pumping shots; one hit a tree Bennie's shoulder brushed against as he fled. The snow was deep but he felt fast; he felt daring and purposeful and somehow he felt certain he would elude Shaw. The ground beneath the snow was now flat and hard instead of bramble, so he was able to pick up speed. Bennie was high-stepping, sprinting toward the wide gray clearing in front of him. The snow was not as deep, he was getting faster, and he glanced back—Shaw was close, but he had stopped, he had his gun raised—and when Bennie returned his gaze to what was in front of him, his feet were free and he was falling.

There was a second of calm—the wind felt different, it was warmer, his legs were still churning, and he was falling with the snow. He felt light and unencumbered. There was nothing to be afraid of. He had no idea what would happen next. He thought he had picked up so much speed, he was flying. Flying away from Shaw. In the instant before hitting the ice at the bottom of the quarry, he was sure that Littlefield would be proud.

4

They'd gotten into paintball because of hunting, and they'd only started hunting regularly after their father died. He'd been a hunter, and he'd also been their biathlon coach. Most people in Maine wouldn't have any idea that there were kids of all ages who competed in a sport that combined cross-country skiing with shooting a rifle—and that these fledgling contests had begun in the late seventies. It had been William Littlefield, Sr.—known as Coach to everyone, including his children—who'd started the Saturday-afternoon races, which were still small-scale but were now happening everywhere: in Rumford, Ogunquit, Bethel, Waterville, Dover-Foxcroft, Brunswick, Bangor, Caribou,

Cumberland, Blue Hill, and on Mount Desert Isle. Pulling his three-year-old twins, Bennie and Gwen, behind him in a plastic sled, Coach had gotten Littlefield on skis at age five. In his twenties, ten years after Coach died, Bennie had earned his fastest times, and his shot was finally steady. Comparing the sport to paintball was difficult: the course was much larger, you followed a track on skis, the rifles were real, and the targets were smaller. It was one of those sports, like iceboating or falconry, that was basic in concept but tricky to execute. After a while—as he kept trying and trying to get better, without noticing any results—Bennie started thinking of biathlon as that well-balanced, perfectly nutritious dinner that took too long to prepare and didn't taste very good. As Coach had said to Gwen and Littlefield and Bennie when all three were still competing: "You each have talent. But to win you need guts and heart." It took Bennie a while to understand what Coach meant by this, and once he did, he quit, and he was the last of the three of them to stop racing. Like Littlefield, he started spending his Saturdays playing paintball instead.

Coach had been masochistic in his own training. After driving trucks at Camp Lejune, William Littlefield, Sr., trained his way onto the biathlon national team, and while he never competed in the Olympics, he finished thirty-fourth in the 1967 World Cup, cleaning all of his targets. He said if he hadn't picked the wrong wax he might have made it onto the Olympic team. That was his story, and Bennie didn't find much point in questioning it.

Later, Bennie learned that Gwen called from New York several times, leaving messages, telling Bennie her flight-arrival time—midday on his birthday—so that he could pick her up at the airport. Littlefield didn't check the messages for several days. At the hospital, Bennie was propped up on pillows, drifting about. The doctor had piped a feed of liquid drugs directly into his arm: first morphine, which helped, then Dilaudid, which helped even more. He had remote controls: a red button in his right hand fed more narcotics, and the nurse call button was within reach of his left hand. He talked on the phone with Julian, who told him he'd visit as soon as things at the restaurant quieted down. Littlefield didn't visit, either—like their father, he hated hospitals—but he called Bennie's room the next day and said *Listen up, it's your brother,* and he told Bennie he'd be feeling better in no time. High on the painkillers, with the static on the line and the certainty in Littlefield's voice, Bennie felt like they were characters in an old-style radio drama.

"That kid, LaBrecque. He's still missing."

Bennie wanted to know the details, immediately, but the shock he felt in his chest made him afraid to ask.

"Bennie, are you there?"

"I'm here."

"LaBrecque got lost in the woods. He might have fallen into the quarry. Like you did. But no one's found him yet."

"People are still looking?"

"The cops. Folks from Musquacook and the island. But he might have skipped town, too. Hard to say right now." Before he hung up, Littlefield told Bennie to get home as soon as he could.

It wasn't the head injury that had him fouled up, or his broken leg. It was knowing that surely he could have died. Waiting to be released, Bennie had a decent amount of time to think about dying. Where was LaBrecque? Had the same thing happened to both of them and only Bennie was saved? In the bed, Bennie was floating, encased in softness, a quiet ocean. Once he even had a vision of raccoon babies, a tight bundle of fur beneath the spruce tree, at the bottom of the ravine. Under normal circumstances, he wasn't one to think much about mortality, but in the hospital he started seeing himself disappear, melting into the snow right beside LaBrecque, the guy he didn't know, with the gray eyes and the large white snowsuit. The way it seemed to have happened was that when Bennie fell off the edge of Keep's Quarry he'd landed in the clean sheets and soft blankets of Parkview Adventist, and suddenly there were round-faced nurses wearing colorful shirts delivering food and checking his blood pressure. Where had LaBrecque landed? Bennie knew his own body was twisted up and broken, but he couldn't feel any of the pain. In addition to the concussion and broken leg, his hip and left shoulder were bruised. When the nurses asked him about the accident, though, the drugs he was taking kept him from the shame he might have felt for being a grown man playing paintball in the first place.

On Helen's first visit to the hospital—the day after his fall, she'd heard about the accident from Julian, at the restaurant—she'd walked slowly into his room, unannounced, and Bennie mistook her for a nurse. He lowered the volume on the TV and brought his arm up out of the covers for a blood-pressure check.

"Hi, Bennie," she said. She was holding one arm behind her back.

"Oh, wow," he said, blinking. Her cheeks were bright from the cold outside. His vision seemed especially sharp—just minutes earlier, he'd pressed the pain button for a surge of Dilaudid, which had settled him, and brightened the room—and he focused on her eyelashes, both above and below each eye.

"I brought you a present," she said, looking down, then bringing her hand out from behind her back and placing a miniature sailboat on the bed. "I don't think this one's a Sunfish. But I thought it was cool. They sell them in the bookstore, in the back, with the kids' books."

He looked down at the boat, with its blue hull and white sails. "It's amazing," he said, dreamily, indebted to her. "You're amazing. I love you."

Helen smiled, but her eyes showed some concern and she took a tiny step away from the bed. It was quiet for a minute before she said, "So things are going okay in here? You're getting better?"

"What I mean is, yeah . . . you're really great for coming. Sorry to . . . well, I'm just kind of out of it right now."

"It's okay," she said. "I'm glad you like the sailboat." She smoothed a spot to sit at the end of his bed, then turned and sat in a chair in the corner.

"You can sit up here," he said. "I won't tell you I love you again, I promise."

She stood up from the chair and sat down on the bed. "You were hunting out there?"

"Well, not exactly. We were playing a game. Shooting each other with paintballs. I'm sure it sounds pretty dumb."

"Kind of," she said.

"I mean, we do it pretty often. We're safe about it. We wear eye protection." He had his ankles wrapped in two constricting sleeves that inflated every few minutes, to make sure his blood was flowing properly. The machine rumbled on, squeezed his ankles, then switched off.

"Do you do it in that kind of weather usually?" She wasn't looking at him—she was picking little pills off the thin hospital blanket.

"No," he said. He wondered if she had heard about LaBrecque, and whether or not to tell her.

She looked up at him. "And you were drinking, too—right?"

"No, not really. Two or three beers."

"We don't need to talk about it now, but . . . I really don't like it. Like, I feel really strongly about it. It's kind of like hunting and drinking? You know?"

"I probably won't do it again."

"Forget it. I just . . . wanted to get that out there."

"Can we talk about something else?"

"It's like . . . the kind of thing you hear on the news. Drinking and hunting."

"It wasn't the beer, believe me. And you don't need to worry about me. I'm really . . . perfectly fine right now." He felt this was true, despite the head bandage, and the leg cast, and the IV in his arm.

After she left, he thought more about what he'd said to her. The Dilaudid was wearing off, but before he gave himself another dose he let himself feel stupid about telling Helen that he loved her. His last girlfriend, Hillary Koeman, was so different from Helen—she was child-like and sweet, and she liked romantic dinners, and they saw each other almost every day and she even invited him to Vermont to meet her family, whom he envied (her parents and little brothers were all prodigies, or close to it, and kindhearted). But when he proposed to her after they'd been dating for six months, she thought it had come out of the blue. She was completely shocked. They didn't break up right away, but it didn't take long—perhaps a month of stalled conversations and half-hearted gestures of friendship.

After he'd first woken up in the hospital, one of the nurses had told him he had "blood on the brain" and that he may have torn his corpus callosum. They said he would be okay after a short recovery, and he agreed with them; his brain felt fine. The only problems came when he felt an itch. He would try scratching it but he couldn't feel his skin. Even worse were those moments when the nurse's aide attempted to give him a back rub—had the doctor called for this?—and as she did he could feel only the lightest touch against his skin. Nothing more substantial. He felt like he was wearing a costume and inside the disguise there was nothing but air.

He wondered about the latest news of LaBrecque. Maybe he had his own nurse, was getting his own back rubs. Bennie called home several times to see if there was any news, and he reached the answering machine.

The nurse's aide had blond feathered hair, long fingers, and generously presented breasts, but in his bed all feelings were being fed to him or released from him through tubes and catheters. Bennie knew there might have been a world out there in which people were sitting in diners, eating real food, walking through the woods, talking about things as though they mattered, but that world felt distant. When the busty nurse's aide left on his second night in the hospital, she bent down close to his face and told him, "It's your job to just float there on your little raft."

He flipped on the TV. He watched but he couldn't concentrate. Animal Planet was often his best bet. Any show about pets and their doting owners. No matter what he watched, his mind often returned to the winter he lived in Brooklyn with Gwen, a year after she'd first moved there, right after he'd dropped out of college. It was almost hard to believe now that he'd gone to the city in his early twenties and worked as a truck driver, moving artwork for an outfit in Queens. The sapphire lights on the truck's dashboard; stopping for eggs and potatoes in Williamsburg; nearly dropping an obscure gilt-framed Monet in a town house on the Upper East Side; napping on the subway coming back from the warehouse; meeting Hillary Koeman while she was taking classes at Hunter College; her fantasies about Maine, which he was happy to fulfill; his proposal and their breakup; accidentally stepping through the side of a crate containing a sculpture made of twigs he was late in delivering to Sotheby's; getting fired; helping Gwen find a new roommate; having Littlefield come down late at night to pick him up and drive him back to Meadow Island; the queasy relief he felt coming up over the Piscataqua River.

Since then, he'd spent time pretending he belonged in Maine. He'd been born there; that helped. After a while, the pretending had melted away. He knew they were real, his financial struggles, his misplaced plans. Being in the hospital—especially when it was nearly time for more Dilaudid, when his room looked dull and shabby—made him think about these realities.

While Bennie was in New York, Littlefield joined the Elks, bought a truck, spent his paychecks on beer and weed. He'd stopped calling their mother, though she would call him from time to time. The day Bennie got back from New York, the harbor looked pristine, the spruce forest and the ground beneath smelled like heaven—it had been raining—and the sky over the ocean went on forever. Littlefield, though, felt like a stranger. He knew his brother was glad to have him back, but Bennie could also sense his brother's wariness. What had happened during their time apart—the things each of them had learned, the failures they'd had—seemed unsettling to Littlefield. Bennie didn't know how to talk about this.

The ceiling in his room at the hospital was white. It seemed wet, like the underbelly of a flounder.

Before he switched the light off for the night, Lynne Pettigrew, a cop from the Musquacook Police Department, knocked on the door and entered his room.

"Bennie?"

"Hello?" he said.

"Can I talk to you for a minute?" Lynne Pettigrew was an old family friend of the Littlefields'; her mother had gone to high school with Coach. Bennie had never gotten to know her well, but their families had spent Easter together once when they were younger. She was of medium height but her shoulders were wide. Her brown hair was cut in a neat bob and she wore wire-rimmed glasses. Bennie knew she'd been a hockey standout at UNH. She coached the Brunswick girls' team when she wasn't policing.

"Sure." He tried to sit up in bed, to look more presentable, but his ankles were still in the pressurized sleeves. It was difficult to move.

"You feeling okay?" she asked.

"Pretty good," he said.

"You probably know by now that Mr. Ray LaBrecque has gone missing. Officers from various towns are helping out with the search."

"My brother told me."

"We're looking in the quarry and all of the woods nearby. We even got the Brunswick guys to bring their dogs down, but nothing came of it. According to your brother and Julian Fischer, it was a pretty wide territory that was covered that evening. Hard to say where he went, exactly, with the storm and all that snow. There's also a chance Mr. LaBrecque left town on his own accord. We don't know yet. He's a friend of yours?"

"No. I knew he was working with Boak and Shaw—Scotty Boak and Craig Shaw—out on Riverneck Island, right?"

"Would you know why he might skip work and leave town after that evening in the woods?" She stood near the bed, holding her black watch cap in both hands.

"No idea, Lynne."

"And you hadn't met him before?"

"Not until that afternoon."

"Okay. Give us a call if you remember anything about Mr. LaBrecque, anything that you might think is helpful. You know where to reach me, Bennie, at the Musquacook station." She placed a card on his bedside table. "Talk to me or Sergeant Thibideaux."

"Thanks, Lynne."

After she left, he called Littlefield, but there was no answer and he didn't leave a message. He was stunned that LaBrecque hadn't been found, especially now that other towns were involved with the search. Dogs, too. It seemed most likely that LaBrecque had left town without telling anyone, which would have been an odd choice in the midst of the storm.

The day before he was discharged was another sleepy one in the hospital. Helen came in the late afternoon, with a small vase of purple lilies. Bennie told her about Lynne Pettigrew's visit, and Helen said she'd heard about LaBrecque's disappearance, but not from her boss, Julian—one of the waitresses had told her. Bennie scooted over on the bed, both of them barely fitting side by side, her shoulder warm against his. They watched Animal Planet for a half hour, a show about cat rescues. When he switched the TV off, Helen said, "It's just . . . I mean, running around with guns? Doesn't that seem crazy to you? In a storm?"

"Can we not talk about this right now?"

"Sorry," she said.

"You know, they're fake guns. They shoot paint."

Helen paused before saying, "But you were scared enough to run off the edge of the quarry. And that other guy had probably been scared, too."

"I wasn't scared," he said. "I was just trying to avoid getting shot."

"Doesn't it sound crazy to you? When you say something like that?" she asked. She and Bennie were still looking at the TV.

"It's a game."

"Pretending to hunt people?"

"Exactly."

She squinted.

"It's not like we're hunting each other. It's like—we're soldiers." As soon as he said this, he knew it was the wrong approach.

"Will you promise not to play that game anymore?" she asked, holding the squint.

He nodded, though he didn't want to promise out loud. He was pretty sure he wouldn't play again—no, he was absolutely sure—but to promise felt dumb. She kissed him softly on the lips, put on her wool hat, and went home.

The next day, Bennie told the nurses his brother was picking him up, but he hired a taxi to get home. He wanted to make a quiet return. After he gave the cabbie directions to the house on Meadow Island, they didn't speak. The guy appeared to be extremely tired, but he stayed within the lines and kept an even speed. His gray beard came down to the middle of his chest. Despite Bennie's concern about the driver's sleepiness, it was the driver who kept glancing back at Bennie in the rearview mirror. After a while Bennie wondered if the guy was curious about his head bandage—a wrap of wide stretchable tape that covered the tops of his ears and went all the way up to the crown of his head. Bennie also wondered how much of an impact the drugs he was taking were having, and if they were making him think the guy was glancing back too often and that the guy looked tired. As the taxi crossed the one-lane causeway to the island, Bennie saw the boats in the harbor—there were only a few, but their colors were overly bright, their hulls too shiny and wet—and for a startling moment, he thought it was a mirage.

But when the cab pulled into the Manse's driveway, he calmed down. He saw the piles of snow that had been plowed against the house, and his brown Skylark and Littlefield's Chevette parked tight against the snowbank. Faint lights glowed in the windows. He realized everything would be okay.

"Fourteen dollars," said the man.

Bennie took a twenty from his pocket, reached out, and let the bill hang over the seat. When the man turned around, his beard grazed Bennie's hand. "Nice place you got there," he said, taking the money, unzipping a large plastic wallet, looking for change. "Nice view."

"It's kind of a shithole, actually," said Bennie.

"You don't say. Seems like a pretty piece of property," said the driver, shifting around to look at Bennie again. He raised his eyebrows with Bennie's change.

A six-dollar tip was too big, so he took the two bills—a five and a one—hesitated too long, then gave back the five. He put the single in his pocket.

"Thank you, sir," said the man.

Bennie felt flooded with feeling: grateful to be home, grateful to be alive, guilty about the disrepair of the old house, ashamed to be called "sir" by someone who had a better job than he did, wishing he'd just given the driver the entire twenty.

"You know, I heard about you guys," said the cabbie. "I know your buddy's still missing."

This irritated Bennie and he was eager to exit the cab quickly, but with his sore hip, the crutches, and the leg cast, it took him a few seconds longer than he hoped. He said nothing. He stepped out into the snowy driveway. The wind brought tears to his eyes. He knew he was thinking foolish thoughts; he needed to get back into bed.

Bennie crutched through the deep snow on the unshoveled walk to the front door, came inside, and went to the kitchen. Even though she hadn't heard back from her brothers, Gwen had flown from LaGuardia to Portland, and when she finally got hold of Littlefield, she convinced him to pick her up. That's when he told her that Bennie was in the hospital. She was incensed, but Littlefield said he hadn't checked the machine right away, and that when he did he'd kept the news from her for her own good—he said Bennie was fine. In fact, Littlefield told her, he was coming home just a few hours after her flight arrived.

Gwen was at the sink washing dishes. She glanced over her shoulder at him, then dropped the bowl she was rinsing in the soapy water. Her hair had grown down to the middle of her back and she wore new glasses with dark brown frames.

"Bennie!" she shouted.

"I got out a little early," he said, gripping the crutches. He put his small duffel on the kitchen table, then relaxed his elbows, letting the crutches sink into his armpits. Ronald, Littlefield's Brittany spaniel, ran across the kitchen floor and flung himself against Bennie's cast, reaching up and scratching with his paws, trying to climb high enough to lick Bennie's face. The dog had always been hyper. He was good for hunting but not much else. He usually slept out in the barn.

"Down, Ronald," said Bennie. He wanted to bend down and pet him, but it would have required too much effort. Gwen shook her hands dry, kissed Bennie on the head bandage, and gave him a hug. "Happy birthday," she said.

"Likewise," he said.

"Look at you, Bennie. You're a wreck." Gwen looked hearty—healthy skin, thick hair, new clothes, the sparkling eyes of an actress. She was polished in a way he'd never seen her. Gwen had always been one who derived a big part of her identity from the strength of her body, her athleticism, her ability to compete, and Bennie knew she'd been trying to translate this into stage presence. She was no longer a competitive athlete, but living in Brooklyn, she went to the gym all the time, and her arms and shoulders were strong. In heels, she was just an inch shorter than Bennie. Hugging Gwen reminded him that he needed to start eating again, in a serious way. In the hospital it had been mostly pudding or oatmeal.

"I mean, you look really bad," she said, smiling.

"I know," he said. "It's mostly the head bandage, though, isn't it?"

She squinted, looking him up and down. "Yeah, mostly the head bandage." He knew she was trying to make him feel better, but still, it worked.

"Where's Littlefield?" Bennie asked.

"He's in the basement." She shrugged. "That's where he went when I arrived." She took her glasses off and cleaned the lenses on her shirt. Since they were teenagers, Gwen and Littlefield had had a hard time sharing space. When Gwen was a junior in high school, she dated a kid from Bowdoin named Max Gates, and when Max came to the house early to pick her up for their second date, Littlefield answered the door (their mother was meeting with her investment club, and Coach had been dead for a few years). Max asked if he could wait for her inside. Littlefield let him in and pointed silently at the purple couch. He pretended to leave the room but stood in the doorway behind the couch and stared angrily at the back of Max's head while Max picked up the newspaper on the coffee table and flipped through it. After a few minutes, Littlefield yelled at him, asking him to stand up and empty his pockets, and then he searched Max's wallet for a rubber.

Littlefield rarely found good ways to express his affection for Gwen—he continued to be rude to her boyfriends until she moved to New York.

Bennie crutched to the cellar door. It was locked. He beat his fist against it and yelled, "Open up." Ronald stood beside Bennie and barked.

There was no response, but he heard faint scraping sounds, like the sliding of cardboard boxes across concrete.

"Bennie, you should get into bed," Gwen said.

He banged again. "It's me," he yelled. "Let me in." He leaned against the door and waited. Ronald barked a few more times, then quieted.

The kitchen smelled like bacon grease and spoiled milk. As he looked around, he heard the scraping sounds in the basement again. "What's he doing?" he asked Gwen.

She shrugged. "He was actually pretty nice at first. He even asked me a few questions about my life when he drove me back from the airport. But as soon as we got back, he went down there." She pointed at the door.

Gwen helped Bennie back into the living room, without his crutches, but just as they started moving, Littlefield's footsteps sounded on the basement stairs. This excited Ronald, who sprinted toward the cellar door, trying to squeeze between Bennie's good leg and his bad one. Gwen tried to hold Bennie up, but it all happened too quickly. He landed on his back.

Gwen crouched at his side, keeping Ronald from licking his face, and Littlefield stood over all of them, in dark blue coveralls spotted with dried paint. He had cobwebs in his hair, and on his right cheek there was a long, thin cut that had scabbed over. Bennie laughed. "You look like a monster."

Littlefield rubbed his hands over his face. "You mean the coveralls? They keep me warm, fuckface."

"What about that cut?"

Littlefield put his hand up to his cheek as though discovering it for the first time. Like Gwen, he had a young-looking face, which was offset by the gray hair at his temples. "I should be the one asking the questions, hombre. You're on the floor."

"Your dog knocked me down," Bennie said. From the floor he could see the windows; sun poked through the clouds.

Littlefield put a rough hand on Bennie's head, below the bandage. "Idiot doctors," he said. "They let you out too soon."

"Ronald knocked me down, Littlefield," he said. He propped himself up on one arm. As Gwen started helping him up, Ronald got a few good licks of his cheek. Gwen pushed the dog away again, then took one of Bennie's arms. Littlefield took the other.

"It must be the painkillers," said Littlefield. "They're too strong for you. What'd they give you?"

Gwen and Littlefield sat him at the table. Sometimes it was better to simply let Littlefield think he was right. He leaned Bennie's crutches against the table before unzipping the bag Bennie had brought with him from the hospital. When he found the bottle, he opened it and shook a few pills into his palm.

"Don't take his drugs," said Gwen.

Littlefield poured the pills back into the bottle. He was still looking at his brother. "Bennie, you should stay home for a while. Don't go into town," he said. Then he started walking to the bathroom. They heard him pour the pills into the toilet. He flushed.

When he came back into the kitchen he said, "Hey, Bennie, get into bed. You're sick."

"Did you just throw out all of my pills?" he asked.

"They're making you dizzy," said Littlefield.

"Yeah, they're also killing the pain," he said. "Painkillers."

"Are you in pain?"

"No, he isn't," said Gwen. "Because he's been taking those pills."

"It's better this way," said Littlefield.

Bennie was too tired to argue. Gwen didn't seem to want to continue the conversation either, so she and Littlefield helped him to his bedroom. Gwen had washed the sheets and neatened his room—the bedside lamp was on, casting a pool of warm yellow light on the glass of water she'd brought him. As soon as Bennie pulled the sheets up to his chin, Ronald came from the other room, leapt up onto the bed, and lay down by Bennie's feet, panting.

"Get off there, you stupid freak," said Littlefield.

"It's okay. I like him there," said Bennie.

"Suit yourself."

Littlefield stayed in the room, and before Bennie fell asleep he asked Littlefield about the night at the quarry. Littlefield laughed at first, saying he couldn't believe he'd run right off the edge. Bennie laughed a little, too, remembering the weightlessness of his body. Then he asked about LaBrecque.

"Yeah," said Littlefield. "They still can't find him. They've had dogs out there and everything."

"I saw Boak and Shaw before I got hurt," said Bennie.

"No shit, Bennie. They were the ones who helped get you to the hospital."

"Where were you?"

"Julian and I were following LaBrecque, up on the north side. He was moving fast. Julian couldn't keep up—he fell back—so it was just me chasing him. Eventually I lost track of LaBrecque, too. I got all the way to Roderick's farm. A hell of a walk." After a few seconds of silence, Littlefield shook his head. Bennie didn't understand: Littlefield had chased LaBrecque all the way to Roderick's farm? It was almost a mile from the quarry. Before Bennie's mouth could open again Littlefield shut off his light and told him to sleep, and then it was as though he was back at the hospital, working slowly through a flip book of dreams.

5

Not long before Coach died, just after Gwen and Bennie turned fourteen, they'd gone out to Cape Frederick. For years and years afterward, this was how Bennie thought of his father, how he dreamed about him: Coach standing on the rocks in his long brown spectator parka.

On that trip to Cape Fred, Bennie had been lying in the way back of the Vista Cruiser with Gwen, who was staring up at the drooping material hanging from the car's ceiling. Littlefield and the family dog, Nixon, were reclined in the backseat. Coach drove and Eleanor, their mother, sat beside him.

Back then, Gwen had short hair, spiked up with

mousse. In middle school everyone thought she was a wiseass. At sixteen, Littlefield hadn't yet made the switch to hard-nosed local; he was still unpredictable, of course, and if he punched you he didn't care if you cried, but otherwise he was good at school and excellent at any sport he tried. He had muscles before most of his peers. He kept a bigger padlock on his gym locker than he'd been issued. The teachers saw him for what he was: smart, determined, stubborn. Everyone called him Littlefield, their last name.

The highway toward the state beaches to the south was a wide smooth road built for Boston-style traffic, though it was often deserted. Someone in the state government had severely miscalculated and there it was, not far from the island, this superhighway. Back then, it felt as though the Littlefields were the only ones who used it. They were headed to Cape Fred for one of their regular visits to the back shore. During the ride Coach was keeping the kids updated on the story the *Press Herald* had been tracking, about a serial house thief whose ritualized break-ins up north were becoming big news. Bennie still remembered this clearly: the paper called the guy the Somerset Marauder. Most of what he stole (jewelry, cash, antiques) he sent to the Christian Scientists in Portland—to their headquarters, the First Church of Christ, Scientist. This was what Coach loved about the Marauder most of all—Coach wasn't a Christian Scientist himself, but he liked the idea of a group of people who renounced doctors and medicine. It was all part of his ongoing battle with his wife, who was a therapist and who believed in such things. She took his teasings well. He deserved a swift kick to the crotch, but she was respectful in holding her line. Even though the First Church of Christ, Scientist in Portland was publicly rejecting these gifts, Coach was cheering the thief's efforts. It was a good rivalry. Eleanor was primarily concerned with making sure the story wasn't scaring the kids—Gwen especially. Gwen may have been a wiseass, but she was prone to nightmares. A wiseass with a delicate heart.

Without turning around, Coach said, "You read the paper this morning? He's still out there." The ice crystals on the window beside Bennie were curved white ferns, and through them he caught glimpses of the plowed snowbanks beside the road. They were driving through the tundra; everything in the world was dead or sleeping. Bennie looked up and caught Coach's eyes in the rearview mirror as he said, "You hear me?"

Bennie didn't respond, not right away, but Coach could see him smiling.

"'Out there'? What do you mean, 'out there'?" said Littlefield. "Those guys on Deer Isle—didn't they get him?"

"Well, they screwed up," said Coach. "He's loose. They lost track of him."

Littlefield coughed out a laugh.

"You think this is funny?" asked Gwen. "This guy's going to get us."

"He won't *get* us," said Littlefield. "He doesn't *get* people. The worst he could do is steal our shit. That's what he does—he's a thief." Littlefield had recently gotten his driver's license, but when they traveled as a family, Coach always drove.

"Oh, he'll get us, all right," said Coach. "And he'll send the proceeds to Portland." He put his blinker on a quarter-mile from the exit, and when they finally turned off the highway, he glided to a stop at the end of the ramp.

"Stop that, William," said Eleanor. "Stop that right now."

That year had been a good one for Gwen and Littlefield and Bennie, biathlon-wise—they were interested in the training (not just to appease Coach) and they were becoming proficient skiers and even better target shooters. Gwen and Bennie were tall for fourteen—Bennie was still shorter than his twin sister by a few inches, then—and despite their awkwardness, Coach was making minor adjustments (pole placement, ski kick, wax, breathing) to help them put it all together. Littlefield, at sixteen, with strong legs, was starting to win races.

Coach went on, "They were taking him to the police, those guys who found him—they were clammers, and they were looking for attention. They made a big deal about how they'd caught the guy, but then they got into some kind of accident," he said. "I think they panicked. They didn't report it until they were sure they couldn't find him."

"Clammers," said Littlefield, cracking his knuckles. "How screwed up is that. What a bunch of amateurs."

"He's a battler," said Coach.

"You're still *rooting* for this criminal?" said Eleanor.

"He's an expert," said Coach. "He's the best at what he does. He made the clammers look like assholes!"

"Stop, William. The man defecates in the houses he ransacks," said Eleanor, and this was true. The paper hadn't reported it, but Coach had heard the rumor. The pooping was an old form of humiliation, a longstanding tradition among house thieves in Maine. A windowsill turd, a reminder of the thief's dominance. This thrilled Bennie and Gwen and Littlefield, of course, and Coach knew it did; he wouldn't refer to it directly, but he would praise the thief, forcing his wife to bring it up as a counterargument. It worked every time.

"Wouldn't that be righteous if he shit somewhere in the Manse? In the Manse, instead of all the other houses to choose from?" said Littlefield.

"And then he could come in and slice me up, too," said Gwen, in a calm voice. "And steal my stuff." Besides the nightmares, she also had trouble falling asleep at night, when too often there was a fluttering inside her head. She'd wake up screaming, which would wake them all up—and as they were falling back to sleep, eventually, Gwen would get up and sit at her desk, practice her drums. She used a drum pad, so it was relatively quiet, but you could still hear the sticks beating against the rubber: *thumpity, thumpity, thumpity, thumpity.*

"Honey, don't say that," said Eleanor. "That's an awful thing to say."

"Coach likes him," Gwen said. "He wants the guy to poop in the Manse, to steal our stuff, to slice me up into little—"

Their mother turned around in her seat and shot a look back at them. Gwen was lying down again, out of view. "No more of this. Don't say things like that. That's just not true."

"Don't worry, Gwen. I'd take care of him if he broke into the Manse," said Littlefield. He bounced in his seat. "I'd take him down with my bare hands. I have to say, though, that's pretty badass, the shitting. I should do that in the next race we go to, after a win." His biathlon jersey was rolled up to his shoulder, and when he saw that Bennie was looking over the seat at him, he flexed. His arms looked like Bennie's arms, pale and hairless, but when he flexed it looked as though he'd slipped an ostrich egg under the skin. When he stopped bouncing and flexing he put his fingers through his hair, spiking it up.

"We don't lock the Manse," Bennie said. "It wouldn't take much for him to break in."

"He hasn't robbed any houses anywhere near us," said their mother.

"Yeah, but he's moving toward us," said Gwen. "He's going by county. Penobscot, Waldo, Knox, Lincoln. Lincoln, right? Lincoln was where they caught him. A few poops each time. That's what they've been saying, right?"

"From now on, you may not watch the news," said their mother. "No more news. None." Then she turned to Coach. "Why bring this up?"

"He's an expert," repeated Coach. "He's a master at his craft. He brings it to the First Church of Christ, Scientist."

"He's a friggin' house robber," said Littlefield. "Watch what happens when he gets to our island. Watch what happens when he runs into the likes of me."

"Enough," said their mother.

"Is he religious?" Bennie asked. No one responded.

"Hey, ass-muncher," said Littlefield. "Why the hell would he be religious?"

"Language!" said Eleanor.

"He gives the stuff to the First Church of Christ, Scientist," said Bennie.

"Oh," said Littlefield. "Yeah."

When they pulled past the crumbling brown sign for Cape Frederick and into the empty parking lot, Nixon started dancing in the backseat, wriggling and slapping the plastic inside of the car with her tail. Littlefield opened his door and she climbed over him, and the family watched her click across the pavement in the direction of the ocean, then bound through the brush to the rocks. They got out and followed her. Catching that first look at the huge view of ocean, Bennie felt heroic, a ship captain exploring new territory, but quickly enough he looked down at all the brittle, wind-beaten brush, like the frayed ends of nylon rope, and the endless shale, common in their part of the state, rocks that looked bored by the repetition of it all. He kept a tennis ball in the pocket of his coat to throw for Nixon.

Already Gwen was pointing to spots along the water's edge in the distance and asking, "Is that one?"

Coach squinted and said, "Nope."

They were looking for light blue herons, a rare bird—though Coach claimed to have seen one on several occasions. He said they were smaller than great blue herons, bulkier and craftier, better fishermen. Gwen didn't know what they looked like, but she was vigilant whenever they went to Cape Fred—even in wintertime, when she knew they wouldn't be there and looked for them only out of habit. In private Littlefield told Gwen and Bennie that he suspected Coach was bullshitting them, that there was no such bird.

Eleanor kept her arms folded on her chest and her knitted purple hat pulled down just above her eyes. She was still annoyed by the conversation in the car. On most of these excursions to Cape Fred she brought her bulky black camera, which hung around her neck. She almost never took pictures.

Bennie had always wanted to shadow his mother at the hospital when she went in to do her rounds, but she claimed it wouldn't be appropriate. He found ways to be privy to her work by other means. If one of them got hurt at home, she would patch them up; she sewed stitches in Littlefield's knee once, and she always knew which injuries were serious and which were not. She was a therapist and a school counselor, but she'd gone to medical school. She hadn't gotten her medical degree, not quite—instead of a psychiatry residency, she got a social work degree. Whenever Bennie was in town with his mother and they'd cross paths with someone she wouldn't introduce to him, he knew the person was a regular client, or someone she'd treated in the hospital. This was an unmistakable tipoff; she was too polite to forgo introductions. When she wasn't counseling at Musquacook Academy she worked on the psychiatric wing at the hospital, and most of these patients looked like normal people, but occasionally Bennie and she would come across someone with sharp, clear eyes who would mutter a few words about the leaves in their yard, and Bennie would be electrified by what was being hidden from him.

Coach looked out at the water and said, "Now, *that* is one hell of an ocean." Eleanor exhaled. Then she said, "It's too cold today." Bennie was throwing the ball for Nixon but the others were just standing and staring at the water, like hunters waiting for a moose to rise from the bog.

This memory came back to Bennie so often in dreams that it arrived in a kind of shorthand: his mother's weary expression, Gwen's pink wrists sticking out from the cuffs of her jacket, Coach and Littlefield standing side by side in their spectator parkas (the kind that covers your ass and encourages you to stuff your hands in the front pockets).

There were thin wisps of sea smoke on the water and a layer of mist just above the dark blue expanse, but otherwise the view was as sharp as it usually was in winter—no islands on the horizon. Cape Frederick curled out to the south, and though its tip was five miles away, Bennie could see snow on the rocks there, and the crisp outline of trees. Otherwise, water dominated the view—a dark blue blanket, nearly black.

They all called Nixon a "prize dog," their euphemism for a dog blessed with enthusiasm but lacking intelligence. Coach had gone north to buy her from a breeder in Millinocket who specialized in Labrador retrievers—Nixon was an easy choice, he said, though Bennie wondered about this. She was fat but still youthfully strong and vigorous, an excellent swimmer, a heroic eater. As a fetcher of tennis balls, she was unstoppable. Sometimes the boys would take her out to the unmowed field by the technical college; they'd put a Nerf football in her mouth and she'd know to run. They'd chase after her, diving at her thick brown body to tackle her, and when she'd fall, slamming hard against the ground, she'd bounce right back up, not knowing the rules of football; she'd keep thundering along, not anticipating the next tackle, thinking only about getting the ball to a safe place where she could chew it. Secretly, Bennie knew Nixon suffered from the high expectations Coach put on her; before he'd married Eleanor he had a Brittany spaniel named Ike who loved to hunt. (Now Littlefield's dog Ronald was modeled after Ike, though Littlefield would not admit this.)

Throwing the ball for her at Cape Fred, Bennie always started with short tosses, warm-ups, getting Nixon wet and accustomed to the exercise. She was an expert at staying on task, and there was something about her dark chestnut-colored hair that suggested stubbornness.

After the warm-ups Bennie threw the ball as far out into the ocean as he could. It fell through the sea smoke to a spot just beyond the single lobster buoy within their sight. The buoy had probably been swept in by a storm—few men set traps during winter, and if they did, they set them in deeper water. Nixon galloped down the shale, then bounded into the waves, swimming with a noticeable wake despite the windy chop, toward the place where the ball had splashed. Her fat made her buoyant, and she was powerful enough that her back stayed well above the surface of the water when she swam at full strength.

As Nixon made her steady way toward the ball, Bennie watched her closely, thinking it was amazing that this animal, *their* animal, who slept on the old purple couch and never barked when strangers came to the door, didn't hesitate to brave the icy water in mid-March.

Nixon must not have seen the ball through the sea smoke, because she went right for the red buoy and bit into it. Bennie was pleased the dog believed him strong enough to throw a lobster pot thirty yards offshore. He found it odd and charming that Nixon was attempting to retrieve the buoy. He was proud of her.

Gwen laughed. "Look at her! How did she fit that thing in her mouth?"

"Good girl," said Littlefield. "Thatta girl, Nixon. Good dog."

Nixon was swimming at her usual rate, full speed. She'd spun a tight U-turn and was swimming back toward shore now, with the red buoy in her mouth. There must have been some slack in the line, because her body made a clear wake, the kind a lobster boat might make, only smaller. But when the line tightened up, the wake stopped.

"Now, we've all heard of a shithouse rat," said Littlefield. "Well, that right there is a shithouse dog. That dog is as nuts as Gwen. Maybe more nuts." Then he raised his voice. "Good dog, Nixon, good dog."

"William, that's cruel," said their mother.

"You don't think Nixon's crazy?" said Littlefield, jabbing a finger out toward the dog, who was snorting at the seawater. "Look at that."

"Apologize to your sister," said Coach.

"A shithouse dog," said Gwen. "I like that. That's exactly what Nixon is."

Eleanor didn't go along with the cheering. She still had her arms folded on her chest and even with her wool hat pulled down, deep lines showed on her forehead. She said, "I don't like this at all—she's going to hurt herself."

Coach was staring at the dog, sternly.

Littlefield said, "Well, it's Bennie's fault. Why'd you throw it all the way out there, ass-muncher?"

"She's swum farther before," he said, but he wasn't sure she had. Then he added, "I wasn't aiming for the buoy."

"She'll be fine," said Gwen. "She'll figure it out." Gwen would do this sometimes—invest her own intelligence in people or animals with lesser gifts. Then Gwen said something that made everyone feel even more uneasy. "She's a prize dog—she'll be fine."

Nixon was bearing down. They saw her clearly: a brown seal in the waves, highlighted by the cherry red buoy, which must have been attached to a stray metal lobster trap—perhaps unattended for weeks, perhaps full of crabs and urchins and sculpin and lobsters, with bricks built into its sides to help it stay on the bottom. Even so, it seemed as though she was covering ground, dragging the heavy trap several yards across the rocky ocean floor. After a few minutes, though, she really didn't seem any closer, and her head was lower in the water. They watched as a tall, thick swell passed over her—a wave that she normally would have risen with, but the tether held her under. After the wave passed, her head and the buoy were in view again. She snorted, loudly enough that the whole family could hear.

"Shithouse!" yelled Littlefield, but everyone else was quiet. Coach was unlacing his brown boots.

"William, what are you doing?" asked Eleanor.

"That dog's going to drown," said Coach. He'd taken off his parka, too, and was unbuckling his belt.

"It's March, William," said Eleanor. "You can't go out there."

"Jesus," snapped Coach. When he yelled, it got everyone's heartbeat going. "You want the dog to die?"

Gwen was starting to cry, so Bennie hugged her. "Come on, you crazy hound," she said.

"Well, I don't want *you* to die," said their mother, who looked confused and startled. Gwen held a similar expression while she took Coach's clothes from him as he disrobed. "Just come back quickly, if you can't get her," their mother said.

"I'll get her," he said.

Coach was naked now, and by the way he moved down the shale, in nearly a run, it was clear he was ignoring the pain in his feet. They'd all seen his body in the bathroom—there was only one upstairs in the Manse, and all five of them used it—but here, his white body cast against the gothic browns of Cape Fred, against the backdrop of black water, he looked like some version of Early Man. He still had most of his Marine Corps muscles. His back and his legs were strong. The family followed him to the water's edge, but even with boots on, they couldn't get down there as quickly as he had. When Gwen and Bennie and Littlefield and Eleanor reached the waves, Coach had already lowered himself in. That was the trickiest part—getting into the water and away from the rocks while the waves came pounding in. He lost his balance when the first wave crested, but he put his hands down on the shale in front of him and took the frigid roller in his face before scooting out into deeper water.

He swam a breaststroke toward Nixon, which seemed to take too long, and when he reached the dog, she was still intent on bringing the buoy back to shore but was low in the water now, just keeping her nose above the surface. When Coach reached her, he ripped the buoy out of her mouth, jerking her head to the side. He threw the buoy overhand behind her, and she weakly started to U-turn again, to fetch the buoy once more—Bennie loved her for this—but Coach grabbed her collar and redirected her toward land. Once they were on course, he didn't need to hold on to her. They swam side by side. For all her diligence, she, like most dogs, didn't dwell on the past. Her owner was swimming beside her, and she had no ball in her mouth. She kept swimming.

Ten yards away, Gwen started cheering them on. "Almost home, almost home! Let's get some, soldier! Here we go, here we go!" Eleanor was silent, gripping the collar of her coat. Nixon and Coach were barely making progress. Coach's stroke had switched to a kind of dog paddle, and his eyes looked unfocused, though his lips were pursed tightly together. Bennie saw the look of one of his mother's patients in those eyes—intent, but lost. Just after they'd started cheering, a wave came over Coach's head, and when it passed, he was gone.

They lurched as a family toward the water, but Littlefield was the first to remove his parka. Eleanor held back Bennie, who grabbed Gwen. Eleanor made a few whining noises, holding on to Bennie and Gwen and watching Littlefield, who charged into the waves and was still able to stand when he reached Coach. Then Littlefield was stumbling back up the rocks with his naked father in his arms—Coach's large turnip-colored body, stark white and wet, his brown hair matted against his head by salt water. His eyes were open and still held that look—as though he knew something crucial was missing. He was coughing meekly, which seemed a good sign. And he wasn't shaking; he wasn't moving much at all.

Bennie took hold of him, too, from the other side and helped Littlefield carry him up the rocks. Eleanor had taken her coat off and had wrapped it around Coach's waist. Gwen had taken hers off and put it around his chest, under his armpits. They assumed this would warm him up, but when they reached the bushes, Coach wasn't responding to anything they did or said.

Even so, his wife spoke to him. "We're taking you to the hospital," she said.

Under normal circumstances, being carried would not have been acceptable to Coach. And going to the hospital would be out of the question. But he said nothing.

"You're sick right now, William," Eleanor continued.

When they got him to the Vista Cruiser, they stretched him out in the backseat and their mother lay beside him. Littlefield started the car. Their mother was hugging Coach in the backseat while the kids took off more of their clothes and covered their parents.

In the midst of this Gwen looked up and said, "Where's Nixon?"

Littlefield hopped out. Bennie had just taken off his sweater and was wrapping it around Coach's shoulders when Littlefield grabbed him by the shirt collar and twisted the cotton in his fists. He said, "You drive the car. You know how to get to the hospital. Once you get him inside, come back for me and Nixon."

Eleanor was hugging Coach, rubbing his arms and his back. Bennie didn't have a license, but he followed Littlefield's instructions. He put the Vista Cruiser into gear and lurched out onto the main road. He knew the basics from the handful of times Coach let him drive on the island. He'd never used a directional signal. They were passing streets he recognized, but everything looked new and large from the driver's side. Within minutes they were gliding to a stop in front of the hospital. A scrawny man in a bathrobe smoking a cigarette stood by the front doors. "I'll get out of your way," he said.

Coach was unable to walk—he was barely conscious—but he still managed to seem angry. His eyebrows were wet, and his hair, which was usually parted neatly, looked like marsh grass, matted down. Bennie opened the back door of the Vista Cruiser and hooked his arms under Coach's armpits to pull him out. Gwen grabbed his legs. They carried him until their mother brought a wheelchair. His calves and his arms were cold and heavy. Gwen went back to the Vista Cruiser to get the armful of clothes they'd draped over him in the car, and she covered him up again.

As soon as Eleanor rolled Coach through the hospital doors, Bennie climbed back into the Vista Cruiser and with one hand on top of the steering wheel he shifted into gear.

On the access road to Cape Fred, Bennie saw them—they were on the shoulder, Littlefield stooped over Nixon. The dog was on her side. Bennie sped up, and when he got to them, he stomped on the brakes, skidding in the gravel. Littlefield picked Nixon up in his arms and said, "Door," so Bennie hopped out and ran around to the other side of the car. He let them into the backseat.

Once Bennie closed the door, he sprinted back around to the driver's side, Littlefield yelling, "Go! Go! Go!"

Bennie cranked the wheel and the Vista Cruiser spun in a neat circle, dipping just slightly into the shoulder before straightening out. "Where?" he shouted.

"Home," said Littlefield. "I've got the stuff to help her back there."

In the backseat, she was panting. Bennie didn't want to ask Littlefield any questions. He didn't want to know how bad off Nixon was. Somehow Littlefield had diagnosed the dog and knew what needed to be done.

When they got to the Manse, Littlefield wouldn't let Bennie into the barn while he worked on Nixon, so Bennie stood just outside the tall wooden doors in the cold. He asked, "How's it going?" and heard a quiet, muffled "Fine" from inside.

It was just after dark when an unfamiliar car pulled into the driveway. The headlights blinded Bennie, who was still leaning against the barn. The car doors slammed. Then Eleanor and Gwen were walking on either side of Coach, all three of them moving slowly. When they reached the barn door, the car pulled back out of the driveway.

"Where's your brother?" said Coach.

"He's in the barn with Nixon," said Bennie.

"Is the dog okay?" asked Coach.

"I don't know."

Littlefield called through the doors. "She'll be fine."

"Aren't you cold in there?" asked Eleanor.

"I'm fine," said Littlefield.

"I'm cold," said Bennie.

"You have enough light?" asked Eleanor.

"It's fine," said Littlefield.

Bennie asked, "Are you all right, Coach?"

"Those doctors are a bunch of assholes," he said. "Every one of them, except your mother."

"She's a psychologist," said Gwen.

Littlefield continued to shout through the doors. He said, "They put you in the tub, Coach?" Gwen and Bennie and Littlefield had all been in the hot tub at the hospital, which they used for hypothermic lobstermen—when their mother worked shifts at the hospital, she'd let them get in if it wasn't being used.

"Yeah, they put me in the tub. But I could have done that at home," he said.

"We were scared," said Gwen.

"Next time, ask me," he said.

"You were catatonic," said Eleanor.

"Well, next time you'll know—don't take me to the goddamn hospital." His voice was hoarse and strained. His face was blanched. He could tell he'd hurt Gwen's feelings, so he said, "Gwen, it's not your fault." Then he looked at the barn doors and raised his voice again. "Come out here, William."

Littlefield unlatched the lock. He opened one of the barn's tall doors just enough to stick his head through. "I need you to sterilize some instruments, Bennie," he said, passing through the crack his Swiss army knife and two small flathead screwdrivers. "Just boil them in water for a few minutes. That should do it."

"Is the dog okay?" asked Coach.

"She's stable," he said. "Just in case, I'm getting her on some mechanical ventilation."

"For Christ's sake, William," said Coach. "If the dog's okay, the dog's okay."

"I might need to manually inflate the lungs, Coach," he said.

When Coach walked toward the barn doors, Littlefield shut them, and they could hear him fumbling with the lock.

"Open up right now," said Coach.

"It's just a joke," said Littlefield. "Take it easy."

"Open the door!" bellowed Coach.

The lock clicked. Littlefield pushed the door open a few inches. Coach grabbed the edges of both doors and flung them open. Littlefield had dragged one of Coach's workbenches over to the warm stove and to the side of the workbench he'd clipped a lamp, which was casting a pool of light over Nixon, lying in a wicker laundry basket. She was panting, and when she saw Coach, she hopped out of the basket and ran toward the door. It was warm inside the barn. Bennie looked at his brother and saw that he did actually look concerned. Not about the dog, probably, but about Coach. He'd wanted to be alone. His eyes were red from crying. Bennie hadn't liked being locked outside the barn, but now it made more sense.

"This dog does not need an operation," said Coach.

"Man, it's warm in here," said Gwen. "I can't believe you locked Bennie out in the cold."

"All right, all right," said Eleanor. "Let's get everyone in the house."

Nixon jumped up and put her front paws on Coach's waist. "Good girl," said Coach.

Littlefield walked back toward the stove, shut its flue, and turned off the light. "The dog's just as tough as you, Coach."

It was just a month later that Coach died; he was only fifty-one. Eleanor said it was his heart. "His heart let him down," she said. He'd been in the backyard building a shed for the lawn mower. Littlefield was with him when he died. The family was blindsided of course—it didn't seem possible that no one would ever hear his voice again, never see him walk into the kitchen early in the morning, rubbing the back of his neck. The boys and Gwen took a break from biathlon. Littlefield spent more and more time away from the Manse working odd jobs—construction and painting and boatyard work—and less time at school. Gwen gave up the drums and started acting in plays. Bennie felt the hours of the day washing over him as if he were impervious to the whims of the world. He saw that his brother was feeling the same way, but they didn't talk about it; they stayed silent. He felt strangely close to his brother then. It was important for Bennie to see Littlefield arrive back from work each day, to see that he was safe.

After Bennie and Gwen had finished high school, their mother moved up to the town of Clover Lake, into a small but well-built colonial on fifty acres, beside the lake. It was Coach's family that was from Meadow Island—he'd grown up in a three-room house at the center of the island, without any views of the ocean. She'd liked living on the island, but after he died she felt claustrophobic, and she knew it would be difficult to stay tied to the community without Coach. She got the sense people resented her wealth and that she was from Massachusetts. Bennie knew it didn't help that she was judgmental about the way locals polluted the harbor and developed the land—she was outspoken about this, and it didn't win her many friends. In the end, it seemed, she felt good about leaving the house to her children, letting them take care of it, as long as she could visit once in a while. Littlefield tried to skip town whenever this happened.

For a while, Bennie continued to keep track of the Somerset Marauder. No one ever caught him. He had a few close calls with the authorities, but he always ended up outfoxing them, and Bennie convinced himself to adopt his father's position. He started rooting for the thief, hoping he'd continue his dominance, elude the cops. Soon, though, the Marauder stopped burglarizing and the southward trend was halted. He never made it to the Manse—he didn't even reach their county—and the newspapers discontinued their stories.

6

Bennie slept for much of the next day. The man in charge of his care, Dr. Miner, had a pinched face but round, kind gray eyes. He'd said leaving the hospital and heading home would be as exhausting as running a marathon. Bennie assumed this comment applied to older patients, but for the first few days back on the island he rarely left his bed or the purple couch in the living room. He dreamt of running races in his cast, with his crutches; after each race ended, another starting gun fired. He wondered if his fatigue had come mostly from the drugs they'd given him in the hospital. In one of the marathon dreams, he was running against dogs, huskies, their paws thundering against the snowpack.

For the first day after Littlefield flushed his painkillers down the toilet, Bennie was okay if he didn't move, but he hated how everything felt, sharp and scratchy and newly awake. The pain was the least of his worries. He stopped drifting around in his head. He got bored. His legs became restless. The world felt drab and pointless. In bed he ran through his memories of falling—especially the instant he landed, before his head hit the ice—and he tried to work backwards from there, trying to guess how he might have contributed to LaBrecque's disappearance. Littlefield had said he and LaBrecque and Julian were chasing each other on the north side of the quarry, and the others—Boak and Shaw—were on the south side. It seemed unlikely that LaBrecque had fallen into the quarry if he and Littlefield were headed in the direction of Roderick's farm, but maybe Littlefield had lost track of LaBrecque sooner than he'd thought.

Between his naps, Gwen came in with a bowl of steaming potato soup on a plastic tray. Ronald stayed up on Bennie's bed when Gwen wasn't walking or feeding him. With Gwen back at the Manse, Bennie was aware of how the place looked; the disintegrating plumbing, leaks cracking the plaster in the ceiling, all the windowsills covered with dust and dead flies. Bennie knew Gwen didn't like that he and Littlefield were letting the family house fall apart, but she kept quiet while he was still recovering from his fall. No one had repaired the hole in the living room or patched the gap in the eaves where the raccoon had originally gained entry.

Their mother called from Florida, where she spent three weeks every winter, on Sanibel Island in a house she shared with her cousin Linnea. Gwen had left the phone next to Bennie's bed when she drove to the supermarket, so he answered it. Their mother wasn't always away on Bennie's and Gwen's birthdays, but the fares had been good—though a few hundred dollars here and there didn't make much difference to her.

She never said hello when she called. This time, she said, "Is this true? Did you fall?"

"I fell, Mom. But I'm fine. The paper didn't tell the whole story." He was still half asleep.

"The paper? There was something in the paper? All I know is what Dora Thompson told me. Why haven't any of you called me?"

"Mrs. Thompson called you? In Florida?"

"Honestly, Benjamin—are you okay?"

"I need to rest, Mom. That's all."

"Do you still have insurance? I'm coming home."

"Yes, I have insurance. You don't need to come home. It's fine. Come back when you were planning on coming back."

"Did I wake you?"

"Yes."

"Dora Thompson said you might have broken your neck."

Mrs. Thompson was a Meadow Island neighbor—they rarely saw her, but she was a prodigious gatherer of information about other people's lives. Eleanor asked Bennie where he'd been treated (Bennie was surprised Mrs. Thompson hadn't told her) and he said the Adventist. She sighed, and he reminded her he'd fallen in Keep's Quarry, and Mid-coast, the hospital that had employed her for years, was farther away. (He refrained from telling her that he'd been unconscious and that they'd been driven into town by a logging truck.)

He told her there was no way the fall could have broken his neck—this of course was a lie—and then he said he was exhausted. She was glad to hear Gwen had flown in and was helping. She was due back in a few weeks, and she told Bennie she would come straight to the house. "That'll be perfect," he said, tired and annoyed by her worry. He knew she didn't want to interrupt her Florida vacation.

"But there's a boy who's missing, still?"

"Who told you that?"

"Dora Thompson."

"He's missing, but he might never have been lost."

"That makes no sense, Benjamin."

"He might have just left town."

"Well, I hope he's okay. Just imagine how *his* mother is doing. Now, Benjamin: I've just sent off a case of oranges and grapefruit. It should be arriving in three or four days. If it doesn't, let me know, and I'll talk to the man I bought them from."

"I'll look out for them, Mom," he said. When he hung up, he was still annoyed, but also oddly relieved to be back in touch with her.

And then he drifted off again. Sleep afforded him something that his waking life didn't. He loved the way his dreams presented situations and interaction that could be both chaotic and unpredictable but that somehow seemed to make perfect sense.

On the third day after leaving the hospital, he no longer felt like lying on the couch. The stillness of the house was making him fidgety. He wanted to shake his head clear, he wanted to stop feeling tired, and he figured that going to the animal hospital and seeing his boss, Handelmann, would help. Most of the pain had subsided, and he wasn't so glum anymore. When Littlefield had first called Bennie in the hospital, he'd told him he was filling in for him at the shelter, so it wasn't as though Bennie needed to get back to work immediately. Still, he wanted to touch base with his boss. He was sure Handelmann would have some petty complaints about Littlefield.

He felt the need to see Helen, too—they'd left messages for each other, but it wasn't until that third day that he actually felt presentable. He no longer felt embarrassed about telling her he loved her, even though it was ridiculously premature. He guessed she understood he was loopy from the drugs. He didn't even care if they had another conversation about paintball. He knew, though, that the topic would be less fun if he was still in obvious discomfort—a victim of war games idiocy—so even though he was wearing a cast, he wanted to be up and around, healthy-seeming, before he saw her.

Gwen slipped a trash bag over Bennie's cast so he could shower. She was sitting on the toilet seat, wearing Bennie's Red Sox cap, still looking glamorous in her new glasses, but more and more she was resembling the stubborn athlete Bennie knew, the old Gwen, the tomboy. She told him she'd called the temp agency in New York and postponed her return indefinitely. There were a few auditions in April she was hoping to attend, but she could decide about them later. Bennie thought this was great news.

After he was done, he wrapped a towel around his waist and Gwen dried the trash bag before taking off the rubber bands. "Littlefield doesn't answer my questions about the night at the quarry," she said. "All he says is that he was following LaBrecque, but then he lost him. It's hard to imagine someone outrunning Littlefield in the snow."

"The visibility was shit," said Bennie. He stepped out of the shower and walked to his bedroom. Gwen stayed in the bathroom.

"Did they fire any shots?" she shouted.

"I can hear you fine," he said, pulling sweatpants on over his cast. "I think he would have told me if he had."

"Have you seen him since your first night back?"

"No," said Bennie, zipping his sweatshirt. He stepped back into the hall.

"That's what I mean. He's being weird. It's like he doesn't want to be around me at all."

"I wouldn't take it personally."

"Why would he be hiding things from me?"

"It's not about you," said Bennie, tying his boots. "He gets in these moods."

"I think it's more than that. He's ashamed about something. There's something he doesn't want to talk to me about."

"Don't you think he would have told us if he'd done something wrong?"

"Of course not," she snapped.

This made Bennie furious. "Maybe he wouldn't tell *you.* But I was there. He's not hiding anything."

"Don't act like Mom, Bennie. Don't be *intentionally* clueless."

It was true that the family often made excuses for Littlefield. It had always been obvious that Littlefield had been Coach's favorite, and their mother would make it easier on Littlefield by covering up his coarseness or selfishness by saying *He is who he is.* Gwen, especially, hated this. But in this instance, Bennie knew that Littlefield wasn't hiding anything from Gwen. Littlefield was just anxious about having visitors, and having Bennie in the hospital for a few days had been hard on him, too.

Bennie wanted to yell at Gwen—he was that angry—but he knew how tough on her Littlefield could be and he didn't want it to seem that everyone in the house was against her. He breathed deeply and then said, "I'll keep talking to him about it, and I'll let you know what I find out."

When Bennie had started the job at Esker Cove, he didn't realize it was going to involve so much animal carnage. His main duties were these: cleaning cages, expressing anal glands, and helping to put dogs and cats to sleep. Just a few days after he'd started the job, he'd wanted to quit, but knowing that someone else was holding the animals when they got the needle would have made him feel like he was chickening out. So he stuck with it. Also, there was the pay, which was fair, and occasionally he got to do other things, like removing a cat from its cage with cat tongs and putting it in a cat bag so he could prep it for an operation. He was in charge of weighing the animals and helping them calm down.

Handelmann looked like the host of a public television children's show. He wouldn't hesitate to euthanize animals, but he never swore, and he ironed his own shirts. Everyone on the island seemed to appreciate him, but he had no close friends, no family, which was rare for a forty-year-old man in the area. Handelmann maintained an emotionless formality much of the time. Because he was a veterinarian with no friends, Bennie kept looking for clues that the animals provided him with a certain kind of comfort and camaraderie, but he didn't think they did. It wasn't as though he disliked the animals, but he showed them no special loyalty.

When Bennie and Gwen arrived, his boss was washing his hands, his back to them. He was clean-cut, tall and thin, with blond hair, creased trousers, expensive shoes.

"Bennie," he said, without turning around. "How's my old soldier doing?"

"Much better, actually," said Bennie.

"How's the leg?" Handelmann asked. He shook his hands in the sink, his back still turned to them.

"Fine."

"They found that other young man yet?"

"No."

"You coming back soon?" he asked.

"Yup."

"Good," he said. "Your brother's a flake. Things are backing up here." Handelmann used several paper towels to dry his hands, then turned and was startled to see Gwen standing in front of him. He extended a hand graciously to her and said, "You must be Bennie's twin." His grin was careful. "But that's odd: you're much too pretty." He turned to Bennie and said, "Assist me with a dog, would you?"

It was Ollie, a black Lab and mastiff combo with tumors in his neck. Ollie's owners had asked that he be put down. Handelmann led the dog into the room, knelt down, took him around the chest, and hefted him up to the lower of the two steel tables. Ollie seemed unusually lethargic. Bennie remembered Ollie as a younger dog, coming in with his owner, Mrs. Samuels, to get heartworm meds. Ollie enjoyed the swamps behind the Samuels house and didn't mind the swarming mosquitoes. You could tell from Ollie's shoulders that he was a frequent swimmer. Bennie held on to him so that Handelmann could give him the shot. Gwen stepped back, sitting down to watch. Ollie didn't have much fat on him but he was at least twice the size of most dogs Handelmann treated. Bennie felt the dog twitch slightly when the needle went in, but his muscles didn't loosen as they did with most dogs within seconds of getting the shot.

"Don't hold on so tightly," said Handelmann. "See if he'll drop on his own."

Bennie loosened his grip and Ollie remained standing.

"One more shot," said Handelmann, so Bennie hugged the dog again, and Handelmann reloaded and stuck the dog a second time. There was no twitch. Ollie stared straight ahead. Again, Bennie stopped hugging to see if Ollie would fall. The dog's eyelids drooped, but he was stable. Bennie rocked him back and forth a bit but he kept his balance. "Jiminy," said Handelmann, tossing the needle to the table and turning to his instrument drawer. He pulled out an even bigger syringe. It was like a small jousting lance, and Handelmann looked like he was struggling to hold it with one hand. Bennie looked over his shoulder and saw that Gwen was crying. With the huge needle, Handelmann drew in the pentobarbital and then sunk the needle into the dog's hindquarters. Ollie made a quiet, low growl. Bennie squeezed him around the neck and shoulders. "It's okay, Ollie, it's okay," Bennie said, which made Handelmann look at him askance. Handelmann said, "Please let go of the dog." When he did, Ollie sat down, but he didn't fall over. He blinked, then started panting. Handelmann pushed the dog's shoulder but the dog didn't budge. "Heavens," he said. He drew more pentobarbital into the needle, and this time he jabbed Ollie with it more swiftly, and Ollie didn't make a sound. Bennie wondered what the dog was feeling, what he was seeing. Handelmann told Bennie, again, to stop hugging the dog. Ollie dropped his head a bit, and as soon as he did, Gwen came to the table and embraced the dog. Handelmann stayed quiet. It was after the third shot with the big needle, the fifth shot overall, that Ollie's legs finally failed; he surrendered his body to Gwen. She tried to ease him down to the table, but his limp weight must have surprised her. The powerful muscles in Gwen's arms tensed, but still, Ollie made a loud sound as he hit the steel. Gwen continued hugging Ollie, awkwardly, and Bennie slid himself to the other side of the table and held on to him from there.

When they were done, Handelmann said, "It might take you a while before you're ready to come back to this, Bennie. You're out of practice."

"Do you even have a heart?" asked Gwen. She was still kneeling on the floor, holding the dog.

"Gwen," said Bennie. "This is what we do all the time." He was embarrassed about her comment, but it was true—he'd somehow forgotten what it was like to kill a dog, and Handelmann seemed especially cold.

"Ollie was in pain," said Handelmann. He pulled the dead dog by the collar, sliding him off the table and into a sling.

"I'll carry him," said Gwen. "This is just horrible."

Managing the crematorium was a big part of Bennie's job. Handelmann tried to help Gwen as she carried the dead dog, and Bennie mounted his crutches and followed them out back. The door to the crematorium was open and Littlefield was inside. Handelmann said, "Look at this. He showed up."

In the middle of the little wooden shed, beside the cinderblock kiln, was a pile of dead animals, and Littlefield was kneeling beside the bodies, waiting to fit the next one into the incinerator. He turned to Gwen. "Just drop that one over there," he said, pointing to the far side of the pile. Once they unloaded Ollie from the sling, Gwen started holding her nose. She asked if she could go wait in the car. Bennie told her he'd be along in a few minutes.

After she left, Handelmann asked, "Your sister. Remind me. Is she married?"

"No," said Bennie. "Unfortunately, though, she lives in Brooklyn."

"Is that right?" said Handelmann, smiling politely. "She's a beautiful girl."

Littlefield said, "You've got no chance with her, bub."

Handelmann shrugged. "I'll leave you to your work here, gentlemen." He closed the door behind him.

"Why be such an asshole?" Bennie asked.

"Just stating facts," his brother said.

It was always better in the crematorium when the fire was at full power; the burning smell was much better than the fetid stink of rotting organs and congealing dog blood. Littlefield had the fire cranked up and the dogs were burning fast. You'd think it'd smell mostly of burning fur, but what struck Bennie always was how much it smelled like any other fire—a bonfire or barbecue—just earthy smoke.

Ollie had struck an awkward pose when he tumbled from the sling—his back was twisted around and his legs were angled wrong. Bennie tried straightening him. Littlefield said, "I can't fit him in yet. He's too big."

"I'm just getting that weird twist out of him."

"Leave him right there. Let go of him."

"Where have you been?" Bennie asked.

"Since when?"

"Since I got out."

He seemed bored by Bennie's concern. "Around."

"You're sleeping in the basement?"

"Gwen needs a bed. She says her room has that mouse smell. And apparently there's a big hole in the ceiling of Coach and Mom's room." Littlefield picked up a boxer by two of his legs and stuffed him into the incinerator, headfirst. "Besides, the basement is fine. Gwen pisses me off."

"She doesn't try to."

"She's nosy. She wants to talk about everything." He kept his eyes on the pile. He picked up a small shaggy mutt next.

Bennie knew it wouldn't fit in the kiln. "Will you slow down?"

Littlefield dropped the dog. "I'm doing okay here on my own, Bennie. I'm doing the work you can't do. Why don't you hit the road? Gwen's waiting for you."

Bennie said, "Hold on a sec. You need to tell me about Ray LaBrecque."

"LaBrecque? Never mind it, Bennie. I chased him, but he lost me. They went looking for him and nothing turned up. That guy has never been in the same place for more than a few days anyway. He probably went back up to Canada." Littlefield picked up the iron poker from the floor and jabbed it into the fire.

"Do you know him?"

"Not really. Some people I know know him, and they don't like him."

"Doesn't it seem weird—"

"Goddamn it—put it to rest, Bennie. I have no idea where he went. What do you think happened? I chased him. It was the game we were playing, remember? And he's good at it—he's damn good at the game. We both got lost. It took me a while to get out of the storm."

When his brother said this, Bennie realized he wasn't sure what he was after. Littlefield was an obstinate prick sometimes, but he was telling the truth. Bennie decided to let him stew in his bad mood—right now, burning the pile was probably the best thing for him to do. He still didn't understand how Littlefield had been outrun by LaBrecque. How could Littlefield have lost track of him? Bennie was often reminded, though—especially in the last few years—that his brother didn't mind being misunderstood.

"All right. Later," said Bennie.

Littlefield poked the fire and didn't look up. When Bennie left the shack and made his way to the Skylark, it was a relief to be out of the confined space of the crematorium, to see the ocean, a snowy field leading to the seaweed-covered rocks of Esker Cove.

He climbed in and closed the car door. Gwen said, "Oh, gross. You smell like dead-dog smoke."

"Sorry," he said.

The car was already warm. She shifted into gear. Bennie told her Handelmann thought she was pretty.

"That guy is completely inhuman," she said. "How can he do that day after day? Seriously, he might not have blood in his veins."

Bennie had been over to Handelmann's house only once. He was extremely neat, and regimented about his workout routine, which he did in his garage, regardless of season. He had a cold way of relating to people, but Bennie knew that he ultimately did a lot of good for the animals. "He's not a bad guy. It's a hard job," said Bennie.

"Man, what a nightmare it was in there," she said. She drove them toward the island and they didn't speak the rest of the way. He loved his sister and he felt the ache of wanting her to move back home.

Just before they got to the causeway, late-afternoon orange light stretched across the snowfields, each long glowing finger distinct against the dark gray shadows. The feeling had been popping up, again and again, since he'd been released from the hospital: everything could have turned out differently. When he'd fallen, he could have easily died. He felt this in his stomach first—a warm glow that spread to his chest and his shoulders and his legs. *I'm alive.*

7

Returning from the animal hospital, Gwen drove on the Weehauk Road, along the Weehauk River, and Bennie asked her if they could stop at the restaurant to say hello. That way she could meet Julian—and Bennie knew they'd like each other. He wanted to find more reasons for her to spend time on the island.

"Eddie's son?"

"Yeah. We've become friends."

"I remember him, kind of. The tall freak."

"He's got other attributes."

"Well, I can't meet him like this," she said. "My hair's been under this hat all day."

"Keep the hat on," he said.

"No dice," she said. She kept on driving when they got to the causeway, past the turn for the restaurant. "Oh, you know what? I forgot to tell you. Helen—is that her name? She called."

"Yeah, Helen," said Bennie. Saying her name brought some warmth to his body, and nervousness. He felt his legs go dead when he remembered how startled she'd been by his head bandage and the big cast. It seemed like she was thinking about the possibility of his death, too, and they hadn't been dating long enough to have to contemplate those kinds of thoughts. He wanted to go to her house, show her he was okay and that it wouldn't be long before everything would return to normal.

The rain was so heavy that Bennie and Gwen couldn't see the harbor, only fog. The water by the road was hammered silver. They saw a bird on the rocks near the far side of the causeway, and Gwen asked, "Is that one?"

"I think it's still too early in the season." Looking for light blue herons was hard without Coach; they didn't know exactly what they were looking for. They knew the birds were stocky and quick and they hunted for fish in the shallows, but otherwise it was a process of elimination.

When they got to the Manse, Gwen parked the Skylark in the snow and helped her brother out the passenger side. For the first time since his return, he thought about all the bills he needed to pay. Littlefield chipped in occasionally to help with the oil bill, but he was always broke. Bennie crutched his way to bed. Plaster from the ceiling above had sprinkled the bedspread. He didn't even brush it off before climbing in. Before he dozed, Gwen came into the room with a small green envelope. "Looks like Helen was here while we were out. She left this." Gwen bent down and kissed him on the cheek, handed him the envelope, then turned and left the room.

Helen had written on a small piece of yellow construction paper, in red ink:

I'm looking forward to seeing you, Bennie.
Sorry to give you a hard time about paintball.
I'm just glad you're okay! Let me know how
and when I can help.
—Helen

He missed Helen more than he probably should have, considering they'd only met in January. He knew it was wrong to postpone seeing her, but he wasn't ready. He still didn't feel quite himself.

A few days later, the same afternoon a case of oranges and grapefruit arrived from Florida, Gwen took Bennie to Dr. Miner's office, where he removed the bandage and took out his stitches. As he peeled off his rubber gloves, the doctor said he was glad to see some color in Bennie's face, and he rested a hand on Bennie's shoulder and told him he was lucky to be alive. There was something about hearing this out loud that made Bennie wish the doctor had kept it to himself. He liked the guy—he'd treated him well in the hospital—but Bennie knew he'd been lucky, he knew it more and more each day, and he didn't want someone else telling him so. On his way out of the exam room he glanced in the mirror beside Dr. Miner's diplomas. They'd shaved his head when they'd put in the stitches. His hair had grown back some, but the scar was plainly visible, a meaty line just above his forehead. The marine cut made him look a little lost. He tried remembering the blood—there must have been a lot of it—but his mind was empty. He thought about his brother, running through the snow, in the opposite direction from where Bennie had fallen. It felt like years had passed since they'd all been at the quarry.

When Gwen pulled up in front of the Manse, Bennie told her to keep the engine running. He scooted across the bench seat toward the driver's side.

"You're not ready to drive, are you?"

"It's an automatic, Gwen. I can do it all with my right foot."

Her eyes looked pathetically sad. Gwen and Bennie didn't often have to explain themselves to each other. She said, "Okay. Just be careful."

She got out, shut the door, and through the window she gave him the same look. He rolled down the window.

"I'm fine," he said.

"I'm glad you're getting better, that's all."

As he pulled away from the house, he waved and she waved back, looking like a parent watching her child swim in the ocean for the first time. It felt odd to be worried about, but he was so happy to have Gwen on the island. He was just getting used to it again.

He had Helen's note in his pocket, and when he pulled up to the restaurant he took it out and unfolded it. *I'm looking forward to seeing you, Bennie.* On second glance, this seemed oddly formal. He felt like a royal jackass for being out of touch with her. She had actually had to drop off a note at his house because he hadn't called her.

He clicked on the Skylark's hazards and fumbled his way out of the car, grabbed the crutches, and hopped up the steps to the side entrance. It was before the dinner rush, though the bar was crowded, and when the loud sounds of conversation hit his ears he realized he didn't want to talk to anyone except Helen. Julian had his back to the bar, mixing drinks, and Bennie thought about the phone conversations he'd had with him since the accident. Julian was unnerved by Bennie's injuries, uncomfortable talking about them, which made Bennie grateful his friend hadn't visited the hospital in person. Julian had been lost in the storm when Boak and Shaw scrambled down into the quarry in the dark to retrieve Bennie after he'd fallen, and Julian said they hadn't known if Bennie was dead, even after they'd found him. Boak and Shaw had carried Bennie out to the South Road, and they flagged down a logging truck to get him to the Adventist Hospital. On the phone Julian told Bennie he was sorry he hadn't been there to help. He'd been on the verge of tears. "It's just—I got so lost. I wish I'd been there to haul you out."

"I made it out okay, right?" Bennie had said.

"I should have been there to help," said Julian.

Vin Thibideaux was slouching at the bar. He was Coach's age—they'd been classmates—and Coach had disliked him, though he'd always been respectful of Vin's athletic talent. Coach talked often with Bennie, Littlefield, and Gwen about Vin's prowess—he'd been the town golden boy: a soccer star, a hockey star, the ace pitcher for the baseball team. Coach said he could have been great at any sport, including biathlon. Vin had a shaved head and a goatee and his cheeks were bright crimson. He looked less like a cop than a strip club bouncer. He was telling one of his stories: ". . . and there she was—she'd just puked on my bed . . ." but then Julian and a few others noticed Bennie had walked in and they turned and Julian smiled, saying, "Looking good, you stud, looking real good."

Julian wore an old dirty sweater and his shoulders were wide. Bennie didn't usually put it in these terms, but when he saw him, he knew it: Julian was the best friend he'd made since high school. He was surprised to see that Julian's eyes were red and his eyelids were heavy. It looked like he'd been drinking or smoking pot out back, which wasn't something he usually did until after the restaurant was closed for the night.

Vin pointed at Bennie and shouted, "Here he is, back from the dead," and even though he thought Vin was an idiot, the whole scene in the bar made him feel at home. Vin looked around at his audience and then pointed again. "This guy wanted to go swimming in the quarry in March. One problem, of course." He raised a finger. "The ice is still about two feet thick." A few guys laughed. Bennie laughed, too, to show Vin he didn't care. (As Vin continued chuckling, Gwen's use of the word "asswipe" came to mind. Before she'd moved to New York, Vin had put an arm around her at a hockey game and told her she should stop over at his house—he wanted to tell her some stories about her dad. He smelled like bourbon, and she asked him how his wife was doing—Gwen wasn't scared of him, only disgusted—and he'd responded: "She's great. She's down in Florida, which is the perfect place for her.")

Vin stood up. He was off duty, but he was still wearing his tight blue cop pants, and a Bruins hooded sweatshirt. Despite his age and the weight he'd gained, he was still strong, sturdy, thick-necked like a work animal. There was one skinny cop in the area, Jim LePage, and one woman cop, Lynne Pettigrew, but most of the others lifted weights and drank beer by the caseful. Coach used to say Vin was laser quick on the ice and that it was difficult to forget what it felt like to get slammed against the boards by him. Coach had also said that Vin had made a play for Eleanor in the early days. She'd rebuked him and married Coach. After that, the two men hated each other. Once Coach died, Vin seemed to pass this hate on to the rest of the Littlefield family. "Come on over here, sharpshooter," Vin said. "Let's play some darts."

"Actually, can I take a rain check on that?" asked Bennie. "I need to touch base with someone in the kitchen."

"Just a quick game, Benjamin," said Vin. He leaned over the bar and grabbed a fistful of darts from a tumbler next to the beer taps and then started walking toward the dartboard.

Julian smiled again and said, "It's great to see you on your feet, man." He stepped around the bar to give Bennie a hug. He squeezed hard, and when he let go he asked, "You okay?"

"Just a little out of it." He had a weird jolt of familiarity standing there in front of Julian, as though he'd been standing in that very same spot having the same conversation just minutes earlier.

"Bennie," Julian whispered. "Come back a little later, so we can talk."

"I will."

"There's a bunch I need to tell you, man." His breath stank of booze.

"Okay, I will," he said.

"You better get going. Vin's waiting for you."

Bennie asked where Helen was.

"She's been working doubles since you went into the hospital," he said, filling a pint glass with Guinness. "I told her to go home, crack a cold one, sit on the couch." Hearing this, Bennie knew she was probably working on some project at home—repainting the living room or building bookshelves. The couch made her antsy.

To get stuck spending time in a bar with Vin Thibideaux was one of the worst things that could happen to you in all of southern Maine. For the next half hour Bennie suffered through a game of darts with him. At first, they threw in silence. Vin was much better than Bennie. Vin stood near the line, his right foot forward and pointed slightly inward, his massive biceps parallel to the ground, his hand holding the dart gently. Then his forearm would cock back toward his eye and the dart would sail wherever he aimed. Bennie studied this form—he'd never been much for darts—but wasn't able to copy him. He managed to hit the cork most of the time, but not once did he hit the number he needed. But Vin didn't laugh at Bennie for being so inept; he was happy to win by a humiliating margin. All the while, he was ordering shots of Jack Daniel's, one after the next.

After taking a commanding lead, Vin said, "I've been wanting to come out to the island and talk to you, Benjamin. Gwennie said you weren't quite ready for me, though." He kept his eye on the dartboard. "But I gotta say, you're looking pretty healthy."

He could tell Vin was getting drunker. "I'm doing all right," said Bennie. "*She* might have been the one who didn't want to see you, Vin."

"Yeah, the Amazon bitch," he said, laughing. He slapped Bennie on the back, hard. Bennie was balanced on one leg, so he had to grab a nearby stool to avoid toppling over. Vin kept chuckling and said, "Son, you okay? I'm just joking. Seriously, though, you seem to be doing all right, considering that nosedive you took. Compared to LaBrecque, I mean. I'd say compared to LaBrecque you're doing great."

"He hasn't turned up yet?" Bennie plucked the darts out of the cork.

"Nope. And the state police aren't calling it a missing person case because the guy was a drifter. He could be anywhere, they say. His motorcycle's gone, too. But you know, Benjamin, they're missing the point. We got two feet of snow in fourteen hours. And we've already gotten seventy-three inches this winter, total. That's quite a bit."

"You had dogs out there searching, didn't you?"

"The staties did," he said, burping.

"Maybe he got out of the woods. Maybe he went back to Tavis Falls." Bennie handed Vin the darts.

"Yeah, Benjamin. Or maybe he got in a spaceship and flew to Uranus." His laugh made Bennie want to shove a flat palm against the guy's face. Vin had dark bushy eyebrows and long feminine eyelashes, and his oversize teeth were framed by his manicured goatee. Coach had said in high school he'd had relatively good luck with women, but Bennie didn't understand how—he was hideous. There was a shot waiting for Bennie on a nearby table, so with the darts in his left hand, he picked up the Jack between his thumb and forefinger and drank it down.

Vin had already gotten the bull's-eye he needed. He had one more nineteen to hit to finish the game. He paused before throwing. He said LaBrecque had come down from Tavis Falls for the urchining work and he'd just started going out in the boat with Boak and Shaw. They'd been planning to spend a few weeks on Riverneck Island, setting up camp there like their crew always did in March.

"The day after you fell, when it stopped snowing I brought your brother out to the quarry to help us look for the guy. Tried to get him to walk it through with us, show us where the six of you had been. Seems like he couldn't remember it too well."

"It was pretty hard to see that night."

"'Pretty hard'?" He turned to Bennie and laughed. "Really? I thought you jumped off the edge of the quarry for fun, Benjamin. Son, you're a stitch."

Vin had a talent for creating moments like this—Bennie had nothing to say. Vin cocked his arm back. He hesitated. Then he turned to Bennie, again, and handed him the darts. "You go. Let's switch scores. I'll spot you the points I've got and we'll play from here."

Bennie couldn't hit the nineteen, and after each of his turns Vin nailed all his spots. He cleared the board before Bennie could hit the only spot he needed.

When they finished, Vin had emptied four shot glasses. Bennie had had three. Each little glass was turned over, resting on the nearby table like a shell game. "Good fight, Benjamin. Good battle." Vin's handshake was surprisingly light and soft. He said, in a whisper, "You know what I think, Benjamin?"

"What's that."

Up close, his greasy nose quivered above his goatee and his breath was foul. "I think—that night—your brother fucked up big time."

"I have no idea what you're talking about."

He smoothed the whiskers on his chin with his hand, staring at Bennie. "I don't believe you."

Bennie was sincerely confused by this. What reason would Vin have to think that Littlefield was in some way responsible for LaBrecque's disappearance? "He was just playing the game, like we all were. But feel free to go after him. I'm sure he'd be tickled. Go right ahead."

This time, the silence didn't last long. "'Go after him.' You're a stitch, Benjamin." He slapped him hard on the back again—luckily, Bennie had the crutches in his armpits, so he was stable—and Vin said, "Pure comedy."

Bennie turned to leave the bar. As he crutched toward the door, he told Julian he would come back later. He heard Vin yell in his direction, "Let's play more darts again soon, Benjamin."

Before going to Helen's, he thought it'd be good to bring her some flowers, so he started heading toward town. He got about three miles down the road before he realized the florist probably closed at five. Queen Anne's lace—or even hawkweed—wouldn't be blooming for months, of course, so he went down to the back shore, down the road toward Sagona's Marine, to see if he could find some sea glass to give her.

There were only two sandy beaches on all of Meadow Island (there were also no meadows, but plenty of woods, and, in the summer, well-cut front lawns). The beach he checked was a place called Singer's Cove, near where Handelmann lived. He parked on the shoulder and hobbled through the woods to get to the shore. The trail was covered with slushy snow and he had to hop carefully in places to avoid getting his cast wet, but he made it down to the beach with a few minutes of daylight left. It took him a while to find one piece of green sea glass—and the edges hadn't been fully worn down—so he decided to look for rocks instead. There were some shiny egg-shaped stones nestled in the sand by the water's edge, which he thought Helen would be keen on. He found a few with white rings of quartz around them—it was a trick to bend down and pick them up wearing the full-length cast and with the shots of whiskey in his blood, but he grabbed them and held them in his hand and looked out at the gray water. Despite the blustery weather, the waves were small. A group of buffleheads bobbed in the swells.

From here—as from much of the eastern shore of Meadow Island—he had a good view of a wide stretch of the bay. The waves spread in the sand by his feet, and the sun had already dipped below the tops of the trees behind him. The beach was gray with a few brilliant squares of orange where the sunlight filtered through the spruce forest, and the sand looked as smooth as eggshell.

As he stared at the calm little waves, it became clear that he needed to finish his conversation with Vin before going to Helen's. No question. He pocketed the rocks, made his way back up to the woods, and returned to the Skylark.

On the drive back to Julian's, he thought about how booming Coach's voice would sometimes become, and how decisively Coach could act when the pressure was high. He seemed able to do the right thing every time. Even so, he didn't take the moral high ground. Littlefield made mistakes all the time, and each time Coach would step in and defend his son—he never made him feel like a fuckup. Which is not to say he didn't lean on him sometimes. Coach could be tough. But Coach was also the only one in the family who seemed to understand why Littlefield was hotheaded, defensive, and impulsive. They all missed Coach, and everyone except for Littlefield talked about missing him, though it was he who probably missed Coach the most.

The itch under Bennie's cast made him squirm, but all he could do was step on the gas. It started raining again, hard. It was fully dark now. There was something appealing in knowing he was about to say something that would get him yelled at, and soldiering forth anyway. He left the car running out in front of Julian's with the hazards blinking. He grabbed his crutches and hobbled to the door, and when he stepped inside, the same crew was there. Vin was still holding court, telling another story—". . . the old guy's sitting in his car, and when I walk up beside him, he doesn't see me coming, and I notice he's dead asleep, so I pull out my gun and squeeze off a few rounds . . ."—but when Bennie came up behind him, he stopped talking, turned around, and grinned. Bennie smiled back without showing his teeth. Vin said, "Hey, hey, it's the comedian." Bennie took his crutches out from under his arms and leaned them gently on the bar. They started sliding toward the floor, but Julian reached over and grabbed them. Bennie sized up Vin's ugly smile, though when Vin saw Bennie's expression up close, he stood up and stopped smiling.

Bennie said, "Littlefield hasn't done a goddamn thing wrong."

Vin seemed drunker now, from the cast of his eyelids and the color of his cheeks. He folded his arms on his chest and smirked.

"And another thing," said Bennie. "Gwen is not an Amazon bitch." As the sentence formed in his mind, as it came from his mouth, he assumed it would sound valiant, but he was immediately conscious of his whining tone.

Vin looked over his shoulder, then back at Bennie, and laughed.

Without hesitation, Bennie swung his cast forward—a swift pendulous leg kick that landed, squarely, between Vin's legs. It wasn't until Vin hunched over and clutched himself with both hands that Bennie realized he'd really done it: he'd hit a cop in the balls with his plaster-covered knee. Three or four guys at the bar sensed the commotion and immediately surrounded them.

Wheezing through clenched teeth, Vin said, "Hummmphttttt." When he finally stood up straight, two of the guys from the bar held his arms and struggled to keep him from swinging at Bennie. Vin said, "Just like your dad was, and your brother—total psychos. You all are." He coughed; his eyes were watering. "Your dyke sister, too."

Bennie felt the anger surge up in him again, and even though he didn't move, there were two guys from the Iron Works behind him who grabbed his jacket and held him back. They didn't know that Bennie wasn't much of a fighter. He'd wrestled with Littlefield plenty, but that was about it.

Julian came around the bar with Bennie's crutches. He took him under the arm and helped him out the front door.

The rain had lightened up. The brackish river smelled faintly of dead crabs and herring. The sound of the water surging through the narrows was calming. Julian said, "What did he say to you?"

"Wow. It's good to be out of the hospital," said Bennie. It was as though the tidal surge matched the pleasant rush of adrenaline in his arms and his torso and his legs.

"Dude, what did he say?"

"He was talking as if Littlefield had something to do with LaBrecque's getting lost. And he called Gwen a bitch," said Bennie, realizing for the first time that he was out of breath.

"Vin'll throttle you, man. You should probably take off."

"Wow, I wasn't planning on doing that. I had something I wanted to say to him—I had it kind of planned out, but then there it was," he said, swinging his cast. "That felt great."

Julian lowered his voice, blinked his boozy eyes, and said gently, "Get out of here, buddy."

Bennie was hoping for a different response from Julian; a slap on the back, maybe, or at least a knowing look. Before leaving, Bennie asked, "What were you going to tell me when I was in here before?"

Julian peered through the back window and scratched his head. "They need me at the bar."

"Come on, Julian. Five minutes."

He slipped his cigarettes from his coat pocket and tucked one behind his ear. "Okay, I'll be right back. Meet me out on the porch. Don't let anyone see you go out there."

The rain was turning back to snow, huge slow flakes. The porch awning was still folded up for the winter, and Bennie sat on a bench by the railing, out of view. The Weehauk was mostly frozen, and the recent rain made the surface look black. The tree branches on the far bank were already white with snow, but the river was still velvety slick. Bennie tried to retrace his thoughts—he couldn't remember exactly what he'd been thinking when he kneed Vin in the crotch. There'd been some recollection of Coach, his righteousness. Coach would have stood up for Littlefield, too. He wouldn't have resorted to violence, but he would have made his opinion clear—he would have bellowed his sincere rejection of Vin's theory. Bennie knew that carrying out his legacy was inevitable—he only wished he could have done it more gracefully.

When Julian finally came outside, he chose to stand. The snowflakes were getting caught in his long curly hair and on the shoulders of his wool sweater. He looked too tired to smile.

"Vin shouldn't have called your sister a bitch. That was out of line," said Julian. He looked down at the deck's wet floorboards. "But dude, I think your brother's in for some trouble."

"Save it, J."

"Do you know who LaBrecque is?"

"An urchiner," said Bennie.

"Yeah. And he's also Martha's boyfriend."

Martha was an old friend—a kind-of family friend—who that winter was a waitress at Rosie's. Littlefield had been obsessed with her forever, though he rarely talked about her, except to Bennie. The first time he'd told Bennie about his interest was on a fishing trip eight years earlier, just an overnight to Green's Island, chasing bluefish, and after several large sips of Canadian Club, Littlefield confessed he was in love with her, that he'd wait for her, as long as it took—and Bennie had said, "Martha who?" because it was unfathomable that Littlefield felt that strongly about anyone. It was only on rare occasions like this one that Bennie could see his brother objectively, as a loner who'd never had a girlfriend. The brothers had strung up a little tarp between two spruce trees even though there was no rain in the forecast, and they sat on the rocks by a fire beneath the high-water mark. They were both looking out at the blackening ocean. Bennie couldn't believe how forthright and romantic Littlefield sounded. He expected that kind of talk from Gwen, or from some movie actor on the big screen. With Littlefield, because it was so shocking, it seemed wholly true. Bennie had no idea that Littlefield had spent any time with Martha since they were teenagers. He didn't know, then, that Littlefield made regular trips to the bar where she worked at the time, the Black Harpoon.

That Martha was LaBrecque's girlfriend was going to make LaBrecque's disappearance more interesting for Vin and others, but Bennie didn't care much to hear this new information. What were the possibilities? Would Littlefield have left LaBrecque in the snow to freeze to death? Not in a million years. Like Littlefield had said, he'd lost track of the guy—LaBrecque had been good at the game.

"The more they find out, the more they'll come after all of us. Especially your brother," said Julian.

"Who cares if they come after us?" asked Bennie.

Julian looked down, sucking hard on his cigarette. "I'm just saying, we've got to help out your brother. Stop kneeing old cops in the balls, okay?"

"I don't think I hit him that hard," said Bennie, but he had a tinge of physical awareness, the feeling of his swinging leg being stopped abruptly, like he'd kicked a wall.

Julian shook his head. "You're an idiot. We've got to look out for each other, man. Don't do stupid shit like that. We've got to circle the wagons."

"Why are you boozing so much?"

"Fuck off, Bennie. It's mud season. This is how it goes."

There wasn't much else to say. He just shook Julian's hand, then gave him another hug and stepped carefully with his crutches as he left the porch and headed to his car.

8

He wasn't slowed by traffic, but he was shocked by how many cars were on the highway. The Maine he knew was getting overhauled, burdened by interlopers and nostalgia-addled white-collar suburbs in the middle of the woods—Cumberland, Falmouth, Yarmouth, Brunswick, old towns with brand-new health stores and woodstove dealerships. Many of the cars he passed had vanity license plates—EX-BRIT, KAYAKR, SOCERDAD, DRMOM—and he weaved in and out of them for thirty miles, all the way to Portland. He got off the Franklin Street exit doing sixty, slowing when he got near the fancy part of town, to the small cobblestone streets. He looked for a parking space, his tires popping along the bumps. He nearly sideswiped a redheaded girl in a jean jacket carrying a snowboard. When she stepped in front of the Skylark, he wasn't thinking much at all about the world outside his head. He was thinking about that bluefishing trip—after the moment the mosquitoes had finally left them when they'd built the fire, and Littlefield had started telling Bennie about Martha. Bennie wondered if there might have been something in his reaction that had irked Littlefield. Maybe Littlefield decided in that moment that no one, not even his brother, was worthy to know his feelings about Martha.

Bennie was considering these possibilities when he saw the snowboard-toting redheaded girl, the back of her jean jacket flashing in front of the windshield. He swerved into the oncoming lane and turned onto Market Street, where he landed, somehow, in an empty spot. The redheaded girl shifted her snowboard from one arm to the other without turning around. Bennie gripped the wheel, breathing hard, the ignition switched off, looking down at his knuckles.

When he got out of the Skylark, it was dicey navigating the cobblestones on his crutches, and the only calming aspect of the moment was the cold air coming up from Commercial Street, which felt good on his head now that the bandages were off. The pain he'd been feeling since Littlefield flushed his Dilaudid down the toilet was finally gone.

As teenagers, Littlefield and Bennie were in constant competition. Both of them wanted to get championship times for Coach during the racing season, and the rivalry continued after the snow melted. The summer Littlefield was fifteen and Bennie was thirteen, most nights before he fell asleep Bennie wished his brother would disappear, join Up with People or get taken up by the derelicts who rode the freight train to Bangor. Littlefield had spent the spring designing something he wouldn't tell Bennie about—he'd lock the barn doors from the inside. All Bennie knew was that Tobey Emerson, a car mechanic from Elmore Farms, had taught Littlefield how to weld, and Littlefield had bought a torch and a mask from him. At the end of that winter, Littlefield brought Gwen and Coach and Eleanor down to the public wharf to unveil his project. Bennie hadn't been invited but he showed up anyway. Littlefield had the thing under a bedsheet, at the edge of the water. The air was humid for mid-June and mosquitoes peppered the air, but the family waited patiently. He tugged at the white sheet, which slipped across the top of his egg-shaped project—a plexiglass and steel pedal-powered submarine he called *Water Dog,* named for the mascot of the island's elementary school; it was what people on Meadow, especially the older generations, called each other. (Coach was a Water Dog, and he considered Gwen and Bennie and Littlefield Water Dogs, though it was a name most kids never used.) The cockpit of the craft, Littlefield announced, was fed air through a hose connected to a dinghy, which needed to follow the submarine's progress as it moved through the harbor. Eleanor and Coach applauded, but they asked a lot of questions. Bennie, too, was skeptical that the submarine actually worked, and Littlefield evidently sensed this: after the unveiling he told Bennie he'd never have the privilege to drive *Water Dog* because it required a special kind of coordination Bennie didn't have.

That summer, Littlefield kept *Water Dog* tied to the town pier, where it listed to one side and collected a thin film of algae beneath its water line. When Bennie asked his brother how it was running, Littlefield told him he was still in dry-land training, preparing for the maiden submergence. When Bennie asked him, again, if he really thought it would work, Littlefield swept Bennie's legs and pinned him on his back, held his arms down with his knees, and put his forearm across Bennie's neck. With his free hand he rapped his knuckles against Bennie's chest. When Littlefield released him, Bennie asked if he could float in the dinghy above during the submarine's first trip and Littlefield said, "No, you've been cut from the team, douchebag. I've got Gwen—she has better eyes."

Water Dog never made it off the pier; that fall, when the town needed to put the floats up for the winter, they dragged the submarine up the concrete landing, then hauled it to the dump. When Bennie told him this, Littlefield shrugged. "That's yesterday's news, Bennie. The harbor's too cloudy, anyway. I'm working on a glider now, and no, you can't help."

Bennie wondered if his brother was going to be an inventor, or a pilot, or an engineer. He never helped Littlefield with his projects, and despite hating him, he had secret faith in his brother. He felt Littlefield was capable of doing whatever it was he pleased.

Rosie's was rarely noticed by the out-of-towners who swarmed the Old Port, even though it was only a short block away from the always teeming corner of Fore and Exchange. Bennie loved its exhaustive menu—you could get pancakes or a bean burrito, a grilled cheese or chicken cordon bleu—though he usually ordered their open-faced turkey sandwich and Hooker Ale. Bennie stepped into the restaurant, awkwardly rubbed his lone boot on the mat, and looked for Martha behind the bar. She wasn't there. He figured that she and the other waitress were probably out back, so he peeked around the dumbwaiter toward the dartboard, but she wasn't there either.

He felt feverish—he needed to see either Littlefield or Martha, soon. Gossip was common, but if you really wanted answers you needed to seek the primary sources.

Gwen and Bennie were in ninth grade when they met Martha, Littlefield in eleventh. Back then their mother still had a part-time gig at Musquacook Academy, which often hired a small catering company to cook for the faculty parties. Martha worked for the caterer. It was 1985, and Martha kept her black hair in a tight ponytail, and she always wore black jeans. Most girls Bennie knew, Gwen included, wore baggy sweatshirts and corduroys. The first night they met her, at Dean Hatcher's house, Martha was wearing a white tuxedo shirt with her black jeans—the party was in its third or fourth hour and she was sitting across the room, staring at Gwen and Littlefield and Bennie unapologetically. Even when Bennie would turn away to say something to Gwen about how they were being stared at, Martha just kept her gaze on them—not looking especially fascinated, but not looking bored either. There weren't any other teenagers at the party. When the dean sat down at the piano and asked people to sing along, Martha came over and sat between Gwen and Littlefield. She was still on the job, but all the adults were so drunk, she didn't care. Her tuxedo shirt was too small—the sleeves were short and the buttons were straining—and her thighs looked strong in her jeans. She was wearing light blue eye shadow to match her eyes. Gwen and Bennie and Littlefield stole glances at her as she looked back in the direction of Dean Hatcher and the piano. Then she said, in a hushed voice, that the dean had "killed seven gooks in 'Nam with his bare hands."

Bennie stared at the dean, a lanky guy in tweed pants and a sweater vest. He was proficient at the piano and he was smiling enormously; he had a toothy mouth like a horse. Bennie squinted and imagined him younger, stronger, a war hero.

Littlefield said, "No fucking way."

"'No fucking way'? Guys have weird priorities sometimes," said Martha, and she explained that Hatcher had fallen in love with a transvestite in Hanoi whose brother had been scalped by the North Vietnamese. The light blue eye shadow gave Martha the look of a gypsy. Sitting near her made Bennie feel skinny and shy.

"'Scalped'?" he asked, looking down.

"He was a spy," she whispered.

Later, when most of the teachers—including their mother—were hammered, nearly yelling the songs, they all snuck upstairs to snoop around. Bennie told Martha he wanted to look for Hatcher's medals. That's when she said she'd made up the Vietnam story. Bennie felt ashamed for being so gullible, but he also felt excited by the way Martha seemed to operate. Rules were big in the Littlefield household: politeness, firm handshakes, integrity, thoughtfulness, and, above all, honesty. Lying got you in big trouble with Eleanor. Martha didn't seem to care about those kinds of things.

After the party Bennie suspected they'd never see her again, but three days later she stole the keys to her father's Caprice, an old orange cab he'd bought at an auction in Westbrook, and she called them, wanting to know if they had any interest in going for a drive.

As usual, their mother had turned out her light at nine; Martha called at ten. Gwen picked up the phone in her room, and then found Bennie. A sleeping parent doesn't need to be lied to; the twins just had to make sure the front door didn't make any sound. As they tiptoed down the upstairs hallway in their parkas, Littlefield emerged from the attic, where he'd been lifting weights.

"What the hell," he said.

"Shut up," Bennie whispered.

In a full-volume voice, he said, "You shut up."

As Bennie and Gwen walked downstairs, though, Littlefield knew to ask them where they were going in a whisper. He followed them out onto the porch.

"That girl Martha, the caterer—she's got her dad's Caprice. We're going joyriding," said Gwen.

Littlefield chuckled and looked away.

"You want to come?"

"No, of course not." It was obvious he didn't like that Gwen was exposing him for being jealous of this late-night plan. Before he went back inside, he said, "I asked around about her. I heard she smells like fish."

Gwen and Bennie met Martha out on the main road, where she was idling without the headlights on. She'd cut most of her hair off. It was the same length as Bennie's. Somehow, she was even more beautiful—with her smooth pale skin and thin dark eyebrows and black hair—than she'd been at Dean Hatcher's party. Her cheeks were red from the heat in the car. Shockingly, there were kids at Bennie's school who wouldn't have even considered Martha pretty because she had too much of an accent. "Where's your brother?" she asked.

"He doesn't want to come," said Bennie.

"Tell him I want him to come," she said.

He ran back to the house, opened the door again without a sound, and went upstairs to find Littlefield. He wasn't in his room, so Bennie crept down the carpeted hallway into Gwen's room, then into her closet. There was a cord hanging from the ceiling that opened a pull-down staircase to the attic. The faint sounds of the radio, "Lights" by Journey, drifted down the hatch. Littlefield was up in the crawl space. He was in the midst of a set of bench presses when Bennie told him Martha wanted him to come. Littlefield finished his last rep, pushing air through his teeth, then setting the bar in its steel cradle. "Of course she does," he said. He put his parka on over his sweatshirt and he and Bennie ran back out to the Caprice together.

Gwen sat up front with Martha, and Littlefield and Bennie stretched out in back. As they crossed the one-lane causeway, Martha lit up a cigarette and didn't inhale the smoke; she just let the haze provide atmosphere. They headed out the Masungun, which was straight and usually empty at night. It was snowing lightly; the snowflakes were being pulled up into the car's grille. In a borrowed car at night in the winter, the next step, they all knew, was finding some way to get wasted.

Martha told them she wanted to try acid. She hadn't yet gotten her hands on any, but she thought it would be perfect for the group. Beer was boring, she said, and it made your breath smell bad. "That's what we do every weekend, right?" she asked, and the Littlefields stayed quiet. She continued. She said that acid was a creative drug, that her father had done it with her aunt and they'd climbed trees for thirteen hours. The Caprice had a red dashboard, which glowed through the smoke.

"Sergeant Crabcakes has acid," said Bennie, but they ignored him. Littlefield stared out the window, saying nothing. Bennie didn't know much about Sergeant Crabcakes except that he was a guy who lived out in Sterling. Kids talked about him at band practice.

Martha clicked off the headlights, slowed down to around twenty-five miles per hour, cracked the windows, and slid the bench seat back far enough that her hands just barely reached the steering wheel. She had the radio tuned to a country music station, the whine of a steel guitar just barely audible. They proceeded this way for a while. Two or three smooth miles. Between streetlights they were blind except for the red glow of the car radio.

Bennie's eyes were open to the darkness. Then Martha clicked the headlights back on. He felt the car leave the road, go over the shoulder onto loose ground. They were in the woods and snowflakes were jittering in the headlights.

Saplings raked the undercarriage. Rocks thumped against the soles of their sneakers. Martha was gripping the wheel with both hands, high beams on, accelerating. Branches slapped the car on both sides. The ground was frozen, but they could feel the different textures beneath—the hollows full of frozen oak leaves and thickets, the rough granite patches, and the ice when they spun through swamps. Martha avoided the big stuff, boulders and pine stands. She said the land east of the Masungun was intermediate terrain. They had no idea how she knew this. The car was tanking along, going faster than they'd been going on the road.

"This is your dad's car?" asked Gwen.

"Yup," said Martha.

"Do you hate him or something?" asked Gwen.

Martha glanced over at Gwen and smiled. "He taught me how to do this."

When Bennie scavenged for a seat belt, Martha said, "Trust me." Gwen had her seat belt on in the front, but Martha didn't have hers on. Bennie found one and clicked it in. Littlefield stayed unbuckled.

She gunned it. Martha looked as though she were trying to pull the wheel from its steering column; her neck, her arms, her straight elbows, her fingers, all tense. Her expression stayed the same. Light from the high beams reflecting off the trees made her face glow.

She turned to Gwen between pine stands, still tanking along, and she had to yell, because of the sounds the car was making as it rumbled through the woods. She said, "This might be what doing acid is like." Then she clicked out the headlights again.

Bennie reached over the far side of the seat and put his hand on Gwen's shoulder. Even though she didn't turn around, she knew what Bennie was saying. He felt glad to have her in the car with him. Not just because they were both scared, but because they were both amazed by what was being revealed to them, and it was good to have a witness. Martha was from a world they didn't know.

There was a small frozen gully just before the Shaw's parking lot, and they hit it at top speed, jetting down and bottoming out before launching off the lip on the far side of the gully, wheels spinning in the air. Finally, Bennie closed his eyes and coughed up a small mouthful of puke. The landing was soft, though—he opened his eyes to the quiet, flat white of the parking lot spilling out in front of them. Martha clicked on the headlights. She slowed down.

Sitting in the car, she gave everyone a code name—Bennie was Hickory, Littlefield was Dickory, Gwennie was Dock—and she tried to get them to shoplift in Shaw's with her, but there were too many people working in the store at that hour, so they returned to the car. They drove to Sterling. Martha asked a few questions about the family, and Gwen told Martha about Coach being dead. They cruised around Sterling for a while before Littlefield spotted the little seafood shack—Sergeant Crabcakes—which was boarded up. SEE YOU ON THE FOURTH OF JULY was written in block letters on one of the boards.

On their way back to the island, they stopped at Cumberland Farms, where Martha bought a twelve-pack of Coors using a fake ID and Littlefield's money. They parked in the empty lot beside the Elks BPO lodge. The heater pumped hot dry air into the Caprice, and the plush seats felt like a living room couch. None of them was tired. Bennie felt like his life was opening up wide.

Littlefield said, "I love beer." The car was lit only by the dim orange sodium lights at the corners of the parking lot, but their eyes were adjusting as they all sipped slowly from the cans. Littlefield continued, "Let's keep driving—let's go to Canada." They let that hang in the air. Bennie didn't know his brother had already fallen for Martha, but he liked how Littlefield acted around her, deferential and hopeful.

From then on, Martha always seemed single but never was. She and Littlefield had kissed the night they'd gone to Sterling—just as she was dropping them off at the Manse, right in front of Bennie and Gwen—and Bennie knew the two of them had hung out a few more times. Bennie wasn't exactly sure why this didn't continue, though he guessed that she realized how difficult he was to talk to, how much of a loner he was. It almost seemed that she and Littlefield came to an understanding: he would never make his affections too obvious or intrusive, and she would never make him feel like a desperate jackass. At the restaurant, Martha was always nice to him, like a cousin. She'd been waitressing at Rosie's for five or six years, and for Littlefield, seeing her at Rosie's was nearly the best way for them to interact. She was available to him, she was flirtatious and accommodating, but at the end of the night, she would stay to close the place down, and he would go home.

When Bennie walked into Rosie's, Sherry Callahan, another waitress he knew, was in the far corner delivering food to one of the tables, so he sat on a stool nearest her station, by the beer taps. The ceiling was strung with white Christmas lights, glowing down on his arms as he rested them on the bar.

Sherry was taller and heavier than most waitresses in Portland, with a handsome face and a quick temper. Her skin was orange in the Christmas lights. She poured him a Hooker Ale. Aside from the large round silver stud in the middle of her tongue, she looked like a mom. "Your brother just left," she said.

"He was here?" Bennie asked.

"Of course he was here. Just like most Tuesdays." Then she started counting her fingers. "He bugs Martha. He drinks. He plays trivia. He bugs Martha again. Then he leaves. In that order."

"Sorry about that," said Bennie.

"Oh, I don't care," said Sherry Callahan. She was trouble—Bennie knew from Martha she had a coke problem and was hell on her boyfriends—but still, as a waitress, she could wax angelic with ease. She was always in control, like a bully. "I'm surprised he didn't know she wasn't working tonight. So, you feeling better?" she asked, sticking a pen behind her mannish ear. "The fall you took, that sounded nasty." She glanced at Bennie's crutches. "Maybe they need to put an electric fence around the quarry."

"No, Sherry. They don't."

"Or barbed wire. Then you wouldn't have ended up in that cast, right?" She smiled and folded her tan arms beneath her breasts. "I'll tell Martha you were asking for her. I like the haircut."

"So Martha didn't work tonight?"

"She went to Tavis Falls," she said. "She'll be there for a few days. With Ray out of town—wherever he is—it makes sense for her to be up there. I think she's got a shift or two back here on Monday." She pulled out another glass and filled it, setting it in front of Bennie, beside his other full pint. "Here you go, Bennie. On the house. Good to see you're out of the hospital."

He ordered the open-faced turkey sandwich, choked it down, watched Nomar hit one out to left center—one of the few home runs the shortstop hit that spring training—and gave Sherry too large a tip before leaving.

9

After leaving Rosie's, he went to Helen's house and parked in her plowed driveway. He hadn't seen her for a week. All of her lights were out, but from the glow of her lava lamp he knew she was in her bedroom. He crutched his way to the porch and rapped on the heavy door. He was nervous to see her, excited, but also worried about how she would react. After a minute or two, she opened the door wearing her bathrobe. Her hair was wet, and in the dim porch light he could see her watery brown irises perfectly.

She said, "You're on your feet."

"I'm on one of them."

"I was wondering if I'd ever hear from you."

"I've been trying to get better. I wanted to get a little better before coming over."

She put her hand lightly on Bennie's head, rubbing his short hair gently with her fingers, avoiding the scar. "They shaved off all your hair." She looked down at the cast, then back up at his face. "Your eyes look good," she said.

"Thanks," he said.

"Aren't you freezing?" she asked. She helped him maneuver himself and his crutches through the screen door. When he rested his weight on his armpits, she said, "You smell like beer. Are you drunk?"

"A little."

"Ah, good. Let's get out the old paintball guns so I can blow a hole in your ass."

"I'm tired, Helen. I can't joke about it right now."

She put her head against his chest and her arms around his waist. When he hugged her, the crutches clattered to the floor. They squeezed for a minute, maybe two. Then she leaned back and he looked at her up close—her shining eyes, the right one holding him captive. He pushed his thumb across her dark eyebrows. He said, "I'm sorry I got hurt."

She said, "That's not the point."

"How about if you stop giving me shit about paintball?"

After a brief silence, she said, "I could probably do that."

"You should try walking in the woods with a gun. It's kind of fun."

She squinted at him.

He nodded. "I know. You're right. It was dumb." All of a sudden he was ready to do anything, or at least say anything, to make peace.

"Can we go upstairs?" she asked. She looked at the crutches. "Do you need a hand?"

"I don't think so," he said, but he hadn't yet tried a big set of stairs. The hopping tired his good leg. He stopped to rest every third step.

They went to her bedroom. The blue light of the lava lamp calmed and comforted him in a way he hadn't been calmed and comforted in what seemed like years. Life before the accident felt far away, but the blue light in Helen's room was real. She asked him to lie down on her bed, on his back. She untied his boot and slid it off.

During their third date, Helen had told Bennie that after she graduated from Bowdoin, where she'd majored in geology, she'd thought about law school, and even medical school—she'd taken a bunch of biology courses, too, though she would have still needed more courses to apply—but cooking seemed like something she could do as a way to see more of the world first. She'd gotten a job doing prep work at a place on the West End in Portland called Vincent's Bistro, and she'd been so fastidious and responsible that the owner was using her as the head chef within three months. The more time she spent at Vincent's Bistro, the more she liked the meditative aspects of the job, and the more she was glad she didn't have to talk much to others while she worked. As time went on, she was less and less certain she could hold a regular job—she liked an hour or two in the mornings to talk to others (she had lived for a while with a friend from Bowdoin), but otherwise she was glad to have much of the day and night to herself, living inside her own head. The job at the bistro ended up having too many social demands, which is why she'd moved to Musquacook and started working at Julian's. Bennie thought about this often—he knew she was unusual. She was so unlike his mother, who even as a therapist couldn't get enough time in the day to share her thoughts. His mother had lots of friends, and she always liked to talk about the complexities of her life. Helen didn't share many of her thoughts with others. He seemed to be the primary person she confided in.

She wanted to see the cast. She pulled his sweatpants down over it, slowly and carefully. "Does that hurt?" she asked.

"Not a bit," he said. He sat up to take off his shirt and she said, "Are you cold?"

"No."

He put his arms in the air and she pulled the shirt over his head. He sat on the bed in his boxers and the cast, and she stood up in her bathrobe, walked to her dresser, and came back with a black felt-tip marker. "I want to sign it," she said.

"Okay," he said. He realized, then, that she was in a more playful mood than he was.

On the upper part of the cast she wrote in small letters:

HELEN

MUSQUACOOK, 3/15/97

"It won't be long before the doctor takes it off," he said.

"I know. I just want to mark the occasion."

She tossed the marker to the floor and knelt on the end of the bed. It crossed his mind that he wouldn't have ever again seen the freckle to the left of her belly button if he'd died in the quarry. She tightened the bathrobe and lay down beside him.

Helen reached down and put two fingers inside the top of his cast and asked, "Does it itch in there?"

"You have no idea."

"I broke my wrist twelve years ago, and I remember. I wanted to chew my arm off." She got up from the bed. "Let me find my yardstick." From inside her closet she pulled out a long metal ruler with a thin layer of cork on one side. When she stuck it down into his cast, a cold tingle rose from his leg to his neck.

She knelt on the bed, the angles of her long body focused on scratching. All of a sudden she looked up at him, startled. "Bennie?"

He didn't answer.

"Does that hurt?"

"Keep going," he said, without breathing.

"You're crying," she said.

"The scratching feels good." He let the tears roll down his cheeks. He put his hand up on her cheek and into her warm hair.

"You must have been scared, waking up in the hospital. Did you know what had happened?" She pulled the ruler out of his cast. He didn't want her to stop, but he figured she had to, sometime. She straddled him, putting her hands up on top of his shoulders. He stopped crying.

"You know, I was just at Julian's," he said. "And I got into a discussion with Vin Thibideaux. And I ended up swinging my cast into his groin."

"Good," she said.

"He's a cop." He wiped the tears off his cheeks.

"I know he is, but he's a jerk, too. Somebody needed to kick him in the balls. You think he'll arrest you?"

"Probably not," he said. "But he'll get me back, for sure. Can you grab my sweatpants?" She reached down beside the bed and handed them to him. He sunk his hand into one of the pockets, grabbed the stones, and held them out to her. In his hand they didn't look nearly as interesting as they had when they were wet on the beach. They looked like rocks he'd found in her driveway. "They were nice in Singer's Cove, when I picked them up," he said.

She cupped her hands to hold them. "They're magnificent." She stood up again and went to her bookshelf, where she kept coins in a white bowl, and she dumped the change into a pile on the shelf. When she put the stones in the bowl, they looked better.

She returned to the bed and told Bennie she'd helped look for LaBrecque out at the quarry. Lots of people from Musquacook and the island had been there, walking the snowfields. Julian had said something about this.

And Bennie tried to imagine it. He knew exactly who would have participated: mothers, lobstermen, volunteers from the library, guys from the town office, George Pettiworth (his old PE teacher), and George's three daughters. Helen said no one really knew where to look. After two days of searching, the rumor spread that LaBrecque wasn't missing at all—he'd gone back up to New Brunswick, where he worked off and on for a logging crew. His motorcycle was gone.

In the light of the lava lamp, he said, "It's good to be back here, in your room."

With her head on his chest, she stretched an arm across his body, her wrist hanging off his hip. After a few minutes, she said, "What do you think happened to LaBrecque?"

He had a picture in his mind of LaBrecque high-stepping through the snow, falling off the quarry's edge, then later, lying still, the snow landing gently on his quiet body. He said, "It's hard to even guess."

"Do you think there's any chance he's still alive?"

"I'm sure he is," he said, almost without thinking. He tried stringing together the images—LaBrecque finding his way out of the woods, returning to Tavis Falls on his motorcycle in the snow, or heading all the way up to Moncton to skid logs.

After another period of silence Helen pulled her wrist off his hip and her soft hand landed on his stomach. It was warm, and she rubbed little circles with her smooth fingers. When the circles turned into squiggly lines, he wondered if she was writing out words for him, a secret message, but he couldn't follow it if she was. The painkillers he'd been taking had kept him from having any interest in sex, but he'd been off them for a week. In the light of the lava lamp, she sat up, then climbed on top of him again, pulling his boxers off, down over his cast, her hair hanging in front of her eyes. She took her bathrobe off. Her stomach and her underwear and her thighs were all as white as the ceiling. She sat up on top of him, but her thigh was getting scratched by the edge of his cast, so she quickly grabbed a T-shirt from the floor and put it between the cast and her leg and slipped her underwear off. He liked that he had never felt lonely with Helen when he was naked in bed with her. He tried not to float away into his own thoughts. He kept looking for her eyes through her hair to make sure she wasn't drifting off, either. He held her waist in his hands. He heard a diesel truck rumble down her street. She maintained a serious, concentrating expression—her eyes half open, her mouth tense. Before they stopped she fell down on top of him, squeezing with all her strength, pushing him down, knocking the wind from him. It felt severe, like tackle football on a cold day. When she finally released him, he asked, "Why do you do that?"

"Do what?"

"Trap me on the bed like that."

"Are you asking why I hug you?"

"I like it," he said. "I just . . . it's sometimes hard to breathe."

"Really?"

"Yeah. But I like it. I just wanted to see if you knew how hard you were squeezing."

"I guess I didn't."

The liquid blue of the lava lamp made Bennie feel impervious—a million miles away from thoughts of the quarry and LaBrecque and kneeing Vin Thibideaux in the balls.

It was around four in the morning when he sat up, opened his eyes, sweating, feeling both hungry and sick to his stomach. She'd turned off the lava lamp and there were no streetlights near her house. She didn't even have a digital clock in her room. He shook her shoulder. "Helen," he said.

"Bennie," she said. She was still asleep.

"Helen, I'm sorry," he said. He couldn't see her, not even her silhouette.

"What is it?" she asked. She groped for his pillow, then his face. She was always kind in the middle of the night, even when he woke her up for stupid reasons, like when he'd walk out to the living room to double-check that he'd turned down the heat.

"I'm sorry," he said, again.

She was waking up now, and so was he. "Why?"

He didn't know what to say, exactly. He'd been dreaming. But he knew he wanted to say something. "I'm sorry, I guess . . . that I haven't told you more about my family."

"What do you want to tell me, Bennie? Should we talk about it tomorrow?"

He reached over and felt that she was propped up on an elbow, facing him. He was still partway asleep, because he had a whole stampede of thoughts. Maybe a good starting place would have been Gwen and her nightmares, and Littlefield and his stubbornness. Or Nixon, the prize dog, and the day Coach saved her, the way Coach looked as he came out of the water at Cape Fred, his hair matted, his body paler than anything Bennie had ever seen, his strong, cold limbs. He could have explained to Helen the feeling of the damp wind on their faces and the thickness of the clothes they spread over Coach and Eleanor in the backseat, or the taste of the salt on his tongue, or the feeling of not knowing, the feeling of wanting to guess what would happen next. Before Coach died, before he saved Nixon, there were plenty of things to say about him—Coach was hardheaded, a lot like Littlefield, but that wasn't the whole story. Their mother was devoted to him, but she would often say that she'd never fully understood him because his family was different, and what she meant by this was that she was from money and he was not. Bennie never worried that his parents hadn't loved each other, but he felt sadness sometimes, looking back, realizing how estranged they were from each other because of their backgrounds, their families. Bennie's mother never came to the Littlefield reunions, which happened every year. Coach disliked Christmas because of the hallowed traditions in Eleanor's family: cutting down a huge tree from their land in the Carrabassett Valley, endless caroling, fig pudding, presents for the dog.

The problem about talking to Helen was not where to start but what to include. What he wanted to explain to her was that there'd be a time, in the not-too-distant future, when she would know him better and understand the subtleties of their family dynamic. He couldn't think of the right way to say it, but he told her, "Littlefield wrote something for my dad's funeral. I don't remember all of what he said, exactly, but I remember being impressed that he had written it and that he had the balls to stand up in front of everyone and read it. Can you believe that?"

"I can," she said in the darkness.

"What he said made everything—for at least a few minutes—seem so easy to understand. It was as though there were certain rules in the world, and the rules he laid out seemed really easy to follow. Everything made sense when he said it. I remember he said something about how Coach was true to himself, and that made things hard sometimes . . . Littlefield probably didn't put it exactly that way, but he made that part of it clear, that Coach had been tough. But he also said we wouldn't have wanted him any other way. Mom didn't want anyone except the minister to speak, but Littlefield did a fucking good job."

"That must have been difficult for him. To stand up in front of everyone."

"It's still hard to believe."

They lay in silence for a minute.

"You know," said Bennie, "I'd like to be true to myself, like Coach was."

"How do you mean?" she asked.

"Not letting anyone down."

Their eyes were slowly adjusting to the darkness. He wanted to say more; he could have said that he really didn't want to screw things up with her, and that he believed he could live up to his potential—the path Coach had set out for him, of being true to your word, hardworking, honest—but when she put her hand on the back of his neck, he decided he didn't need to enumerate. She curled up against him and said, "It sounds like it might be good for you to talk to him—tell him some of this."

He nodded, but he knew he wouldn't talk to Littlefield about Coach's funeral. After a few minutes he said, "You know, when I think about my fall that night, and everything that was involved in saving me . . . well, maybe LaBrecque didn't make it out, Helen. All I know is that Littlefield didn't do anything wrong." They stayed awake for a while longer, listening to the steel chime of the bell buoy near Esker Point. As they neared sleep, Bennie thought about turkey hunting with Coach and Littlefield, all of them dressed in camouflage, trudging through the cold mud and brambles to a spot far from the road, huddling together against the same tree, Coach teaching them the difference between a cluck, a cackle, a yelp, and a purr, all of them waiting patiently together for a tom to parachute down from one of the pine stands.

10

The next afternoon, when he drove back from Helen's house to the Manse, Bennie was relieved to see Littlefield's Chevette parked by the side door. He sat in the Skylark for a few minutes as snow slowly covered the windshield and made it dark inside the car. He looked at the backs of his hands, their red chapped knuckles.

He hopped to the oak door, exhausted. It was locked. Bennie pounded on the door. He'd been in charge of the Manse for three years and had never locked it. Growing up they'd never locked it, either.

After Bennie shouted and pounded for a minute or two, Littlefield finally came to the window beside the front step. His hair was combed neatly and he'd shaved. His shirt was wrinkled but otherwise he looked well rested and calm. He opened the door a few inches and said, "I'll meet you by the porch. I want a cigarette." Then he closed and relocked the door.

The snow had lightened, but it was still falling steadily, and Bennie tried to concentrate on the task at hand—walking on crutches through six inches of new snow—without getting angrier. He met his brother by the porch.

Littlefield was sitting on the wood box, his thin frame leaning over his knees, halfway through a cigarette. Ronald reclined in the snow, licking his paws. Bennie stood leaning against his crutches, out of breath. He said, "Okay, now should I ask why you didn't let me walk through my own house?"

Littlefield reached down beside the wood box and picked up their two old Daisy pump-action BB guns. Keeping the cigarette in his mouth, he handed Bennie one of the guns. He started pumping the other one. "Vin Thibideaux. He keeps coming around. We've got to keep the doors locked."

Bennie took the BB gun and held it loosely in one hand. He felt ridiculous. These were guns he'd seen in the back of the closet, but he hadn't used them since he was eleven or twelve. "Couldn't you have just let me in? We still could have locked the door, Littlefield."

"He's already been here twice. I don't want to give him an inch. He could have been hiding behind a snowbank or something."

It wasn't an argument Bennie would ever win, so he said, "Right." Littlefield finished his cigarette, then brought the little BB gun up to his shoulder and looked through its sight.

Bennie knew where he would aim—the birdhouse nailed to a birch tree fifty feet beyond the stone wall at the edge of the yard. Littlefield squeezed the trigger and an instant later they heard the hollow knock on the front of it. Ronald went bounding across the yard, not breaking through the crust of snow, looking for the wounded bird. He got to the birdhouse, circled it, barked twice, then ran back toward Littlefield.

"What if Vin drove up to the house now?" Bennie asked. "He'd find us back here, right?"

"Maybe. Then I'd shoot him in the ass." He pumped the gun again, raised it to his shoulder, and squeezed the trigger. Again, the pellet knocked the birdhouse. Ronald sprinted toward the far end of the yard.

"Where's Gwen?"

"God knows."

Bennie shook the gun in his hand and heard the rattle of pellets. He raised it to his shoulder and lined up the sight. Without hesitating he fired. They heard the same hollow knock. They kept shooting—alternating, listening for the knock against the birdhouse, watching Ronald race across the top of the snow. The dog would never get tired. Bennie relaxed. All he thought about was the gentle squeeze of the trigger and the birdhouse above his sight. It felt like the afternoon was stretching outward in a comforting, enveloping way. Neither brother seemed disappointed that the target was easy to hit, and Ronald seemed invigorated by the game. After alternating shots six or seven times, Littlefield put his gun down and lit another cigarette. Bennie asked him, "Where's LaBrecque?"

"I can't fucking believe you."

"Do you blame me for asking?"

"I just can't fucking believe you're still talking about this."

"It seems like you might know where he is."

"Think about the snow we got that night—what was it, two feet? We're all lucky we got out of there in one piece."

This was something Bennie felt deep in the center of his chest: he knew they'd lifted his unconscious body from the bottom of the quarry, they'd carried him out, they'd brought him to the hospital. They'd saved him. In a nighttime blizzard, you couldn't get much luckier than that. Bennie had even tried to call Boak and Shaw from the hospital to thank them, though he hadn't reached them.

"What you should be worried about now is that Vin Thibideaux will keep coming around," said Littlefield. "He's all riled up."

"You heard I kneed him in the balls?"

"Yeah, I heard that."

Bennie looked for a smile on his brother's face—or any other look of approval—but Littlefield didn't seem to think it was particularly remarkable that Bennie had done this. He turned toward the back door, unlocked it, and held it open for Bennie. Ronald squeezed past them.

After Bennie had walked inside, he asked, "You know LaBrecque is Martha's boyfriend, right?"

"Of course I do," said Littlefield, who pushed the door shut behind him.

The back hallway was full of fishing poles and empty bottles of antifreeze and cross-country skis and ski poles, so Littlefield took Bennie's crutches in one hand and grabbed his other arm as Bennie hopped through the dark house to his bedroom. At the end of the hall Bennie turned on the light, but Littlefield reached across his brother's body and switched it off. "No lights," he said. "And don't let your girlfriend park in front of the Manse."

All Bennie managed to say was "Will you tell me if you find out anything, Littlefield?"

"I will," he said.

Bennie collapsed on his bed, on the scratchy wool blanket, tired from the drive and from the sleepover at Helen's. He didn't even take his one boot off. Soon he heard the front door open and close. He pressed himself up from the bed and looked out the window to see Littlefield walking to the Chevette. He kept looking until its headlights blinked on and Littlefield drove away.

The summer after Bennie graduated from Brunswick High, he and Littlefield spent a week on Cuxabexis Island in the middle of Penobscot Bay with their uncle Theo, working the stern of his lobster boat, helping him haul, bait, and set traps. Theo wasn't their uncle, exactly; he was Coach's second cousin. They worked long days and went out with him at night, from party to party. Bennie and Littlefield had felt like minor celebrities—Theo was a popular guy on the island, especially with single women his age, and it seemed everyone wanted to meet his "nephews." At the end of each night Theo would drive Bennie and Littlefield to his cabin in the middle of the island, down a winding dirt road, tunneling through the mossy forest. Littlefield and Bennie slept on a mattress on the floor in the basement.

Sleeping side by side was something they were used to, from family trips; Gwen refused to sleep next to either of her brothers because she was such a light sleeper and both of them talked and moved around a lot at night. Bennie and Littlefield no longer hated each other like they had when they'd been competing, when Coach was alive. Bennie felt that they had an unspoken understanding now, that he and his brother would look out for each other. Gwen was working at a summer camp in Standish, getting ready for her first year at Vassar, but Bennie and Littlefield had no special plans for the coming year. Lying on the mattress, they could see the moon through one of the little windows near the basement ceiling. It smelled like earth and woods and new carpet. Their first night on the island Littlefield told Bennie, "I'd be happy living out here. Way out in the middle of the ocean."

"I think I'd miss home too much," said Bennie. They were both lying on their backs, wearing T-shirts and underwear under the covers in the dark.

"Out here, though, you wouldn't have to deal with any of the bullshit."

"What bullshit?"

"The bullshit. Stuff like taxes and . . . I don't know . . . lots of cars driving around and . . . people getting in your business."

"Meadow is an island, too."

"Yeah, but it's kind of a bullshit island. You can drive to it."

"I think they probably pay taxes out here," said Bennie.

"Uncle Theo doesn't."

"Well, you could probably stay on the mainland and not pay any taxes, too."

"Whatever," said Littlefield. "You know what I'm talking about. All that crap you need to deal with. It'd be simpler here."

Bennie looked across the room at the window, which framed the moon and the clouds racing by. He wondered if his brother, whom he knew to be smart in school, was acting dumb just to trick him. But he liked listening to Littlefield's voice, which sounded like his own in many ways. They sounded more alike than they sounded like Coach or anyone else, though Bennie thought of Littlefield's voice as a little deeper and less tentative. They drifted off to sleep.

Bennie awoke later—it felt like hours later, but he wasn't sure—to what sounded like conversation. He blinked his eyes but he couldn't see anything; the moon was gone. He waited to hear what Littlefield was trying to say.

"Hug me."

"What?" Bennie asked.

"Hug me," he said again.

"Are you awake, Littlefield?"

"Hug me," he said, and he grabbed Bennie's arm. His grip was loose.

"Why?"

"Hug me," he said. His voice was pleading—not insistent, but close.

It had been a while since he'd given his brother a hug. He figured it was an easy enough request to satisfy. He leaned over and gripped his brother's far shoulder and tried to give him a light squeeze.

This woke him up. "What the fuck?" Littlefield said, and jumped off the mattress. "What are you doing, Bennie?"

"You asked me to hug you."

"Jesus, no," he said. "I didn't ask you to hug me! Damn! What are you, a homo?"

"You must have been dreaming."

Littlefield paced around the basement, scuffing his feet against the carpet. "Jeez, my head's spinning."

The conversation ended there. Bennie didn't expect Littlefield to tell him what it was he'd been dreaming about; Bennie didn't even have a good guess. They didn't laugh about it the next day, and when Bennie tried bringing it up a few months later, just as a joke, Littlefield shook his head and smiled dismissively. "I didn't ask you to hug me, Bennie. You misunderstood me. That's just you being a fruitcake."

This was the push and pull with Littlefield—Bennie knew how much his brother depended on him, but he also knew how Littlefield needed to consider himself self-reliant. Bennie probably had some of the same inclinations himself, though whenever he talked with Gwen, she sympathized with Bennie's frustration.

"He can be so selfish," she had said during her first week home, for Christmas break. "He thinks he's the only person in the world who lost a father."

Bennie agreed with this. Littlefield *was* incredibly selfish, and he kept most of his opinions and judgments to himself, unless he was angry and he wanted to punish you. But Bennie reminded himself that when he and his sister were in high school they'd had friends, people outside the family who'd looked out for them. Littlefield had depended solely on Coach. There were entire days in the fall when the two would go off alone into the woods to track deer. He and Coach would walk slowly through the forest if the tracks indicated that the deer had been walking, and they would run together, Littlefield following their father, when they saw that the deer had picked up speed.

Vin Thibideaux came by the Manse four times in the next twelve hours, but each time Bennie kept the house dark. Vin would leave his police cruiser idling, come to the front door, knock, look in the windows on either side of the door, knock again, then return to the car, which labored in the deep snow as it left the driveway. Bennie hid in the shadows of his bedroom.

The next day Helen called Julian to ask if she could skip her lunch shift—she said he was annoyed by this, but he allowed it—and Bennie picked her up in the Skylark. They drove out the Masungun Road, to Church Road, to a dirt road where they could access the snowfields and woods near the quarry. Bennie waited for the shock of recognition, a flicker of memory to illuminate his trip to the hospital, but everything along that route felt new to him. The wind was ripping through the woods from the east, the drifts were shifting, and the snow on the branches was dusting the road. They parked on the shoulder nearest the corner of the old stone wall—the same place they'd all parked the night Bennie had fallen into the quarry.

"You won't be able to get down there on your crutches," said Helen.

"I want to give it a shot," he said. From the shoulder, Helen climbed down into the ditch, deep with plowed snow, then scrambled up into the field, trudging toward the woods north of the quarry, sinking in up to her thighs. She turned around and looked at Bennie, who was still up on the road. The wind blew hard at his back.

"The ground's really uneven here," she said. "I don't think you should come. I'll be right back. I just want to cross the field, get a sense of the area." Bennie knew in the summertime the terrain was a maze of rocks and blown-down trees and brambles.

"The cops have already searched here, haven't they?" he asked.

"I thought you agreed this was a good thing to do," she said.

"What are we looking for, exactly?" He poked at the dense snowbank beside the road with one of his crutches.

"I'm just going to walk to the far corner, over there. It shouldn't take me more than twenty minutes." Helen pulled her hat down over her eyebrows and zipped her jacket up over her chin.

But Bennie knew why they were out there: to find LaBrecque's body. It was true the police had looked, but with nearly four feet of snow, there was plenty of acreage that had probably been neglected. It would have taken a hundred men several weeks to prod every nook of the quarry woods, and the prevailing opinion was that LaBrecque had left town on his own. As soon as Helen suggested that they come to the quarry and the surrounding snowfields, though, Bennie knew that he, too, was starting to wonder if Littlefield was telling the whole truth.

Bennie sat in the Skylark, listening to WBLM, staring at the knob on the glove compartment. Every few seconds, he glanced up at Helen, at her back, as she moved steadily through the drifts. He'd get lost momentarily in a song, then he'd look up and see Helen. The farther she got, the less he liked the idea of her exploring the woods by herself. He'd left her alone in the cold with thoughts of the chase, and of the dark snowstorm. When she reached a thicket of pine trees, he opened the car door and stepped back into the wind whipping along the icy road. "Helen!" he yelled. "Helen, come back!" She was ducking under branches; she stumbled, and he wondered if she'd bend down and check to see what she'd stumbled on, but she kept her head up and continued trudging through the drifts. He yelled again and still she didn't turn around. He watched her red jacket disappear and reappear as she moved through the trees, and soon she was out of sight entirely.

He stared at the place where he last saw her, the hard smooth trunks of beech trees, until all he saw was an abstract weave of overlapping, muted colors. His eyes watered in the wind, so he stepped back into the car. For the next forty-five minutes, he looked through the windshield at the spot where she'd disappeared. He hoped she was walking in a straight line from the quarry, toward Lindonville. He imagined she was steadying herself on the trees as she moved forward. He wondered if her suspicions about Littlefield were growing. Did she still believe Bennie, deep down, when he said he knew Littlefield had done nothing wrong? He was sure she was winded and her legs were growing weak after walking through the deep drifts. This would help her know what Littlefield and LaBrecque had gone through.

But it still nagged him, why she cared so much. Did she have her own curiosity about that night at the quarry, or was she simply trying to help him, trying to provide him with a better understanding of his brother?

She might have come to these woods only to confirm for herself how foolish winter paintball was. Maybe she was still trying to figure out if he was a good boyfriend. With Helen out of view—somewhere beyond the beech trees—he remembered how little he knew her.

He closed his eyes and saw her falling, the wind gusting: a broken ankle, blood coming from a gash on her temple. He got out of the car again and screamed her name a few times. Yelling at the top of his lungs on a cold windy day in the middle of an open patch of fields beside a deep forest only made things worse.

The songs he listened to in the car while he waited were "Learning to Fly," "Space Cowboy," "Purple Haze," "Lucy in the Sky with Diamonds," "Red, Red Wine." Each one seemed to go on forever. He was surprised by how repulsive, slow, and stupid these songs sounded.

He was still staring at the silver trunks of the beech trees when Helen reemerged, first just a blip of red, then her entire jacket in view. For another few minutes he watched her labor through the deep drifts. When she was closer, he jumped out of the car. "Helen!" he yelled, waving. She waved back. When she got to the edge of the road, he tried not to show too much concern. "Are you freezing? You were gone for longer than I thought you'd be."

"I'm boiling," she said. "That's hard work, walking through the deep stuff. My feet kept getting tangled." She brushed the clumps of snow off her pants and knocked her boots against the tires. When she climbed back in the Skylark, she took her hat off and steam swirled from the top of her head. "There's a lot of land out there," she said. Despite the sweat in her hair, her cheeks and her nose looked cold, and her eyes had been tearing from the wind.

"I was shouting, trying to get you to come back," said Bennie.

"Calm down. I can walk through the woods by myself."

"'Calm down'?" He felt anger rising in his chest. "I don't want someone else getting lost in the woods, Helen. Is it all right with you that I don't want that to happen?"

"Listen. Don't worry about me. Right now there are just two people we need to worry about. Ray LaBrecque—that's for sure. He could be anywhere."

Bennie had never heard her talk like this, and it was pissing him off. "Oh, really, Nancy Drew? And who else do we need to worry about?"

"I was going to say your brother. Your brother is acting weird. But you know what? *You're* starting to worry me even more."

"Oh, really?" he yelled. "Well, maybe we need to make a deal. I promise not to give a shit about you if you promise not to give a shit about me."

"Deal!" she yelled back.

They were both breathing heavily, staring straight ahead, watching as the windshield fogged. Bennie blasted the defrost fan. After a minute or so of not talking, Helen said, "Ray LaBrecque's girlfriend—she's in Tavis Falls right now?"

Bennie nodded.

"Maybe we should go up there," she said.

This wasn't her way of exposing his foolishness. She wanted to help him. Bennie clicked the windshield wipers on and put the car into drive.

11

It took Helen less than five minutes to throw some clothes in a boxy suitcase. They drove across the island to the Manse, and Helen stayed in the car while Bennie crutched his way through the snow to the oak front door.

When he stepped into the kitchen, Gwen was standing at the electric range, stirring a pot of soup. Ronald was sleeping near her feet. A sharp smell of burning plastic floated in the air.

"What's on?" Bennie asked, unbuttoning his jacket.

"Holy shit," she said. "Thank God you're back." Her face was pale and her eyelids looked heavy. During the previous week—ever since she'd returned to the island—she'd continued wearing nice clothes, but she was pulling them out of her luggage and the house didn't have an iron. She'd started keeping her hair in a loose braid, which made her look more like herself—scattered, impetuous, just like she'd been before she'd moved away. She dropped the spoon into the pot and walked over to him. Standing close, she whispered, "Is Littlefield totally nuts?"

"Is he here right now?" Bennie asked.

"He's gone."

"Why are you whispering?" He felt immediately defensive of Littlefield, even though he often felt a similar frustration, a similar annoyance with his brother.

"He slept in the cellar last night," she said, this time in her normal speaking voice.

"He does that sometimes."

"Well, when he left this morning, I went down there. I broke in."

"You shouldn't have done that, Gwen."

"Besides that big lock on the cellar door, he put up another door at the bottom of the stairs—it's got a big new lock."

"So you couldn't get in?"

"No, I got in. I crowbarred it off its hinges. The dog was going crazy while I did it—it's like he knew Littlefield would be pissed."

Bennie looked down at the kitchen floor, at the splatterings of pasta sauce on the linoleum, and at Ronald, who seemed in the midst of a dream. His legs were twitching and he was whimpering quietly. Taking the door off was a bad decision on her part, but still, he was curious to know what she'd found. "Well?"

"He's got a cot down there, and his empty soda cans," she said. "Isn't that creepy? He's got these two big doors with locks and that's it. Oh, and a bucket he's been pissing in."

"Great," said Bennie.

Bennie didn't know why he'd lock himself in the basement, but Littlefield had always been cautious. Recently he'd gotten anxious about identity theft. He rarely used the U.S. mail—if he had something to send, he hand-delivered it, even if it meant driving to Augusta—and he never gave out his Social Security number. Though Bennie didn't do these things himself, he considered this behavior quirky, not worrisome.

Gwen glanced out the window at Helen in the Skylark. "Is she waiting for you?"

"We're going away overnight. If he comes back, tell him I was the one who broke in," said Bennie. "It'll be better for all of us."

"You can't leave right now, Bennie."

"I'll be back tomorrow."

"He doesn't talk to me at all. He came up here to eat last night—he just stood at the fridge and bit into that block of cheddar cheese I bought. It's got these grooves in it now, from his teeth. Then he drank from the carton of orange juice, and he took a few cans of root beer. I said hi, and he said hi, and then he just headed back downstairs."

"That sounds like him," he said. "Why don't you leave, too? Spend the night at Jenny Tollefson's house."

"I don't think Jenny lives on the island anymore, Bennie. I haven't seen her since eighth grade. Do you really need to leave tonight?"

Bennie peered down at the stove. "Did you burn something, Gwennie?"

"I think there was macaroni down there in the burner," she said, frowning at the electric coils. "What I really want is for Mom to come back."

He buttoned his coat. He didn't want to admit it, but this was true for him, too—he wanted to see his mother. "I don't want her to freak out," he said.

"You know, she can handle it. She's been through worse."

Gwen used a spatula to dredge for the spoon she'd dropped in the soup. Before he left he asked, "Did you ever meet Ray LaBrecque?"

"I don't think so," she said. "Why?"

"Vin Thibideaux will be coming around. He'll ask questions. I just want to know what you know."

"How would I know anything?"

"You talk to people."

"Only you, Bennie," she said, shaking her head, stirring the soup. "When I come back here, you're the only one I talk to. God, I hope Vin doesn't come around when you're not here. That guy gives me the creeps."

"Just keep the door locked. You can talk to him through the mail slot if you need to." He gave her a hug. He knew she hadn't heard what he'd done to Vin at Julian's, and that was fine. He'd tell her when he got back, if he needed to. He walked back outside, through the snowdrifts to the Skylark.

Helen had tuned the radio to a classic rock station and had moved into the driver's seat. She had her green sunglasses on even though it was still snowing. Her face was bright and giddy. Before she shifted into gear, she leaned over and kissed him, and put her hand on the back of his neck.

They seemed to have recovered from their argument—maybe she was good at moving on, not holding a grudge. It was amazing, really, that someone like Helen—confident and stubborn, beautiful and seemingly sane—was helping him. She was interested in finding out more clues about LaBrecque's disappearance, but she also seemed to like sitting beside him; she put up with his insecurities and his other troubles, his lack of direction. Other women, he knew, thought he needed work. Helen seemed to recognize he was a mess, but a worthwhile mess, somehow. Maybe she was one of those women who liked to take on projects, wanted to solve the man they were with. Most guys—if they knew that was happening—they'd run. Bennie was happy to be considered a project, especially by Helen. They'd talked about his ambitions, about how he'd started college but hadn't been able to stick with it, about how he'd liked studying physics and European history even though he'd never learned how to apply the knowledge. She seemed patient.

Lewiston was an easy drive from Meadow Island, less than an hour.

Helen wanted to show Bennie her old house on their way to Tavis Falls, and she knew her mom would be at work. As they crossed the Androscoggin, Helen gripped the wheel with both hands, staring intently at the road and the cars around her. Along the way, they'd passed a few gift shops in the middle of nowhere, and the sight of them—in wintertime, each with a dozen or so cars parked in front—made Bennie wonder about all the people, none of whom he'd ever meet, who traveled up to central Maine to buy lobster-trap coffee tables. For much of the drive, they didn't speak, listening to Cream and Hendrix and Creedence Clearwater Revival at low volume on the radio.

Mrs. Coretti lived in a raised ranch on a busy road in the center of town. When they entered, a frail white-haired poodle stood up from its little dog bed and hobbled over to greet them.

"Baby!" said Helen, getting down on her hands and knees, putting her face down against the dog's scrawny neck. As Helen nuzzled him, he turned his face up toward hers and began licking her nose. "You want to give him a hug?" she asked.

Bennie reached down and picked up the dog, who was as light as a newspaper. He'd been shorn recently; you could see his pink skin and sun spots through the white hair on his back. Bennie gave him a gentle squeeze, and he heard a quiet growl gathering in the dog's throat.

"Go ahead and check out my room upstairs. I'll take the old boy out for a quick pee."

At the top of the stairs, the first room Bennie saw had a neatly made bed with a thick mattress, an uneven stack of *Lewiston Sun* newspapers at its foot, and a book called *Reinventing Your Inner Comanche Princess* on the bedside table beside a shriveled set of very used earplugs and an ashtray full of menthol cigarette butts. The next room was the carpeted bathroom; the end of the hall was what Bennie knew immediately was Helen's room. It was early afternoon but the bedroom was dark and smelled slightly different than Helen—it smelled like high school. He sat down on her bed, a soft mattress on the floor. The shades were drawn, and as his eyes adjusted he could see the titles in her bookshelves: Spenser and Marlowe next to some Lloyd Alexander fantasies and manuals for Dungeons and Dragons. On the same shelf, beside a snow globe from New Hampshire, the King James Bible. Also, books about witch hunts, whirling dervishes, butterflies, the Ottoman Empire, and American Sign Language. On a small bookshelf in the corner, she had all of Encyclopedia Brown, Tintin comics, and the Chronicles of Narnia.

He felt immediately willing to leave his family behind, to join forces with Helen. He wanted to run away and escape into the books of Helen's childhood. He could even imagine a future when he'd adore the dog. It felt urgent—he wanted to hold on to her; he didn't want to make a series of small mistakes that might lead, eventually, to a breakup. It had happened before, but he didn't want it to happen this time.

Above the bookshelves were posters thumbtacked to the wall—the Cure, Billy Idol, the Eurythmics. Also, three old high school posters from the plays she'd been in. At the far end of the room was a large framed photograph of the poodle wearing a necklace made of small red felt hearts. He felt, for a moment, like he was being watched, sitting on her bed with her high school stuff on display.

He knew she'd acted in plays back then, and he tried to imagine it, but it was difficult: Helen had a tendency to be so withdrawn, so private. He wanted to go back in time, pay the two-dollar entrance fee to Lewiston High School's transformed cafeteria on opening night, to see Helen as Josephine in *H.M.S. Pinafore,* Helen as Hermia in *A Midsummer Night's Dream,* Helen as Lucy in *You're a Good Man, Charlie Brown.*

And then there was her time at Bowdoin College, only twenty minutes away—but it must have opened up a whole new world for her. Maybe she tried to be in plays there but wasn't good enough; maybe it was college that had forced her to be shy.

He lay back and stared up at the glow-in-the-dark constellations on Helen's ceiling and, squinting, tried to see them as actual stars in the sky. He wanted to block out all other thoughts, but his mind drifted back to the island. He saw Vin Thibideaux's ugly face, his shaved head and fat nose. Then he thought about LaBrecque running through the woods on that starless night, and Littlefield, panting, moving from tree to tree for balance, determined to make it out of the storm.

Hearing her coming up the stairs, he closed his eyes. She'd taken her shoes off and crept across the carpet; she crouched over him without making contact. She kissed his forehead, then his nose, then his cheek.

He felt numb.

"You okay?" she asked.

He opened his eyes and saw her body arched over his. He felt hollow in his chest, a deep, searing regret: there were so many times he could have reached out to his brother. When he'd returned to the island from Brooklyn. Earlier, too. When Littlefield didn't have any friends in high school. When Coach died. Bennie didn't know how to explain this.

The urgency to be absorbed by Helen returned, and he pulled her in close, wrapping his arms around her. "I think I'm letting my brother down," Bennie said. "I should have never let him get so far away."

She shook her head. "It's really not your fault," she said.

"I think things are going to get worse."

12

The town center of Tavis Falls was a few miles west of the interstate. On the left side of Augusta Street as you came into town, a diner called Wendell's was set back from the road with a gravel parking lot out front. They stopped there so that Helen could pee and they could get something to eat.

There weren't many folks in the diner at four o'clock. Three guys at the counter, two of them reading the paper, one of them with his head just a few inches above his plate, eating mashed potatoes. All of the booths were empty. While Helen went to the bathroom, Bennie sat in one of the middle booths, sliding across the vinyl seat to the window. The snow hadn't let up; the sky was still dark gray and the air was white with flakes. He looked outside at the field behind the diner and heard snowmobiles.

There was only one waitress in the diner, a thin-faced gray-haired woman in her fifties. She wore her hair in a ponytail. When she came to fill their water glasses, he saw that both of her forearms were tattooed—a deer and an eagle. She nodded hello. She tapped her index finger on the paper placemat when she saw he was looking for a menu. He said, "Thanks," and she didn't respond.

The men at the counter weren't speaking, either. Bennie was glad when Helen returned from the bathroom. The diner posted a list of the winners of the town's tomato prize on the wall outside the ladies' room, and Helen reported her findings: a guy named Chester Millbridge had won the tomato prize for seven consecutive years, from 1922 until 1928. Then Molly Magavern unseated him, the first woman to win the prize.

The men at the counter were eating silently, and while they didn't turn around, Bennie knew they were listening. When the waitress came to field their order, Helen looked around for a menu, so he tapped his finger on her placemat, and she said, "Oh."

The tattooed waitress held her order pad and pen but remained silent.

Helen asked, "The tomato prize. Is it for size or quality?"

"Weight," said the waitress.

"Right. I guess quality would be harder to judge."

"Nowadays it's rigged, that prize. My cousin always wins it. He owns the scale." The skin underneath her eyes was dark and sagged deeply. She stared at them.

"Hmm. That's too bad," said Helen.

"The pecan pie any good?" Bennie asked.

"Nope," said the waitress.

"What's good?" he asked.

"Hamburger. Fried clams."

"I'll have a hamburger," said Helen. Close up, the tattoos were that long-ago shade of green: an eagle with its wings spread, holding arrows in its talons. The deer was standing proudly with a wide rack of antlers.

"I'll have some apple pie," said Bennie.

"Don't have any," said the waitress.

"Pumpkin?" he asked.

"Nope."

"What do you have for pie?"

"Pecan," she said.

"All right. I'll have the pecan."

"She just said it's not any good," said Helen.

Bennie looked up at the waitress and she returned his gaze, plainly. "You want it?" she asked.

"Sure," he said.

She turned and walked through the swinging doors to the kitchen. After she left, one of the men reading the newspaper got up from his stool, put a few bills on the counter, and started walking toward the door. He stopped beside their booth. He had neatly parted black hair, long sideburns, and the clean look, clear eyes, and straight smile of a Cumberland County politician. He was wearing a turtleneck, and aside from his sideburns he was clean shaven.

"Hello," the man said. "You folks passing through?"

"Kind of," said Helen.

"Vacationing?" He clasped his hands together. His face looked chapped from the cold, which made his smile stand out. He seemed happy, but there was a hint of aggression in his cheer. Bennie was glad to let Helen do the talking.

"Not really. We're here to see a friend," she said.

"Are you in town for supper?"

Helen looked at Bennie, then back at the man. "We're here for the evening," she said. "But we'll be with our friend."

"Well, bring your friend along to the Grange. We're having a gathering," he said. "A Saint Patrick's Day event. Lots and lots of folks—everyone I know, and some I don't. We'll have dinner, talk about some important issues. Issues important to everyone, not just us here in Tavis Falls, and those of us in my group."

"Sounds good," said Helen, in her quiet voice.

"Try us out. The name's Arthur Page."

They introduced themselves, and he gave them directions to the Grange. Helen asked him if he knew Martha.

"I don't know any Marthas in this town, but who knows, there might be a Martha or two. I don't know everyone. I'm relatively new to the area. What I can tell you is that if you're visiting for the evening, you can't go wrong. Afternoon's a good time as well. Enjoy the beauty of the world, my friends. It's a gift." He looked out the window beside the booth, at the snowy field. The snowmobiles were still whining in the distance.

The waitress arrived with food. "Move it, Art," she said. "Let these people eat."

He smiled and said, "She gets a little cranky, but she's a good soul. Aren't you, Evelyn."

She ripped their tab from her order pad and placed it facedown on the table.

"Pecan pie," said Arthur. "Finest kind."

Evelyn rolled her eyes. She said, "Art's from Massachusetts."

"See you tonight," he said, putting his hand on his heart and smiling again. Then he walked out into the snow.

The pie tasted like Aunt Jemima syrup and soggy bread. Evelyn was resting on one of the stools. Bennie asked her, "You know that guy pretty well?"

"Art? Sure," she said.

He asked her what his "group" was.

She said, "Beats the hell out of me. Some kind of gladhanding, I'm guessing. You see, people come from out of town, say they like it here, and then next thing you know they're trying to change everything to how they *really* want it to be."

The man reading the newspaper at the counter laughed.

Helen chewed her burger. With a full mouth she asked, "You ever been to one of Art's meetings?"

"Nope," she said. "He's giving out free food, though."

"You know Martha?"

Evelyn looked at Helen skeptically. "I know a few Marthas," said Evelyn. "But none of them is a Martha anyone would ask about."

Helen seemed to think about this for a brief moment, then she nodded.

When they walked outside the temperature had dropped but the clouds were still hanging low in the sky, and what was falling now was that light, icy snow that sometimes falls for days at a time.

They drove into town, carving troughs in the deep snow, and parked on Main Street near the small green bridge that spanned the St. Jeremiah River just north of the falls. Portland had a big influence on Brunswick, and on their island as well. Inland Maine was a world apart. Tavis Falls was only thirty minutes from Brunswick, but its dark storefronts and boarded-up mill buildings were good reminders of this difference. As they walked down Main Street, the town felt like a shadow of the original model—maybe the mill had once brought color to the place, but now, especially in the new snowfall, everything felt muted and gray. The shops that had probably opened in the fifties were still there, and though they looked like they'd been closed for years, Bennie and Helen saw dim lights in the back of the shoe and hat store, and someone in the window of Wheatcroft's Hardware arranging a bundle of snow shovels. The most active-looking storefront was Hilldreth's Barbershop and Newsstand. The windows were clean, and someone had shoveled the walkway and the steps leading up to its door.

The metal rack by the door inside Hilldreth's contained no local papers, only *Car & Driver, Penthouse,* and *Juggs.* The barber said he'd heard of Martha Doyle—but then he said, "Doyle? Are you sure it's Doyle? I knew a Martha Pinkham. Married to my brother's friend Jason Pinkham. He's in lockup." At the Shell station—where Bennie also asked about Martha and received a barely noticeable shrug in response—they bought a copy of the *Jeremiah Bulletin.* The lead article, "EAST HANCOCK LIKES IT INDIAN STYLE," reported on the grand opening of an Indian restaurant forty miles away. They stood out of the cold while Helen read Bennie the story, which was full of quotes from the restaurateur such as, "We will be serving Tikka Massala, Korma, Vindaloo, and other savory dishes." She flipped through the rest of the paper and saw no mention of Ray LaBrecque, the search, nothing. In the Events Calendar, Arthur Page's gathering at the Grange was listed in bold type.

"If the party's big enough, I bet someone'll know Martha," said Helen.

"Or how to find her," he said.

The Grange was on the other side of town from Wendell's Diner, on a bend in the road, at the top of a hill. There were no other cars parked in the lot, though there was a dim yellow light above the entrance illuminating neatly painted, gently curving black letters. TAVIS FALLS GRANGE. Bennie put his arm around Helen and he hopped with her through the snow to the door as she carried his crutches. Someone had plowed recently. The door was unlocked.

They stepped inside, the dry heat warming their faces, and saw a long hallway, golden light coming from a small overhead globe. The wood floors were clean, freshly varnished, and the walls were unadorned. They turned in to the first room, a kitchen, immaculate and foodless—Bennie checked the ancient refrigerator and it was not only empty but spotless. The place felt solemn and well cared for, alive, and all Bennie could say was "This wasn't what I was expecting." Helen ran her hand along the steel countertops, well worn and polished. The kitchen was connected to the main room of the Grange—the meeting hall—which had three podiums near the back, each draped with purple velvet, fringed with gold tassels. Otherwise, the place was empty. The size of a small basketball gymnasium, the room had tall windows, but the radiators along the walls kept the room warm, almost hot. They shed their jackets and stood in silence in the room, smelling the varnish. Then Bennie put his arm around Helen again and they headed back to the kitchen. Beyond the counters and the old gas stove there was a small door, which took some effort to open—the doorknob was loose—but once the latch clicked free, they walked inside. It was a tiny room with a single window and a little bed. There was no radiator so it was cooler, but they kept the door open to the kitchen.

The dark blue light from the snowstorm had filled the room, and Helen and Bennie sat down on the bed. For the first few seconds all they heard was the quiet sound of their breath. Out the small window the spruce boughs were heavy with snow. He pulled her closer, then he shut his eyes to the little room, to its simple and spare perfection, to the waning light of the afternoon. After a few seconds he felt her turn toward him, and when he opened his eyes he saw that she was looking at him in a casual, familiar way. At first this made him feel uneasy—to know that she was in Tavis Falls for him, to help him, even though he himself didn't know exactly why they'd come—but this feeling passed, and he gave in to the warmth of her body and her wet-looking eyes and he thought to himself, *This is it, it's happening, my life.*

They watched as the daylight faded. He no longer felt hidden from Helen; he knew she could see him as clearly as she ever would. Since falling into the quarry, the world had been flooding into him, unfiltered. He felt more awake, as though the brightness of the world had intensified, and despite the trouble with his brother, and with Vin, all he could feel was gratitude. His leg was still healing, but he was thankful for his arms, his hands, his fingers—where his skin touched Helen's it was very warm, and the heat from the kitchen was now coming in through the doorway, but there was a small crack in one of the windowpanes, so when the wind picked up outside, swirling, rushing through the nearby trees, there was a thin draft on their faces.

Helen said, "Maybe we shouldn't ever go back to the island," and while he knew she didn't really mean it, he thought about the possibility.

Then they saw stark white light spread on the trees outside. A car. Helen's face was flushed and her eyes were shining as they stepped into the kitchen. Arthur Page and a woman who appeared to be his wife were knocking their boots on the steps outside the door. They entered the kitchen, both wearing blue knit wool hats pulled down over their ears, both smiling as though the snowstorm was too exciting to bear. They were carrying large trays covered in tinfoil, wearing oven mitts.

"Ellen! Bennie!" cried Arthur. "Fantastic!"

"Helen," said Bennie, nodding his head in her direction.

"Helen, of course," Arthur said, setting the tray down on the counter. "This means a lot to me, that you found your way here."

He introduced them to his wife, Nancy Page, who said an almost whispered hi to them, and after Arthur put the two racks of lasagna into the oven, all four of them walked into the main room to set up chairs and tables. They made space for fifty people. "Who knows how many will come," said Arthur. "But it's always best to be ready." He was wearing a button-down blue oxford shirt tucked neatly into his jeans; Nancy, too, was wearing jeans and a light blue shirt, and though she didn't speak, she was jittery with anticipation—you could see it in her eyes and her dry red cheeks and easy smile. Whenever Arthur made a comment, she would nod in agreement. When they'd finished setting up the chairs and tables, Arthur and Bennie and Helen sat down while Nancy went to the kitchen to check on the food.

Bennie asked Arthur if he knew Ray LaBrecque.

He said of course he knew him. He was a quiet kid, but even so, Tavis Falls was a small enough town. He asked how Bennie knew him, and he said he didn't, really, he just knew LaBrecque had gotten work on one of the islands down near Meadow, and that now he seemed to be missing.

"Got a job on the coast? I don't think so," he said, laughing. "He goes to school with my son. They're not exactly friends, but they play on the same basketball team." He stood up and pushed a few chairs neatly against the tables.

"Maybe we're not talking about the same Ray," said Bennie.

Arthur sat back down and put his hands on his thighs. "Ray LaBrecque. His parents live up the hill, on the other side of the falls?"

"I think the Ray I'm talking about was raised by his uncle," Bennie said, straightening chairs on the other side of the table.

Arthur didn't seem to be listening—he said the LaBrecques were a good family, and that he wouldn't be surprised if they showed up for the program at the Grange that night.

Helen stood up and walked to the kitchen to check how Nancy was doing. Bennie asked Arthur what the "program" was, exactly, and he said Bennie and Helen would enjoy it—it would involve talk of peace and humanity and spirituality and destiny.

"Wow," Bennie said, nodding.

"Thanks for backing me up, son," he said. "I don't suppose you could help hold a placard or two during my presentation? It'd be nice to have someone on the 'outside' assisting me."

"A placard? Like a sign?"

"Thank you, son. Wonderful," he said.

Two young couples entered the hall, and Arthur leapt up to welcome them. The two men looked as though they'd spent the day sleeping in a ditch. They were probably brothers—both were wide-chested and wore canvas pants with lashes of oil and dirt at the cuffs, and their red beards were the same hue. At first glance the young women accompanying them looked alike, too. All four were crimson-cheeked from the cold. One of the men said, quietly, "This where the free dinner is at?"

"Sure is. I'm Arthur Page." He extended his hand and the two men extended theirs reluctantly in turn, and the two women nodded with gentle smiles. None of the four said another word—they didn't introduce themselves and just stood in the back, waiting.

Just as Bennie was resigning himself to an awkward evening with the two ditch-sleepers and their wives, listening to Arthur prattle about world peace in this pristine wooden hall in the middle of the Maine woods, the doors opened and the crowd arrived. He looked for Martha, a desperate scan from face to face in the sea of new bodies. The throngs entering the Grange must have inspired confidence in Arthur, although nobody seemed to know why they were there. Bennie couldn't wait to hear Arthur's opening pitch. There were other "insiders"—earnest-looking, bright-eyed, well-groomed men and women carrying more trays of food—but most of the assembled crowd weren't a part of Arthur's organization. They looked hungry, tired, and drunk. The divide was easy to notice. There was Arthur and his wife and his well-scrubbed friends. Everyone else was forming into smaller groups, and most of them looked like those first two: unshaven, large, and hungry. Helen and Bennie camped near one of the radiators.

Arthur approached. He appeared less jolly and self-assured. He said, "I think we will probably have enough food."

Helen asked, "You must have advertised?"

"I put a small announcement in the paper. And I put up a few signs at the rec center. And at the sawmill." He looked around. "Looks like word spread at the sawmill best."

Behind Arthur was a man in a green baseball cap with a case of beer under his arm. He'd ripped a hole in one end of the cardboard and was passing the cans around.

An eager line formed for food. Arthur's wife had driven into town to pick up a dozen pizzas, and she returned just in time; all the lasagna was gone, and the loud line curled out the kitchen and well into the hall. People who'd made it through the kitchen were starting to sit down. Helen and Bennie brought their plates to a table with two older men. The guy on their left had short-cropped hair and a long gray beard. They were playing cribbage and drinking cans of Busch.

When they sat down, Bennie asked, "How's the grub?"

They didn't respond, but when the man with the long beard finished moving his pegs, he said, "Sorry, what?"

"I was just asking how the food was."

"Quite good," he said. "Not as good as the beer, but quite, quite good."

"Kind of weird to be eating lasagna on Saint Paddy's Day, but it's free," said the man sitting directly across from them. He raised his beer and said, "Cheers," then tipped it back, finishing it. Skinny and oddly tan, he had two packs of Marlboros in the breast pocket of his blue flannel shirt. He reached down into the red cooler at the base of the table and brought out four more cans, sliding two across the table for Helen and Bennie.

"Thanks," she said.

It was a fast-paced game; they didn't study their cards and they didn't look at the board when they moved the pegs. Bennie agreed with the man with the long gray beard: the beer was good.

When the deal switched, Bennie asked, "Ray LaBrecque—you know him?" The words came out of his mouth more quickly than he'd wanted them to, but the two men didn't seem to mind.

The bearded man smirked and peered across at his opponent. They both started laughing. Bennie joined in, just a low chuckle.

"My name's Zander," the man with the beard said. "I'm a cousin of the LaBrecques'. A distant one, thank God. This guy here"—he squinted, slowly and dramatically pointing at the skinny man in the blue flannel—"that's my second cousin Ray LaBrecque. We call him Dog." Dog nodded. "And that guy over there, the drunk guy with the green hat, he's Ray LaBrecque, too. They call him Sid, for some reason. Why do they call him Sid?"

They all looked over in Sid's direction, at the table beside them. Sid was laughing and drinking from a bottle of Dr. McGillicuddy's Mentholmint Schnapps. The tendons in his neck were strained.

"His dad's name is Paul," said Dog.

"Yeah," said Zander.

"But everybody calls him Sid."

Zander looked at Dog, waiting.

Dog shrugged. "Even though his name is Ray."

"Anyway," said Zander. "There are probably four or five Ray LaBrecques in town."

"Seven," said Dog, and he seemed pleased with this correction.

"Seven Ray LaBrecques," said Zander, smiling, pulling on his beard.

Dog glanced at the cribbage board before looking up at Bennie and asking, "You wanted to know about Ray LaBrecque?"

"Oh," Bennie said. "There was a guy named Ray LaBrecque from up this way, I think—anyway, he was down on the island a few weeks ago. Meadow Island. That's where we're from."

"That's Little Ray," said Dog. "He's Big Ray's nephew. He's been away for a few weeks."

"Yeah, I heard that, too," said Zander. "Some folks are looking for him. He'll turn up, though. He's a tough kid."

"He ain't lost," said Dog. "He's just off doing his thing."

"Big kid. Strong and hardworking. Goes up to New Brunswick a lot."

"They like him at that logging camp, seems so. He's a big strong kid."

"He's bigger than Big Ray, ain't he, Dog?"

"Ray Junior's pretty big," said Dog.

"Yup, Ray Junior might be bigger than Little Ray, probably. Fatter, anyway."

Dog looked at them. "Fatter. Definitely."

Zander asked, "What was he doing down there, anyway?"

"Sea urchins," said Bennie. "He was looking for sea urchins."

Zander told them he'd seen Ray a while back, during the cold snap in February, flushing out the radiator in his cousin's truck. That's when Ray had told Dog he planned to go to the coast for a fishing job.

Dog and Zander had more to say about Little Ray: he rode his motorcycle all year round, he went up to Canada often in the winter to trap marten, he'd been the hard-charging center for the hockey team—they recalled the game against Lewiston when he netted five goals—

and he dated a beautiful girl. They spoke in tones reserved for the kid you shake your head at, smiling, knowing you've never been quite so lucky.

"He got lost in the snow," said Helen. "It was dark and snowing hard."

"I've heard some people are worried." Dog scratched his neck. "But I've got a feeling the big fella's got everyone fooled."

"Little Ray's still got to be bigger than Ray Junior," said Zander. "Even though Ray Junior is fat."

"Ray Junior just sits around, listens to classical music, and collects disability," said Zander.

"I'd take Little Ray over Ray Junior any day," said Dog.

"Well, one thing's decided. You're the Ray LaBrecque who drinks the most beer," said Zander. "You're the drunkest Ray LaBrecque."

"Not drunker than Sid," said Dog, aiming his hand toward the table beside them.

"You're the drunkest Ray LaBrecque who's not an actual *drunk,*" said Zander.

"I guess so," he said, raising his can of Busch. They both laughed.

"Little Ray, yeah, he's a good kid," said Zander. "Raised right. Both his parents died, but his uncle's a good man."

"Little Ray's girlfriend—she's here," said Dog. "She's right over there." He pointed across the room.

"Martha," said Zander.

"Sweet kid," said Dog.

"Irish," added Zander.

She was standing, collecting the paper plates from her table. "There she is, that's her," said Zander. She looked calm and easy in her movements, and Bennie watched as she dumped the pizza crusts from one of the plates into a teenage boy's lap. She kept a straight face but everyone around her was laughing. She was wearing a Patriots T-shirt over a long-sleeved shirt, and black jeans. To see her there in the Tavis Falls Grange, looking like herself—the same black hair and thin face—amid an assembly of strangers made Bennie feel like he was watching a movie. It made him feel old. Helen squeezed his arm. For her, seeing Martha must have felt more real—they'd never met.

"Yup, that's her," said Zander.

Arthur was getting ready to speak; he was standing behind the middle of the three podiums draped with purple cloth. People were talking and laughing and the noise in the hall had become riotous. There were a few tables where men were passing around large plastic bottles of LTD whiskey.

Arthur tapped a knife against a glass, but no one could hear him, so he started waving his arms, still holding the glass and the knife. That didn't work, either. He tried yelling above the racket. His mouth was moving, and no one else seemed to notice. Finally, he set the knife and the glass on a nearby table and put his fingers in his mouth and whistled. The crowd quieted down, slowly at first, and then, as though Arthur were about to lead them in a hymn, the Grange was silent.

"Hello," said Arthur. "Welcome."

There was a spattering of murmured replies.

"I suppose you'd like to know why we're all gathered here," he said.

A few tables away, a man raised a handle bottle of LTD and said, almost inaudibly, "We know why we're here." This got a few laughs, but mostly people were whispering to their friends, asking what it was the drunk man had said. Across the way, Martha had her arm draped around an older woman sitting next to her.

"What's that?" asked Arthur, with a smile. No one answered, so he continued, "Anyway, I'd like to talk about why we're all here. And I don't just mean here as in here at the Grange. I mean here in the sense of being *here,* if you will, on Earth, and *here* in the sense of doing what we're doing."

Bennie was already starting to feel embarrassed for Arthur, but everyone remained quiet as he continued.

"The question I'd like to ask each of you is *why.*" He lingered on this last word.

After a few seconds of silence, a red-faced, curly-haired woman across the room said, "Why *what*?"

"Why here, why now?" said Arthur, calmly.

There was more silence, so Arthur spoke up again. "I mean, why are we here together? What brought us here tonight?"

A few tables over, one of the woodsmen said, "He drug me here," and he pushed the guy sitting next to him. The two men were framed by one of the tall windows with dark panes; snow blew against the glass.

"Okay, out of companionship," said Arthur, clasping his hands together. "Some of you were convinced to come here by your friends."

"He's not my friend," said the man, shoving the guy next to him again. They laughed.

"Why else?"

Zander shouted, "For the food and the beer. Saint Paddy's Day!" He raised his can, and nearly everyone in the hall raised a glass or can and cheered.

"Yes, of course," said Arthur. "There's nourishment for our bodies, yes. What I'm getting at, though, is the deeper meaning of why we're here. How about fate? Do you think there might be something steering us all down the same road?"

"He drug me here," the woodsman said again, and he pushed his friend a third time.

"I met a young gentleman named Bennie tonight," said Arthur. "And he's kindly volunteered to help me in my presentation."

Helen leaned over and whispered, "You did?"

Bennie had no other choice than to stand and crutch his way up to the front of the hall. A slick sheen of sweat covered Arthur's face as he looked out at the audience. Bennie saw Martha, who didn't seem surprised by his presence in the hall; he nodded in her direction, and she laughed, shaking her head. Arthur handed Bennie a stack of white cardboard placards. The one on top had the word GOODNESS printed on it in big block letters.

"Life can seem confusing," Arthur said. "We don't always know the meaning of why we're here, but we know we're here. And we want to know the meaning, don't we?"

The man who spoke next stood up and addressed Arthur with an even, well-mannered voice. He was probably in his sixties and was wearing a red checked wool jacket. His face looked banged up, but his silver hair was thick and neatly combed. "No one told us this'd be a church occasion, Mr. Page. It's Saint Patrick's Day, right? I'm drinking a toast to you and your assistant up there, friend."

The crowd started cheering. Bennie wanted poor Arthur to let everyone know with a thunderbolt of purpose and conviction why they were all gathered in the Grange. The GOODNESS placard wasn't helping. The ugly man with the neat silver hair sat down, but the crowd was still clapping, or tipping back beer cans.

"You bring up an interesting point," said Arthur, raising a finger thoughtfully. He nodded his head a few times and meted out another dramatic pause. "I was there once myself, in your same shoes, turning my back on the serious questions." His eyes darted over at Bennie, and then he quickly flipped through the placards Bennie was holding. He pulled one out that said QUESTIONS? He had all eyes on him now. "I was there. Letting my life burn along like a wick through a candle. Oblivious and undecided." Arthur's face was stern. He turned back to Bennie and pulled out a different sign. Bennie glanced down at it—it read PEACE.

"This is what we're all after, right?"

The crowd agreed, quietly.

"And this?" he asked, taking away the PEACE sign and revealing one that said LOVE.

Whistles, applause, laughter. Someone yelled, "I don't suppose you have a 'BEER' poster in there, do you?"

Arthur smiled in a sportsmanlike way. He looked down at his shoes for a moment, and the crowd quieted again. Then he continued in a gentle voice. "When you feel this resistance—this resistance to good and pure things in the world, you know who's responsible, don't you?" He let the question linger in the hall for a second or two before wiping sweat from his forehead and turning again toward Bennie. From the back of the stack Arthur pulled out another placard and placed it in full view. The crowd gasped. Three or four men stood up and threw empty beer cans, which fluttered before landing at Bennie's feet. He peeked over the front of the placard and saw the word SATAN. Below it was a well-rendered drawing of a devil, with horns and seething eyes, a triangle tail and a pitchfork.

Arthur needed to yell now to be heard, and his voice was growing hoarse. He was smiling, desperately. "If you think this is nothing but a joke, then the joke's on you. I'm sorry to say this, but Satan is alive and well. You can turn your back on him, though, my friends! Put the devil out of work!"

Those who'd been throwing beer cans earlier had started to crumple them up for better loft and aim, and the poster Bennie held was getting pelted. He held it in front of his face. He felt someone grab his arm. He turned and saw it was Helen. "Just put the posters down, Bennie," she said, covering her head.

She led him away from the front of the room; Arthur had his arms folded across his chest and stared confidently out at the people in the hall, not watching Helen and Bennie as they left. They found Martha in the back of the room, near the kitchen. "Is this what it's always like here?" he asked.

"I can't believe it's you, Bennie," she said, the lights from the rafters reflecting in her light blue eyes. Helen put out her hand and introduced herself, and Bennie was pleased when they seemed to show a warmness toward each other. Helen told her they'd met Arthur Page earlier in the day, when he hadn't seemed like such a nut, and Martha laughed. She said almost everyone in the Grange knew he was a kook; they'd come for the party and the free lasagna.

When they moved into the kitchen, where it was quieter, Helen didn't waste time; she told Martha they were in town because they were concerned about her. Bennie told her they'd been to the snowfields; he told her how deep the snow was, and how tangled the brambles were, and what it must have been like to run through the woods during that storm. If Ray had been out there, said Bennie, there was a real chance he'd gotten hurt.

She shook her head, then looked away. "No," she said.

" 'No'?"

"He'll hitchhike into town tomorrow, just watch. Or he'll drive back on his motorcycle. He's done this before. I know he'll come back and laugh at me for getting upset."

"You really believe that?" asked Helen. Bennie worried that she was being too direct.

"Or he's off sea urchin diving," Martha said. "That definitely could be what he's doing. Especially because I told him I didn't want him to go, so that's probably exactly what he's doing—and he's hiding from me because he knows I think it's dangerous."

Bennie wondered if everyone in Tavis Falls was delusional and unwilling to accept the truth, or if there was something truly extraordinary about Ray LaBrecque—that he was impervious to harm, blasting along on a motorcycle through the wilds of Canada.

"You don't think there's any chance he's really missing?" asked Helen.

When Martha's tears came, she hid her face in her hands. He could see how exhausted she was. He hugged her. Helen, too, put an arm around her.

"Just because I'm crying doesn't mean I don't think he's alive," said Martha, shaking her head, with red eyes.

The shouting started up again in the other room. Through the doorway they saw five or six men gathered in a tight semicircle up by the podium, yelling at Arthur and Nancy and another of Arthur's cohorts. It was loud, but so far people seemed to be keeping their hands to themselves.

Over the noise Helen said, "Come back to the island with us, Martha. We can look for him. We can go out to where the urchin divers are and check if he's there. We can search the snowfields. We can figure out what happened."

"I don't think I can handle seeing Littlefield right now," Martha said.

"You won't have to," said Helen. "You can stay at my house."

Martha seemed embarrassed to have cried in front of them. When she pulled her sweatshirt on over her head, scooping her ponytail out of the hood, she smiled again. Helen made another plea to Martha—she told her they'd keep looking for Ray as long as it would take.

"Why did you guys come all this way?" she asked.

"We want to help you," said Bennie.

"There must be heat on Littlefield," said Martha. "And that probably won't go away until we find Ray." She paused. "Well, I need to be back at Rosie's on Monday, anyway. And my car doesn't have snow tires."

Bennie was amazed by the matter-of-fact way Martha approached the issue of Littlefield. He wondered if she would start asking, at some point, if he and Helen suspected Littlefield's involvement, too. For now, though, her concerns seemed more practical.

Before they left, Bennie told them he wanted to give Gwen a call with an update. Helen and Martha went out to warm up the car, and Bennie squeezed past a loud group of kids who were finishing the pizza, eating it directly from the boxes. The phone was mounted to the wall in the corner. He pressed his back against the warm wall, staring at his fingers as he dialed the number. When it started ringing he watched the group of junior high kids attack the leftovers, the boys in faded jean jackets, the girls in ski parkas.

When Gwen picked up, she didn't say hello.

"Gwen?"

She whispered, "Bennie, you've got to come home. Now."

He was staring at the back of a teenage girl's head, at the way her short blond hair brushed the collar of her ski jacket. He asked Gwen what had happened. She didn't respond, so he asked her again. She said, softly, "He's here."

"I need a few more details, Gwen. Why are you whispering?"

"You've got to come home," she said. What she said next he could barely hear. "The guy who's been missing. Ray. He's here. In the Manse."

Bennie knew the phone was in his hand, but otherwise he couldn't feel anything except a dull pulse somewhere deep in his head. Two of the boys in jean jackets started wrestling with each other—laughing but grappling, hard. One of them backed into him and with his free hand Bennie shoved them and they toppled over. The boys continued wrestling, but everyone in the kitchen was looking at Bennie. He said to Gwen, "We're coming. Are you okay?"

"Hold on," she said. She'd taken her mouth away from the receiver and he heard her talking to someone else, but he couldn't make out the words. Then all he heard was the dial tone. He called back. It was busy. He called back four times, and each time: busy.

He weaved through the crowd to the door and crutched out to the Skylark. Martha needed to get a few things from Ray's trailer, so they drove out to the ridge above town, fishtailing on an unplowed county road. Ray lived behind a snow-covered blueberry field. Martha left the car and high-stepped through the drifts, up a short flight of stairs, inside. A light blinked on.

In the dark, cold car Helen asked, "Did you talk to Littlefield?"

"I talked to Gwen," he said, swallowing hard. "She says Ray LaBrecque is alive. He's at our house."

"He is?" she shouted.

"We shouldn't tell Martha," he said. "Not yet."

After a long silence she said, "We can't do that."

"Gwen didn't tell me what was going on," he said. "She didn't say anything. I don't know what's happening back there. We need to see for ourselves." He leaned over and hugged her, and over her shoulder he saw the light in the trailer blink off and Martha's silhouette jogging back down off the hill, and then she was clicking open the right rear door of the Skylark, throwing her rucksack on the bench seat, and scooting in.

13

Driving back from Tavis Falls in the dark snowstorm, nearly getting hit by a hulking plow outside Lewiston, catching glimpses of the cars that had spun off the road, Bennie tried to discern what Martha was thinking about. She probably wasn't worried about the road conditions—she'd never been timid about driving—but he wondered what she really thought had happened to Ray. Was there any part of her that truly believed he was alive? She'd always been able to judge every instant, every situation, with cool eyes. He was silent behind the wheel while Helen and Martha talked about the old, tiny kitchen at Julian's. They compared other aspects of their jobs—apparently the cooks at

Rosie's got a decent share of the tips, which was something Julian had never offered. Martha told Helen she was crazy to agree to such terms, and Helen said she was probably right.

"Bennie, you drive like my grandfather," said Martha.

"It's snowing pretty hard," he said. "Did you notice that?" He found himself slipping back into his teenage persona, intimidated by Martha, deferring to her judgment.

"When it snows, you've got to show the road who's boss. Let me drive."

"We're almost there," he said, weakly.

"We're only about halfway. Come on. You're making me nervous."

After they pulled over, Bennie ended up in the backseat. Martha didn't hesitate to start passing cars right away, scooting out into the oncoming lane, weaving back and forth between pickup trucks. Bennie closed his eyes.

By the time they got back to the island, it had stopped snowing and gotten much colder. Bennie didn't want to arrive at the Manse with both Helen and Martha—he didn't know what he might find there—so he asked Martha to drive them to Helen's first. Bennie would pick them up in the morning.

As Martha collected her stuff from the backseat and Bennie got back behind the wheel, Helen stepped out into the cold and kicked her way through the snow to his side of the car. He rolled the window down. She leaned in. Their noses were nearly touching when she whispered, "You don't think we should come back to the house with you?" He stared at her dark eyebrows, her uneven eyes, then down at her mouth. He tried to see her whole face, but she was too close. Her breath was a little sour. She said, "Wouldn't it be better if we all went?" He put his hand up on her cheek and drew her toward him. They kissed. She squeezed his hand and turned toward her house. He wanted to say something to her, but sitting there, looking at her, he was quiet. He was hoping she'd understand what the silence really meant—that he wanted to be with her, but that he needed to go to the Manse alone. As she walked into her house he wished he'd been able to say the right thing.

It was midnight when he got home. Only one light was on—the living room light—and there was smoke coming from the chimney. He sat in the car with the engine running and smoked two cigarettes before stepping out into the cold. He'd had the same pack of cigarettes in the glove compartment for weeks; Helen hated smoking. The sky was clear, with only a few wispy clouds highlighted by the moon. He had a vague image in his mind of Ray's corpse, wrapped in a bedsheet, hidden in the bathtub.

As he hopped through the unshoveled snow in front of the Manse, he heard Gwen's laugh—loud guffawing, unabashed. As surprising as it was, he was relieved to hear it; he hadn't heard her laugh like that since the beginning of her visit. He knocked twice then pushed against the door—it was still locked, but Gwen came to open it almost immediately. She stuck her round, flushed face out into the cold, grinning. "We've been drinking a lot of beer," she said. Her hair was still in a loose braid and she was wearing an oversize white T-shirt and shorts. Ronald was wagging his tail beside her. When Bennie crutched inside, Gwen tried to jump up into his arms. Ronald barked and scratched at his cast. Bennie hopped backward once on his good leg to keep his balance, and Gwen hugged him and laughed, and again she said, "We've been drinking a lot of beer."

"Let me get my balance," he said.

"He was sleeping, but now we're drinking beer." She hugged him again. "Happy Saint Patrick's Day."

"Is Littlefield here?"

"I'm sorry if I scared you on the phone. I was freaking out then. But I'm beginning to see how amazing it all is." She took him by the hand. "You'll like him. Here, come. Come into the living room."

He followed Gwen through the kitchen (they had the thermostat cranked up to what felt like eighty degrees; he usually kept it at sixty) and into the living room. Sitting by the fire, slumped in the wicker rocking chair, with his head down and his eyes closed, a blanket pulled around his shoulders, was Jamie Swensen. Swensen was a biathlete from Brunswick Littlefield and Bennie had known in high school. Bennie hadn't seen him in a while, and he looked different—his curly brown hair was longer, covering his ears and the back of his neck and stopping just above his closed eyes. He had a thick bandage on his head, like a bandanna, and a small spot of blood had soaked through, where the bandage covered his temple. The upper parts of both of his arms were heavily bandaged, too, as was his waist, just above the belt of his jeans. His hands were wrapped in white bandages, the individual fingers fat with gauze. His cheeks were ruddy and he reeked of beer.

Bennie stood a few yards away and said to Gwen, "You must be absolutely shitfaced. What's Swensen doing here?"

"I'm sure it's a relief," she said with wide eyes. "I mean, that he's alive."

Bennie pointed. "That's Swensen."

"I know it's . . . weird. I guess you don't remember meeting Ray."

"That," he said again, "is Swensen."

She shook her head.

Then he spoke directly to Swensen. "What the hell, man. Tell my drunk sister who you are." He tapped him on the chest.

"Careful," said Gwen. "He's pretty fragile right now."

Bennie turned back toward Gwen, who seemed both concerned and ready to keel over. He looked at Swensen, whose eyes were still closed, and tipped Swensen's head back. Swensen blinked open his eyes. His expression was inscrutable, and then he scowled, but the scowl quickly faded to a vague look of discomfort.

When Bennie pinched his nipple and twisted it, though, the scowl returned. "Damn it, Bennie," he said. "You were supposed to go along with it."

Gwen looked confused. "Ray?"

"Maybe you should go," said Bennie, looking closely at Swensen's head bandage.

Swensen asked, "What's up, bro? I haven't seen you in *too* long." He unwrapped the gauze on his fingers and said, "Man, it's hot in this house." His tongue seemed like it was causing him problems; his words slurred. "When you coming back to train?"

"Swensen, what the hell are you doing here?"

"Oh, man." He smirked, but then he looked at Gwen, who was moving slowly toward him, staring into his eyes.

"Have you been fucking with me?" she asked.

Swensen picked up the bottle near the rockers of his chair and drank a few gulps before Gwen grabbed it from him.

"Have you been?" asked Gwen. She folded her arms on her chest and stood over him. There was a long row of empty bottles lined up by the fire. Swensen unwrapped the bandages on his hands, then looked up at Bennie and Gwen.

"Talk," said Bennie.

"Yeah," slurred Gwen.

"Okay, okay," he said. "We were over at Lackey's house—me and Lackey and Nate Langholtz and Nate's dad and Vin Thibideaux, and we were all drinking, putting up some good numbers, you know . . . it's Saint Paddy's Day. Just a bunch of dudes, sitting around."

Bennie remembered these guys—Lackey and Langholtz—from Brunswick High. They were basically unobjectionable, except that they were fairly dumb, and usually got swept up by whatever prevailing wind happened to be blowing. Bennie was sure things hadn't changed much for those two. Swensen, unfortunately, was the kind of good-natured guy who was unwittingly influenced by their stupidity. And Vin Thibideaux—it wasn't surprising that he and Nate Langholtz's dad were in on it, too.

"Thibideaux, he was the one who said your sister was back in town," Swensen continued. "You know, and I'd always heard she was cool.

Dude, you probably don't want to hear this . . ." He leaned in closer to whisper to Bennie, though Gwen was close enough to hear. "Your sister—she's mint!" He grinned.

Bennie glanced at Gwen. She still looked stunned, but she stayed quiet.

"Go on," said Bennie.

"Thibideaux said I should come over and say hello. He said he'd been coming around, trying to see if you were okay, Bennie, but that he hadn't seen you yet. He said you'd think it'd be funny as hell if I came over—"

"Wrapped up in bandages?"

"Yeah," he said. "He said you'd all be fooled." It seemed Swensen was slowly realizing that what he had done was not as hilarious as he'd hoped it would be. "They just told me to call myself LaBrick."

"LaBrecque," said Bennie.

"Right. LaBrick. Say my name was LaBrick, and say I'd been lost since that night you got hurt, Bennie."

"Why are you hanging out with old guys like Vin Thibideaux and Nate Langholtz's dad in the first place?" asked Bennie.

"They had the beer," said Swensen.

Gwen's face was aglow with sweat. She was still staring at Swensen as he unwrapped the bandages, shaking her head, smelling like perfume and Rolling Rock.

Bennie asked her, "This is what you were talking about when we spoke on the phone?"

She put her head in her hands. "I'm such an idiot."

"No, you're not," said Bennie. "There are a lot of assholes in this town." It was exactly the kind of idea that Vin Thibideaux and his buddies, all of them sitting around swilling beers, would come up with.

"I'm sorry," said Swensen. "I had no idea I was messing things up. They said you'd be fooled. The fake blood . . . that was Langholtz's idea."

Bennie couldn't believe how tanked Swensen was. Gwen collapsed on the purple couch and put a pillow over her head.

"You never heard about LaBrecque?" he asked.

"No," Swensen said.

From beneath the pillow, Gwen cried, "Why would that jerk do this? Nate Langholtz? We had the same homeroom, for Christ's sake."

"It wasn't Nate," said Bennie. "It was Vin. Vin's an idiot. And he hates our family."

"Gwennie, we were having a good time, right?" said Swensen, sadly. He picked up another half-full beer by his feet and started drinking it. This time, Gwen stood up from the couch, walked over to him, and plucked the bottle from his lips.

"Not really," she said.

"I didn't know I was going to piss anyone off," said Swensen, standing up from the rocking chair.

"If you're wondering why I was being nice to you," she said, "it was because I thought everything was going to be okay."

"Man, I'm confused," said Swensen, scratching his armpit. Gwen seemed to be realizing he was a difficult guy to get mad at. "But wasn't it a good time"—he lowered his voice—"when we were kissing on the couch?"

She slapped him softly across the face. Swensen smiled. She slapped him a second time, harder, torquing her waist like a tennis player. This got Swensen's attention. He stopped smiling for a minute but continued looking admiringly at her. He said, "You've got some serious power. Check out those arms." Then he stood up and asked, "Hey, should I go get us some more beers?"

"No," said Bennie.

"Come on, guys. Let's just hang out for a little longer," said Swensen.

Gwen and Bennie looked at each other. Then Bennie said, "We've got more in the crisper drawer."

They all drank Rolling Rocks for another hour or so. Bennie was surprised Swensen hadn't heard about Ray LaBrecque or the accident. But Swensen lived with his folks on River Road in Brunswick on the banks of the Androscoggin, and they didn't involve themselves much with town. Each time Swensen finished a bottle, he handed it to Gwen, who was lying quietly near the fire and added it to the line. Swensen continued talking about how his shooting had been improving; he was hitting his targets on full rest and was feeling more confident about his accuracy during the races. Swensen was a big, strong guy, but he was an oaf—he didn't have the necessary control during a race to clean the targets. He wasn't the kind of Brunswick kid who told lies when he was drinking, but with the bandage on his head it was difficult to take him seriously. By the end of the night he'd probably passed nine or ten empty bottles to Gwen to add to her line, which had started to curve around the coffee table.

"I'm going to bed," said Gwen. Since she'd arrived from New York she'd been sleeping on the purple couch, so by saying this she was asking Bennie and Swensen to leave. She got on the couch and slipped inside her sleeping bag. She wriggled around, then pulled her pants out of the top of the bag and set them on the coffee table. Ronald was curled up on one end of the couch. "Get down, Ronnie," she said softly, and she nudged him, and he slinked to the floor.

"Hey, Gwen," said Swensen. "I'm sorry. I liked talking to you, back when you thought I was LaBrick. I didn't mean to piss you off."

"I guess it's okay," she said. "But just remember, I didn't mean any of what I said. Or . . . what I said to you I was saying to someone else. Someone I thought you were."

Swensen's cheeks, and his eyes, were ablaze. "Okay," he said. "It's cool."

He stayed in the rocking chair after Bennie switched off the lights. Bennie let people sleep over at the Manse often, anyone who didn't want to drive off-island late at night.

Just after Bennie collapsed into bed, he heard Gwen get up. She stumbled into his room with her sleeping bag wrapped around her shoulders. She sat down on the bed near his feet. "I think Swensen passed out," she said. "He didn't say anything when I walked past him in my underwear."

"What did you expect him to say?"

"I don't know," she said, glancing over her shoulder. "I think he likes me. Does he have a girlfriend?"

"Swensen? No," he said. "But you've got to remember—Julian's the one for you."

"I told you. I knew that kid back in high school. He's a hippie."

"He's grown up. He's tall. He's a good cook."

They were silent for a while. The storm window beside Bennie's bed was rattling. He could feel cold air streaming in, by the sill.

"We drove over to Tavis Falls, where Ray is from," he said. "We met Martha at this Saint Patrick's Day Bible thing."

Gwen pulled the sleeping bag more tightly around her shoulders. "Saint Paddy's Day Bible thing?"

"Martha is Ray's girlfriend," he said.

He saw it unfolding in her eyes—she was realizing that Littlefield was probably wrapped up in something that would not end well. He hadn't been able to think it himself, but he recognized it in her eyes.

"You know, it was easy, when I saw Swensen. It was easy for me to believe Ray was alive. Littlefield and I had a long talk earlier today. Not about Ray, about other stuff. Acting, my life in New York. And Littlefield told me he wants to get out of Maine. He was being normal, Bennie. It's the most I've talked to him in a long time. He was being nice to me. It was easy, really easy. I guess I was just wanting to believe Ray hadn't been badly hurt. When Swensen showed up, I believed it." She lay back on the bed by Bennie's feet. She sighed. "Those bandages on his hands looked pretty stupid. But come on, you might have believed it, too."

"Probably."

They lay in the quiet for a while. Bennie kept his eyes open even though he couldn't see anything. Then she said, "I'm worried about our brother."

"Where is he?"

"I haven't seen him since this afternoon."

"Well, it *is* Saint Patrick's Day," said Bennie, but the fact that Littlefield had been nice to Gwen—chatted her up—meant to Bennie that he was probably on his way out of town.

14

During her senior year at Vassar, Gwen drove to the island from Poughkeepsie. When she arrived, Bennie was already in the kitchen to greet her, and they walked together into the living room, where Littlefield was waiting quietly on the purple couch, staring at logs burning in the fire, dressed in a brown tweed jacket, a white shirt, and a red tie.

"Oh, shit. Should I be wearing a dress?" asked Gwen. She had on jeans and a T-shirt and a thin red parka.

"We're late," said Littlefield.

"We'll be fine if we leave in a few minutes," said Bennie. "Get up and give your sister a hug."

Littlefield sighed. "Kiddo, did you even pack a dress?"

"Well, hello and good to see you, too," she said.

He stood up and hugged her. "If you want them, there are some clothes in the back closet."

"Since when do you give a shit what I wear? And what about Bennie? Shouldn't he be dressed up, too?"

Littlefield shrugged. He stood up and strode to the kitchen, returning with a pitcher full of water. He poured it on the fire. Thin rivers of ash streamed from the hearth.

"Oh, man," said Bennie. "What a mess."

"You're the one who started this fire. We can't let it burn while we drive to Mom's."

Bennie walked toward the back hall closet. "I'll go put on a tie."

Eventually they crammed into Littlefield's truck, sitting three abreast, Gwen in the middle. Knowing they'd be late, Littlefield insisted on driving. His studded tires were noisy on the dry road, and he kept the window rolled partway down so he could smoke.

Eleanor had been living off the island for only a year; Bennie knew she hadn't yet found the friends she was hoping to find and she was spending too much time at home. She'd invited Bennie and Gwen and Littlefield to Clover Lake for the anniversary of Coach's death. It had been eight years.

Gwen started to tell her brothers a little bit about how things were going at Vassar, and Bennie knew she was being careful: Littlefield had never had any interest in going to college and was critical of any lifestyle he considered leisurely, especially when he was actually working (these criticisms vanished when he wasn't). Bennie also wondered if Gwen didn't like talking too much about her studies because she knew Bennie had dropped out of Orono after a year of being bored with most of his classes. So she talked about her new interest in acting. She said it was a demanding major; she had workshops during the day and rehearsals at night, and she also had to find time to write papers. She said her director was a genius. He'd been on the faculty for twenty years, but he also worked occasionally Off Broadway. "He says I'll do well in New York."

"Sounds like he wants to sleep with you," said Littlefield.

"Why do you have to say things like that?" said Gwen.

"I'm sure you're good at acting," said Littlefield. "I'm just saying you should be careful. You've got to watch out for guys like that. Think about it. He teaches girls. At a girls' college."

"Vassar's been coed since the sixties," said Gwen. "And so what if he wants to sleep with me? He thinks I'm talented."

Littlefield laughed, and Gwen frowned and furrowed her brow, but then she started laughing, too. She punched Littlefield in the arm. "You're such an asshole."

"It's true," said Bennie. "You *are* an asshole."

"Just make sure," said Littlefield, "after you fuck him and he gets you a role in a play down in New York, that you set aside a ticket for me. I'd like to come down and see that."

"You'd come down to New York to watch a show?"

"Of course. And afterward I'd take a ride around Central Park in one of those horse carriages."

Gwen shook her head. "You're such a butthole."

"No. I'm serious. Okay, maybe I'll just hire a taxi and have it run me around town. Either way, if you fuck your teacher and get a role, I'll come down for it."

"And if I don't fuck my teacher but still get a role?" said Gwen. She sneezed.

"Sure."

"You could always go see her in a show at Vassar first," said Bennie.

"Yeah, you could, too, retard. I'm just saying, I'm waiting for her to make it to the big leagues," said Littlefield.

"You sound like Coach," said Gwen. She sneezed again, then opened the glove compartment, where she found a few Burger King napkins. "Are these clean?"

Littlefield nodded. Gwen blew her nose. "Did you ever notice that I sneeze when you smoke in the car?" she asked. "Do you care?"

"The thing about Coach," said Littlefield, blowing smoke out the window, "is that he'd want to come. He'd want to be at every goddamn play you were in—at Vassar, in New York, wherever. You put on a puppet show behind your couch, he'd want to be there. But he wouldn't leave the island to do it. That's why I'm different. I'll come to New York after you fuck your teacher. One hundred percent."

At dinner, Littlefield was less talkative. Gwen carried the chicken into the dining room from the kitchen and placed it in front of Littlefield for carving. No one spoke directly about Coach, except Eleanor, who said that it would have pleased him to see everyone together. Gwen started talking again about her theater activities, though instead of talking about the brilliant director, she told their mother about the play she'd been writing—a side project, really, but something she was trying to work on for at least a few minutes every day. Her focus within the major was acting, but she was getting credit for an independent playwriting project, too. She didn't want to discuss the details, but she mentioned it was set on an island, and it was about two brothers—a basketball coach and a hockey coach—and their competition with each other, both of them trying to recruit the same kids, both of them in love with the same woman.

"You know, your dad didn't have a brother," said their mother, wiping her mouth with a cloth napkin.

"It's not about Coach," said Gwen. "It's made up."

"What's it called?" asked Bennie.

"I'm not sure," she said. "I've been calling it *Coach.*"

Littlefield chuckled.

"What's so funny?" asked Gwen.

"If you're drawing from your experiences with your dad," said

Eleanor, "I think that process can be very difficult. If you want to talk with me about it, I'd be happy to."

"Never mind. Forget I said anything about it."

"You don't need to be rude to me, Gwennie," said Eleanor.

"Just lay off, Mom," said Bennie. "It's not a big deal. It's just a project she's working on."

"I'm with Mom, actually," said Littlefield. "Stick to acting, kiddo. I don't think Coach would be too pleased to know you're using him to please that big-dick teacher of yours."

Gwen's mouth hung open. She slapped the table, rattling her plate.

Eleanor said, "William!"

Bennie shook his head, looking down. "Nice one, man."

Gwen stood up, her face red with anger. "Since when are you the only one who knows what Coach wants? That's such bullshit!"

"He's dead," said Littlefield, calmly. "He doesn't want anything. He doesn't care. Which means I was wrong. You can go ahead and write about Coach, and you can enjoy your teacher at Vassar, Mr. Big Dick. There's nothing to worry about. The world is your oyster."

Gwen picked up her glass and threw her milk at Littlefield, splashing it in his face. "You're a fucking turd," she said, and walked out of the room.

"William, go to your sister. Apologize to her right now," said Eleanor.

Littlefield wiped his face with his napkin. "What a baby."

"Go find her, Littlefield," said Bennie.

"There's nothing I can say that'll change things," said Littlefield. "She's in her own little world."

"You don't need to be so harsh to her," said Bennie.

Eleanor began to cry. "This is not what I had in mind when I planned this dinner."

"God, Mom," said Littlefield. "Why do we need to pretend that everything's the same? You put out the nice china and everything, but it's a joke. Isn't it obvious?"

"I don't know what you're talking about, William."

Bennie put his arm out, as if to hold his brother back. "Just stop being an asshole, okay?"

"No!" yelled Littlefield, standing up. "I will not stop being an asshole! I hate coming here! I hate pretending this family is *anything at all* without him! You people are insane!"

They heard Gwen call from the other room, "*You're* insane."

"Nobody is insane!" screamed Eleanor, with tears on her cheeks.

"Whoa, Mom, are you okay?" asked Bennie.

"I want everyone to sit down right now," said Eleanor. "There will be no more yelling. You are not insane. I want you to eat your chicken. It's getting cold. Sit down, William. Gwen, come back in here."

Almost instantly, Gwen returned to the dining room and sat down. There was a point in every family meal—even upsetting ones, like this one—when silence arrived. Everyone chewed, looking around at each other. A few minutes passed.

Bennie was the first to speak. "Hey, Mom, did I tell you? I've started to repair the plumbing. In the Manse. It's not as bad as I thought it would be. But still, I think it's going to take a while."

"Thank you, Benjamin. This is good news. Are you helping, William?"

"I'll tell him when he starts to make big mistakes," said Littlefield.

"Thank you, William."

"I'll help, too—when I'm around," said Gwen. "Maybe after graduation."

"Thank you, Gwen," said Eleanor. "I'm glad to hear this. Your father would be happy to know you're working together on the house."

"Hey, kiddo," said Littlefield, his mouth full. "You really shouldn't make plans to come back to the island after you graduate. We need you to go to New York. We need you to be a star." He swallowed, then stood up and collected a few of the dishes, bringing them out to the kitchen. When he returned, he was carrying a plate of Eleanor's cookies and a pot of coffee.

After another period of silence while they ate dessert, Eleanor said, "I have something I want to say, and I don't want any of you to argue with me. Okay?"

Littlefield shrugged. Gwen said, "Okay, Mom. What is it?"

"He loved you three more than anything. He loved you so, so much."

15

It was four a.m. when they heard the pounding. Bennie woke up, convinced Gwen was having a nightmare. But a voice was shouting, "Benjamin! Open the door! Benjamin!"

He sat up in bed. Light from the moon, reflected off the snow outside his window, was making the walls of his room glow. Everything felt luminous and liquid and blue. At first he thought he was in the hospital, or deep inside a snow cave. Then he heard the voice yell, "Get out here! I know you're there!" That got him to turn his bedside light on, and then he had a better sense of where he was and what was happening. Ronald was barking in the kitchen, snapping his jaws.

Bennie pulled on a sweater and sweatpants and hopped around the corner from his bedroom into the living room. Gwen was staggering from the purple couch to the front hall closet, where she rummaged for a baseball bat. She gripped it in both hands and went to the front door. Without hesitating, she flung it open and there was Vin Thibideaux. Ronald continued to bark. Bennie stayed out of view, far enough from the light of the fire.

"Mr. Thibideaux?" asked Gwen.

"Hey, Gwen. I'm on police business," he said. He was wearing a black wool cap but no jacket—just a Patriots T-shirt and jeans. The dog stopped barking.

"I'd like you to quiet down, Mr. Thibideaux," she said.

"Where's your brother?"

"My head hurts," she said. "Please quiet down. Do you know what time it is?" The bat rested on her shoulder, but she still held it with both hands. "It's the middle of the night."

Bennie was standing in the corner of the room with his back pressed against the wall so he couldn't be seen.

Vin tried to take a step inside the door, but Gwen poked him in the belly with the bat. She didn't put much into it, but her aim was impressive. He stumbled back.

"Let me talk to Benjamin," said Vin.

"Wow, you stink," said Gwen. "Is everybody in this town drunk?"

"Everybody in the goddamn world," he mumbled.

"I've got a question for you, Mr. Thibideaux," said Gwen, poking him again with the end of the bat. "Did you send Jamie Swensen over here?"

He smiled, then pushed the bat away with a quick swing of his forearm and stumbled into the kitchen. It was dark enough that Bennie just saw his thick outline, a big bear up on hind legs. When he made his way into the living room, Gwen jumped on his back and put him in a quick headlock. Ronald went crazy, grabbing Vin's pant leg, tugging it back and forth. Vin tried to shake Gwen off his back but couldn't, and they tumbled onto the floor, near where Bennie was hiding. It wasn't long before Vin was on top of Gwen, pinning her arms while Ronald snarled and tugged. Gwen thrashed her head back and forth, but Vin held the rest of her body still, and then Bennie jumped from the shadows and hurled himself at Vin, cast and all, bashing him to the floor. Vin knocked over the long line of empty beer bottles. "What?" he cried. The only light in the room was from the smoldering fire.

Swensen was in the back hallway, dead asleep on the runner carpet.

"Grab the bat, Gwen," said Bennie.

They were grappling on the wood floor—Bennie had one of Vin's arms and was trying to crank it toward the middle of his back, but with his other arm Vin was pulling Bennie's good leg up toward his chest. Bennie told Gwen to hit Vin with the bat if he wouldn't let go.

Gwen had the bat held high. "You guys are too tangled up," she said. "Want me to call the cops?"

"I'm the cops, you assholes," said Vin, who was now on his back, everything tensed, his face a reddish purple. He turned his head to the side and vomited on Bennie's hand. A hot, raw smell filled the room, like the carcass of a freshly slain animal.

Gwen said, "You're not a cop. You're a fat, gross, pigheaded turd. You went to school with my father and I know how stupid you are. Rosebud whiskey? Is that what you've been drinking, Mr. Thibideaux?"

Vin stopped struggling. His face was slack, still purple. He burped, then relaxed on his back. He was winded. Ronald let go of his pant leg, walked up to the puddle of puke, and sniffed it.

"No!" yelled Gwen.

Ronald scampered over to the purple couch, hopped up, and curled into a ball on the far end.

"I'll get some paper towels," said Bennie, pushing himself up from the floor, workmanlike, shaking the warm puke off his hand.

"I'll get them," said Gwen.

"No," he said. "You stay and break Vin's kneecaps if he tries to get up."

She held the bat like a samurai sword. "You used to have a crush on my mom," she told Vin.

As Bennie hopped out of the room, Vin retched again, curling onto his side.

Coming back from the kitchen, he flipped on the overhead light. They all squinted in the brightness. He tossed the paper towels at Vin. They bounced off his chest and rolled into the fireplace. Bennie stared down at him, disgusted by the old, drunk cop. He felt some relief, too. For the moment, he had no reason to fear him.

Vin got to his knees while Gwen kept the bat cocked and ready. But he crouched down and vomited a third time, a small amount that spattered the puddle he'd already made. "I've got to get home," he said.

"Run along," said Gwen.

Vin tripped on the door jamb, then struggled to his feet and ambled through the mudroom, through the door, and out into the yard. He stumbled in the deep snow and fell on his side. He pushed himself up, glanced back at the Manse, then walked in a curved line to his cruiser. As soon as he started it, he revved the engine, spinning in the snow, and nearly sideswiped the stone wall. When he made it out of the driveway, though, his headlights disappeared quickly. The house felt calm again.

Swensen stumbled into the living room wrapped in a blanket, rubbing his swollen eyes. "Who was that?" he asked.

"Your buddy," said Gwen. "Mr. Thibideaux."

"That guy knows how to party," said Swensen.

16

When Bennie left in the morning, Gwen was asleep on the purple couch. Swensen was snoring in the hallway, lying on his stomach, his arms and legs spread wide.

Bennie arrived at Helen's house just after nine. She was peeling an eggplant and Martha was sitting next to her at the kitchen table. Helen didn't say anything when Bennie pulled a chair up next to her; she just continued to peel. He knew Helen was expecting news—perhaps even good news. But all he said was "Hi." He took off his hat and scratched the top of his head.

"They're due in sometime tomorrow," said Helen, slicing a long thin peel from the fat eggplant.

"Who?"

"The fucking urchiners," said Martha. "That's when Ray was supposed to get off the island." She was hunched over, holding her hands in her lap. She looked exhausted.

Bennie suggested they go down to the docks, ask around, see what kind of information they could gather. It was possible they'd find someone who'd seen him, heard his plan. If he wasn't lost in the snow, maybe there were other answers. It was a desperate idea, and Bennie could tell Helen was upset that he'd even suggested it, but without Littlefield or any other leads, there wasn't much to do. He could tell Helen knew by then that Gwen had been wrong: Ray LaBrecque was not alive and well at the Manse. She put the eggplant down. Martha said, "Let's get going."

Bennie called Julian to see if he wanted to come along. He said it was a dumb idea, but if they were going he wanted to captain the boat. "We need to get the heat off your brother," Julian said. "Where is he, by the way?"

"I haven't seen him for a few days. Gwen saw him yesterday, though."

"Maybe he took off?" asked Julian.

"I doubt it," said Bennie, but earlier in the morning he'd been concerned enough to call Skunk Gould's trailer—which is where Littlefield always spent his drunken nights—and Skunk hadn't seen Littlefield for a few days, either.

Bennie and Martha and Helen arrived at Kearney's Lobster Cooperative a few minutes before Julian, and stood in the cold beside the stacked green wire traps. Bennie had called Handelmann from Helen's house about using his outboard, and Handelmann consented immediately, though he warned Bennie to bring a shovel, because the boat would be full of snow. Handelmann kept his boat at the lobster co-op;

a few of the guys who fished out of Kearney's had pets that Handelmann cared for, and they let him tie up to their wharf in the off-season.

Julian arrived in his Silverado, which had dents in the front panels and the hood from driving into the back of his barn, which is what he'd done a few times late at night after drinking at the restaurant. Julian was carrying fishing lines—hand lines—and while this annoyed Bennie, he realized it was probably not the worst idea. Looking for information about Ray's whereabouts and trying to find the urchiners was likely a fruitless mission; at least they could troll for mackerel along the way, which, during the wintertime, would also be fruitless, but it would give them something to do. Again, it looked from the color of his face as though Julian had recently swilled a few beers, though he wasn't drunk, just slightly subdued. He hadn't seen Martha in a while, and though Bennie feared he might say something inappropriate, Julian didn't; he just said hi and bowed his head.

Then everyone became businesslike, getting the boat ready to go. Martha carried the shovel as they walked down the hill to the wharf. She told them that even though she'd been working in the area for a long time, she'd never spent time on the ocean. She was from Maine, of course, and she'd been to Old Orchard Beach, and out on the Peak's Island Ferry in Portland, but that was it. She had always liked to make comments about how different she was from them—she hadn't grown up in a house on the water, she'd never gone to college, she didn't have family money to fall back on.

Julian didn't seem to know what to make of Helen outside the restaurant; he was careful with her. It was hard to make small talk with her in general, but at the restaurant especially, she was focused on her job. And Julian was her boss. Julian was wearing an Eskimo jacket with a fur-lined hood; even though Helen was tall, Julian looked like a giant next to her. When he took out his cigarettes and offered her one, she shook her head. He handed Bennie one without offering first, but he shook his head, and Helen caught the exchange. She said, "He doesn't smoke," though she knew he did on occasion. Julian didn't say anything, which surprised Bennie—Julian was normally a loudmouth, especially given an opportunity to tease Bennie.

After Martha finished shoveling, Bennie started the engine, which needed a few pulls and a lot of choke. Once it fired up, it revved obediently. They let it idle for a few minutes. Julian took his seat behind the wheel, folding up his long legs between the thwarts. It was a small aluminum boat, the kind in which balancing weight is important—too much on one side, when the chop was coming at a bad angle, could flip it over. They all stayed in the middle, Martha and Helen on the forward thwart, facing aft; Julian at the helm with Bennie beside him. As soon as they got moving, the snow that Martha hadn't been able to reach under the thwarts, beside the riveted seams, swirled up around them and off the stern.

Julian didn't need to ask; he steered a course to Riverneck Island. Two miles would take them twenty minutes. They picked up speed between the long swells, but there was chop coming from the north, which brought big wings of spray over the bow. Whenever Julian slowed to lessen the spray, it seemed they weren't making enough headway. But then he'd speed up and they'd get soaked again, although they were already wet, so it didn't much matter. Bennie used an old Clorox bottle cut in half to bail seawater out of the bilge, off the stern.

They were halfway across the channel when Bennie caught up with the bailing and Julian asked him to take the wheel. Shifting weight while at full speed in a heavy chop crossing a deep body of water in a tin boat is tricky, but they moved slowly; he scooted over to sit where Julian had been sitting while Julian reached behind the seat to get the hand line. He said he wanted to troll. They were going much too fast, the water was too deep, the chop was too rough, and mackerel were scarce in wintertime—but Julian thought it was a good time to cast a line. Bennie wondered if Julian had swilled more than just a few beers. Bennie kept his hand on the throttle and didn't slow down.

After letting out enough line so that the bright-colored tackle was no longer dancing on the surface, Julian tried to tie the other end to the boat, but Martha reached over and tapped him on the shoulder, putting out her hand to take the line. Julian seemed glad to know Martha was interested in fishing, too.

There were two lobster boats tied to the stone pier in the deep-water inlet on the eastern side of Riverneck Island. As soon as the pier was in sight, Martha started hauling in the mackerel line. It was almost flat calm once they got inside the northern point; the wind was still blowing, but there were no swells and the tide was nearly high.

Riverneck Island didn't have many trees; its shore was all loaf-size granite rocks leading up to the field. A developer from Boston owned the island, though he never visited. He left a few head of sheep there to keep the grasses short, and for a few years he'd been letting urchiners stay in the shack at the top of the island—the change in usage gave him a deal on his taxes.

At first, Bennie planned on scouting out the shack on his own, but Martha and Helen climbed off the boat onto the pier and started walking up the well-worn sheep trail, brown in the snow. Bennie was slow on his crutches, and Julian hung back with him. The islands in the area didn't usually get much snow, but Riverneck had plenty. They were making their way uphill to the only stand of spruce trees, at the top of the island, beside the shack, and they saw one of the men in the far distance sitting down between two trees in an orange rain jacket. When they got closer they saw he was naked from the waist down except for his boots, shitting. His back was to them. He wiped his ass, stood up, and walked into the shack.

"My kind of place," said Martha.

"Do you want to wait outside?" Bennie asked Martha and Helen.

Helen shook her head dismissively and walked toward the door. Julian stepped in front of her; he wanted to be the first to enter. He knocked and no one responded. Then they heard someone shout, "Who's there?"

When Julian opened the door, hot air struck their faces—a heat laced with the smell of feet, whiskey, and dead fish.

"Julian here," he said.

The shack was one large room with a woodstove on the far end heating a wide cast-iron pot. The floor was covered by dry mud. In the corner there were two triple-decker bunk beds, and in the center of the room two men sat playing cards beneath a kerosene lamp hanging from the ceiling by a chain. One of them was Shaw—whom they'd battled that night at the quarry—and the other was Avery, the kid who'd stopped paintballing and let Ray LaBrecque take his place. Avery had lost most of his hair and had shaved the rest of it down to stubble. He didn't seem to recognize Bennie. The short stocky urchiner in the rain jacket who'd just taken a shit on the lawn was pulling up his jeans near the bunk beds. He turned around; it was Boak, who, along with Shaw, had helped get Bennie to the hospital.

Helen and Martha and Julian and Bennie stood drenched in a tight group near the doorway.

The urchiners looked at the newcomers as though they'd just emerged from the depths of the ocean. Martha and Helen had their watch caps pulled down and their jackets zipped up.

"We're looking for Ray LaBrecque," Bennie said.

Boak said, "Well, he isn't out here." He sat down at the card table.

"Who said you could tie up to our pier?" asked Shaw. He stood up.

Boak stood up, too, and said, "Take 'er easy, Shaw." Then he turned toward them. "We haven't seen him since the night we went to the quarry."

Shaw said, "We've been short a man ever since."

Martha stepped between Julian and Bennie and said, "Is that all you care about, fuckface?"

"Quiet down, cunt," he said, brushing his hand calmly over his crew cut.

Martha tried charging him, but Julian grabbed her arm.

"She'll rip your head off, Shaw," said Avery, laughing.

"Why didn't you take better care of him?" asked Martha.

Boak said, "No one could see a goddamn thing that night." He looked at Julian and Bennie. "You two could tell her that."

"You're all fucking wrong," said Shaw. "I just think it was an easy way for him to skip out on work. I bet he took off for New Brunswick."

"Don't you get it?" asked Helen, in a steady, quiet voice. "He's missing, and there are people who care about him. Don't speak that way to Martha." Before leaving, Martha looked back at the men; she seemed to want to say something else, but then she dropped her chin and turned for the door.

Bennie's crutches slowed them up, but they moved purposefully down the muddy path, across the snowy field. When they boarded and Bennie was just about to cast off, he saw a squat figure in a raincoat coming down the trail. It was Boak. Julian cut the engine and when Boak reached the pier he said, "I'll cast off your lines. It's tricky to get pointed the right way in this wind." Martha was sitting on the forward thwart, and he addressed her from the pier. "Ray was a good worker. Tougher than Shaw, when it came right down to it. I wish I could tell you where he was now." When Bennie handed him the line, Boak grabbed Bennie's arm and with his face close he said, "Your brother went off in the same direction as LaBrecque, before you fell, but that's not telling you anything you don't already know, is it?"

Bennie wanted to throw him off the pier, but instead he just stepped into the boat and let Boak push the bow out in the right direction.

They still had an hour or so before it got dark. Helen put her arm around Martha; they huddled together on the forward thwart. The spruce trees on the back shore glowed orange and purple in the late-afternoon light. The swells had lessened a bit—now they were three or four feet high and endlessly wide. The wind had died, so when the sun started setting over by Sheep Island, the light was catching the crests of the waves and giving the channel incalculable depth, and in those last minutes before it got darker, before the water turned black, it looked as though the ocean went on forever. Helen and Martha had the late-winter light on their faces, glowing, looking like they'd just descended from the clouds. Bennie was glad to have a simple task ahead of him for the next few minutes. All he had to do was watch Helen and the ocean behind her while they crossed the channel.

The water was a full unknowable world. From across the boat he caught Helen's eyes. She looked like she did when they'd gone out on the Sunfish six weeks earlier, when they were strangers to each other. The sun coming over the trees made her skin look peach-colored, and her hair peeking out from under her watch cap was blown back toward her neck. Martha set the line out again—it was evident from the ride over that the mackerel weren't biting, but Helen gave her room to fish. Helen didn't smile, though Bennie could tell she was thinking about the ocean in the same way that he was, looking at the water's glinting edges, frigid and infinite. This was a comfort. She'd probably heard what Boak had said to him. He was sure now that she believed Littlefield was to blame for LaBrecque's disappearance. Maybe everyone in the world believed this now. He wanted to talk to her, to tell her again there was no way Littlefield had done anything wrong, but he wasn't sure he could form the right words. His faith in his brother wasn't changing, he insisted to himself; he was just cold and tired. His mind felt sluggish.

When they came into the harbor, Martha started hauling in the line, winding it toward her chest. As they made the final turn, just fifty yards from the dock, she brought the jigs up into the boat, tucking their hooks into the wound-up line.

The harbor was still and silent. All other fishing boats, the scallopers and sea urchin divers, had been done for the day hours ago. The tin boat was again sheltered from the wind, but now that the sun was setting, the raw air crept up the cuffs of Bennie's jacket. He could tell by the way Martha moved from the float to the ramp to the pier that her first priority was to warm up, though beyond that, too much was unclear. The light was going fast—the orange hue he'd seen on Helen's face was completely gone from the world, and though it wasn't snowing, there was a dark blue heaviness to the air that made it seem snow was minutes away.

"I hope Littlefield's home by now," said Helen.

"Me, too," said Bennie.

As they stepped off Handelmann's boat and looked up at the spruce forest, the land around them felt uncharted, untouched. Their bodies ached from the cold.

17

Nixon lived to be fourteen, which was a decent age for a large Labrador retriever—a big-headed chocolate Lab who was an expert at knocking over the kitchen trash can. She'd eaten a lot of extra food in her younger years. Whenever leftovers remained on the table—and no one was around—she would pull the tablecloth with her teeth, sending the pot roast (or turkey or fish stew or spaghetti) to the ground, where she could devour the evidence before anyone in the house responded to the sound of dishes crashing to the floor.

When Nixon was ten, several years after their father had died and Eleanor moved off the island, Bennie and Littlefield took the dog to the field by the technical college, and they brought a baseball and a bat. Since they'd entered their twenties, they only came out to the field once a year, for a game they called Man Versus Animal. Unlike the old days, the field was now well cared for—the maintenance crew at the college had mowed it recently—which made Man Versus Animal fast paced and exciting. This is how it went: Littlefield hit the ball, and Bennie stood in the field with a glove and tried to get it before Nixon did. The dog always got a good jump, so Bennie needed to chase down the fly balls, get under them, and reach up and swipe the ball out of the air before Nixon could jump up and catch it in her mouth. Ground balls were almost always snared by Nixon; she could charge toward the incoming ball and field nearly any bounce.

On that particular afternoon—late fall, just after the Cincinnati Reds had won the World Series—Bennie was feeling spry. He knew he was gaining an edge. Nixon was still energetic but on the decline, and Bennie was twenty—stronger and quicker than the last time they'd played (an autumn ago, after the previous World Series). Nixon had put together an impressive streak. She'd won each of the last four years, beginning in '86, when the Red Sox collapsed against the Mets in the Series (that had been a tough year for Bennie—first the Red Sox loss, then humiliation in Man Versus Animal a few days later). But Bennie felt powerful. He'd eaten a good breakfast. And this year he'd found an old pair of soccer cleats in the closet. The field was slightly damp, but his feet felt sure in the grass.

Littlefield always promised to hit the fungoes in a random pattern, mixing in pop-ups, line drives, hard grounders, and fly balls. While Nixon and Bennie never knew where Littlefield would hit the ball, both man and dog took an aggressive approach, lining up side by side in the field only twenty yards from Littlefield. Gaining possession of the ball gave you a point, and the first to four was declared the winner.

After warm-ups, Littlefield smacked two balls high in the air, both of which Bennie fielded easily. He tracked the ball as it fell into his glove, out of Nixon's reach. Then came a towering fly ball, well over both of their heads, but it hung up in the wind long enough that Bennie was able to chase it down, his quad muscles burning. He caught the ball over his shoulder. If it had hit the ground, Nixon would have gotten to it first—she was running wild circles around him, impatient with the game, ready to get her teeth on the ball. Littlefield hit a sharp grounder next, and with Bennie and Nixon playing a little too deep—because that last ball had been hit over their heads—Nixon was able to outsprint Bennie, getting to the bounding ball with ease, snapping it up in her jaws. She took a few jaunty laps around Bennie, wheezing with the ball in her mouth—it looked like she was smiling—and Littlefield cheered. Littlefield rarely showed allegiance to either Bennie or Nixon during these contests, but he encouraged displays of arrogance.

The next few balls were grounders, too, and Nixon got to them easily, dashing through the short grass, getting the ball lodged far enough back in her mouth that she coughed. The score was three to three; the next point delivered bragging rights for an entire year. Bennie checked to see that he didn't have clumps of dirt caught between his cleats, and he bent over to stretch his hamstrings. After three grounders in a row, Bennie was guessing that Littlefield would smack a ball high in the air. But if Littlefield hit another grounder, Bennie couldn't afford to let Nixon take the lead, so he took a few steps closer, and he stayed up on his toes with his glove at chest level, ready to spring into action as soon as the bat struck the ball. Nixon took a few gingerly steps toward Littlefield, too, all of her muscles tense and ready.

Bennie heard the crack of the ball against the bat and tracked the line drive as it hit the dog cleanly between the eyes—*thwack!*—and while she stayed on all fours, her face looked puzzled, panic-stricken. Bennie had never seen Nixon like this. Her whole body quivered: her head, her chest, her legs, her back. She didn't go after the ball, which had landed a few feet in front of her in the grass. Bennie's first worry was that someone was watching, that their cruel treatment of this innocent animal would be witnessed. Littlefield dropped the bat and jogged out toward Nixon, and for a few seconds the two brothers stood in front of the dog and waited for her to notice the ball. She didn't look hurt, exactly, and she wasn't whimpering, but something was clearly wrong.

"You okay, girl?" asked Bennie.

"She's definitely not okay," said Littlefield.

"You hit it right at her," said Bennie.

"I know I did. I was trying to get it over your head. I guess I didn't get under it enough."

Nixon was panting, a slick of drool oozing from her gums. Then she lay down in the grass, rested her head on her paws, and stopped shaking. She was down for a few seconds, then she stood up, walked over to the baseball, and picked it up gently. She lay back down, panting, with the ball in her mouth.

"That's four to three," said Littlefield.

"Oh, for fuck's sake," said Bennie.

"That makes five straight years of Animal dominance. Animal wins!"

"How can this be an official victory?" asked Bennie, but he felt immediately ashamed for complaining.

Littlefield sat down next to Nixon, scratching her back. Nixon rolled over, giving him access to her stomach. When Littlefield rubbed her stomach, she stretched out and yawned. "This is one for the ages. I hit it as hard as I could, and she still fielded the ball, knocked it down, then picked it up cleanly. If that's not championship caliber, I'm not sure what is."

Bennie sat down on the other side of Nixon and gently rubbed her ears, looking into her calm eyes.

The seizures recurred for the next four years. They didn't know how often she suffered them, but every month or so Bennie or Littlefield would see her stop in her tracks, shake, froth at the mouth, and lie down. The first time Gwen witnessed this, she ran into the kitchen, where her brothers were eating breakfast, and she asked them to help her carry the dog to the car so that she could take her to Dr. Guilford (this was back before Handelmann started the Esker Cove Animal Hospital and Shelter).

Littlefield had said, "That's not necessary."

"She's convulsing!" cried Gwen. "Come and see. She's not well."

When they got to the living room, Nixon was sniffing around the couch, looking for crumbs. Gwen knelt down and hugged her. "I guess she's okay."

"She's just hungry," said Littlefield.

"Do you know why she'd shake like that?" asked Gwen.

"Like what?" asked Littlefield.

"Like she's in a trance. Like she's completely out of it."

"I have no idea," said Littlefield. "She's an old girl."

Bennie had wanted to say something else, something about what had happened in the field by the technical college, but it was clear Littlefield felt otherwise. Bennie followed his brother's lead, and the two never spoke about the origin of the seizures—to each other, or to anyone else.

18

On their way back from the pier, they stopped at the only gas pump on the island, outside Scandling's Citgo (which sold bait in the summer and cigarettes, coffee, nutty bars, Donettes, and minature pecan pies in the winter). After putting a few gallons in the Skylark, Bennie went inside to pay. He opened his wallet but had no cash. He knew he'd had forty or fifty dollars when he and Helen returned from Tavis Falls, and he hadn't spent any money since then. He glanced again inside the empty billfold. He knew Littlefield had taken it. Littlefield borrowed money at will, without asking—he considered everything of Bennie's public domain. Sometimes he'd return money, too. This time, he'd cleaned out the wallet. Bennie couldn't be sure when he'd taken it, but it had to have been in the last few days. The most troubling part was that he didn't leave a note. As unpredictable as Littlefield could be, he always left notes, especially if he took money. Bennie returned to the car and asked Helen for a twenty, and as he went back inside to pay for the gas, he wasn't angry. He started to think it might be a long time before he saw his brother again.

Local kids built their bonfires on Kinney Beach, a seldom-used public park that faced the mainland, just down the road from the Manse. During the entire week after their trip to Riverneck Island, not long after dark each night, a snake of headlights jittered through the woods past the Manse down to the beach parking lot. It was state tournament time for the basketball and hockey teams at Musquacook Academy and Brunswick High. By eight o'clock they were lighting the bonfires, the lot was full, and cars were parked in the ditches, backed up for a quarter-mile.

After coming back from Riverneck, Bennie brought Julian and Helen and Martha to the Manse—everyone had wanted to stay together. He'd forgotten that he'd been scheming since Gwen had arrived to find an occasion to have her meet Julian. They all stumbled into the house, frigid, their noses running, their clothes still wet. Helen made a beeline for the shower. They'd noticed smoke coming from the chimney as they approached the house, so Bennie and Julian and Martha rushed to the hearth. Gwen was taking a nap on the purple couch, sleeping off her hangover, but they didn't spot her right away as they entered the room. Julian peeled off all of his layers, including his T-shirt and jeans, and he was doing jumping jacks in his Snoopy boxer shorts when Gwen awoke. Martha and Bennie were taking off their wet clothes, too. Gwen reached for her eyeglasses on the coffee table, put them on, blinked, and sat up.

Martha spotted Gwen and said, "Gwennie!" Gwen wiped the drool on her chin with her forearm before standing to hug Martha with the sleeping bag wrapped around her waist. When the bag fell down to her ankles, she stepped out of it and jogged from the room in her underwear. She called over her shoulder, "I'm going to take a quick shower."

"Helen's in there," called Bennie.

Gwen returned, all six feet of her, and for an endless second or two, Gwen and Julian were facing each other in their underwear, staring. "I think I met you a long time ago," said Gwen.

"Yeah, I think so," said Julian. He stepped forward to shake her hand, but he slammed his toe against the rocking chair. "Son of a cocksucking whore!" he yelled, grabbing his foot with both hands. After he hopped a lap around the chair, he let go of his foot and took Gwen's hand. "Ouch," he said. "It's good to see you again."

Gwen smiled, then padded back to the purple couch and slipped into her sleeping bag.

Once they'd all warmed up, Helen cooked pasta and they sat at the kitchen table in candlelight. Julian poured himself a half glass of whiskey and drank it down, then poured himself some more. The screaming at the bonfires was loudest when they were first lighted. From the kitchen window they couldn't see the fire itself, but they could see a glow above the trees, sparks arcing through the air. In high school, Bennie had gone to these rallies. Most of the kids took off their shirts and danced around the orange blaze, and the brave or drunk kids would swim, then come back to the fire, but all along, everyone would be screaming at full pitch. Every year Littlefield was one of the kids who swam. He wasn't like the other swimmers, the heroes of the school, but he would swim anyway, and he yelled the fight songs as loudly as anyone. Inside the group the screaming filled their heads, filled their bodies, and the sound swirled with the heat coming off the fire. Nothing could be hotter, or louder, as they bounced up and down, screaming, feeling their eyelashes singe.

As the kids at Kinney Beach began their screaming, everyone in the Manse ate quietly, making only the sounds of slurped noodles or the scrape of a knife on toasted bread. When the kids started the Water Dog fight song, Gwen said, "This one's my favorite." Bennie looked at Julian, shaking his head, as if to say *these kids aren't as loud as we were,* but Julian was staring down into his tumbler, listening. It was a simple chant, a call and response:

I know a Dog!
I know a Dog!
He wants to *eat* you!
He wants to *eat* you!
He's very, very hungry!
Very, very hungry!
A big mean Water Dog!
A big mean Water Dog!
Fight, fight, win!
Fight, fight, win!

Bennie had heard the song almost every year since he was little, and during the last few years it made him feel homesick, even when he was sitting in the kitchen at the Manse. This time, it made him want to tell the kids to quiet down and grow up. Everyone at the table smiled faintly, the light from the candles flickering in their glassy eyes.

After the fight song ended, the mood in the room was light, but Helen looked at Bennie in a particular way, the same way she'd been looking at him for the last few days. It was as though she was trying to convince him with her eyes to take charge of the situation in a more commanding way, though she also knew that there was very little he could do. He stood up and started washing dishes.

Helen spoke up. She rested her forearms on the table and addressed the group: "So, are we just waiting for Littlefield to come back? Then what?"

"I want to be in one spot for a while," said Martha. "Ray will find me here . . . when he comes back." Helen and Gwen nodded. "And when Littlefield gets here," she continued, "maybe he'll tell us more."

Julian stood up. "You guys, I can't stick around. I've got too much to do. Sorry." He grabbed his coat and headed for the door. Helen squinted at him skeptically. Bennie followed Julian and caught up to him just as he was stepping out into the snow.

"Wait up."

"Ben," Julian whispered. "I just can't deal with it. What the fuck is going on? We all know he's dead."

"No, we don't."

"This kind of shit happens, man. I can't sit around and dream that it didn't. Those girls are freaking me out."

"Just stick around, Julian. I need your help. I think Littlefield has taken off."

"Well, that's fucking dumb of him. It's just going to make him look more guilty." He picked up a clump of snow, pressed it into a compact ball, and gunned it at the Skylark. "I'm out, Ben. I've got to leave."

When Bennie came back into the kitchen, Helen asked, "What's his problem?"

"He's got to get to the restaurant, to check up on things," said Bennie.

19

For the next three days, they went off-island each morning to search the snowfields near the quarry. They knew the state police had brought dogs in for the search when Bennie was in the hospital—but still, Martha kept saying there was a chance they'd missed something. Just because the police had stopped their search didn't mean they'd scoured every inch of the woods.

Bennie knew that Littlefield's time away—while Helen and Gwen and Martha were searching the snowfields for clues, waiting for him to come back—was just making everyone more and more suspicious, and making it harder for everyone to believe looking in the woods for LaBrecque was worthwhile. They all knew that hearing from Littlefield was now more important than anything else.

Still, after each visit to the snowfields, Bennie would check in with their various sources—Julian's prep cook Hud Kenneally, Sherry Callahan at Rosie's, the harbormaster Jake Riley (he was often too drunk to make much sense of), the warden at Cape Frederick, and whoever would pick up the phone at Skunk Gould's trailer. Helen called Vin Thibideaux down at the police station, and she said he sounded sheepish when he talked to her; he told her they didn't have any information about Ray's whereabouts and that his missing motorcycle was still the best evidence that he'd gone back up to Canada. After each of these visits or calls, it became increasingly difficult to report back to Martha, to find a new way of saying nothing. They avoided talking about Littlefield or Ray by name. In the Manse they focused on other topics, like how Hud was doing at the restaurant now that he'd taken on more responsibilities in Helen's absence. Sherry Callahan made for good conversation, too: her charm, the blunt way she had of insulting you. Martha trusted her to call them if Littlefield came into Rosie's; even so, they wanted to call Sherry because it gave them something to do.

Each day, Helen and Bennie walked down to Singer's Cove. Even then, they didn't talk about Littlefield or Ray or the snowfields. They parked the car and he followed her down the dark tunnel through the spruce woods, the floor of the forest still deep with snow, the smell of the ocean filtering through the branches, their needles, the lichen on the bark.

One early evening after searching the snowfields, Helen and Bennie spent nearly an hour sitting in the snow above the rocks and sand, watching light fade from the sky. There was a bird that had been there since they'd arrived—it was standing in the shallows. It was stout, bigger than a seagull, and had sturdy legs. They watched it scout for fish, just ten yards from where they sat. When they were getting ready to leave, the thought struck Bennie.

He whispered to Helen, "That's a motherfucking . . . that's a light blue heron." He was sure of it. He wanted to jump up and cry out, but he didn't want to scare away the bird. He pulled Helen in closer.

She knew that Gwen and Bennie looked for them, that they'd been keeping an eye out for the bird for years. "Wow. Really?"

Littlefield had told Bennie on several occasions that he'd never heard of the "light blue" variety of heron and that Coach had just made up the name. Bennie looked it up in the World Book and found no reference to light blue herons, and while he knew Coach was given to such pranks, he also knew the search for the light blue heron was not one of them. Coach may have gotten the name wrong, but the bird they looked for definitely existed—Coach had described it specifically and with reverence.

The heron was standing in the sand. It had a long beak, white and blue-gray feathers, and a black tail, just as Coach had told them. It didn't move much as it stared at the surface of the water. The small waves that spread on the sand, then retreated, didn't bother it, and Bennie and Helen's presence didn't either. As the tide came in, it took a few steps closer. At dusk the cove turned dark blue, as though they were inside a big tent. They'd been there with the bird for nearly an hour. Bennie leaned in to Helen, closing his eyes, feeling her warm shoulder against his. After a few minutes, when he opened his eyes to the grays of Singer's Cove, he expected the bird to have lighted from its spot in the shallows, but it was still waiting there in the near darkness.

"You know, your friend Julian's a real jerk. He really should be helping us."

"He's got other things going on," said Bennie. As soon as he spoke, he didn't trust his own knee-jerk defense of Julian.

"I don't buy it. The restaurant is fine without him. He does nothing except drink and sit behind the bar. I think he's just heartless. You've seen what a wreck Martha is."

"What do you expect him to do?"

"Just what we're all doing. He should be with us at the house. We should all stay together."

Bennie agreed with this.

Helen continued, "I also wanted to say . . . I know these last few weeks have been incredibly hard for you, Bennie. You know, you're not wrong to believe in your brother."

He felt angered by this—not at Helen, exactly, but at her need to say this out loud. "I don't need you to tell me that," he said.

"Relax."

"It just seems like no one is talking straight with me. Like everyone believes Littlefield is evil but they can't say it to my face."

"I don't think he's evil."

"Well, what do you think?"

"I honestly don't know. I barely know Littlefield."

"I can read between the lines."

"Jesus, Bennie, what do you want from me?"

"Just let me believe what I believe."

"That's what I just said. I want you to know you're doing the right thing."

After sitting for a few more minutes, feeling less defensive, he took Helen's hand. Even when they stood up to brush the snow off their pants, the heron didn't move from its spot. They left while they could still find their way through the woods.

Back at home, Gwen told Helen she'd gotten a few calls from the restaurant; nothing serious, but Hud Kenneally, the guy filling in as head cook, wanted to check in with her about how things were going. Helen was reluctant to return the call, so Bennie picked up the phone and dialed. He talked to Hud, who had plenty to say. When Bennie hung up, he said, "Yikes."

"What?" asked Helen. "What is it?"

"It seems like Hud is really, really excited to be running the show while you're away."

"Oh, God," said Helen. "Just don't tell me anything else." She held her hands over her ears.

"It sounds as though everything's fine," Bennie said, smiling. "He put up a New York Yankees banner behind the stoves. And he's doing pigs in a blanket, corn dogs, and baba ghanoush appetizers. That's all." Hud had actually told him this.

"You're lying!" cried Helen, reaching across the couch, trying to grab Bennie around the waist. He hopped to the other side of the rocking chair. "Don't worry," he continued. "Free corn dogs after every Derek Jeter spring-training home run isn't costing the restaurant too much." She leapt over the couch and grabbed him as he tried to escape.

They ended up on the couch, wrestling; she got the inside position and forklifted him onto the floor. He landed—*thud!*—on his elbow and hip. In his cast it took him a while to get back up, but when he did, he grabbed her wrists and pinned her to the couch. Her legs were kicking dangerously close to his crotch. "Uncle!" she yelled, but when he let her go, she shoved him hard and he landed on the floor again. He could tell she was worried she'd hurt him, so he faked a grimace, then grabbed one of her feet and tried to yank her down beside him, but she was well anchored and held her ground. Finally, she let him return to his seat on the purple couch, calmly. "Sounds like Julian's really running a tight ship over there," he said.

Waiting, in the abstract, was something that seemed a lot easier to do than it actually was. On the third day they sat together in the living room, Bennie started to wish Coach was around to provide a game plan or enforce the rules. What rules they needed, he wasn't sure, but Coach would have known. He would have known how to reach Littlefield. He would have known exactly what happened to Ray. He wasn't delicate, or sensitive, but he probably would have known the right things to say to Martha, too.

After Helen and Bennie's wrestling match, they all ate and napped, off and on, for the next couple of hours. Whenever someone would finish a bottle of beer, Gwen added it to the long line by the fire. They were all awake—Martha in the rocking chair, staring at the bottles, Helen and Bennie down on the rug beside the fire, and Gwen sprawled out on the purple couch. The sun had gone down so it was dark in the room except for the light from the fire, but still, everyone's face was in clear view, orange from the firelight. Helen put more logs on.

Out of nowhere Gwen asked, "Hey, Martha, when did you meet Ray?" The question worried Bennie; he didn't want her to say anything that she wasn't ready to say. But Martha seemed almost relieved when she heard this. She looked down at her bottle of beer and smiled. She shifted her body in the rocking chair and told them that over the years she and Ray had crossed paths many times—they'd always known each other's families—but the first occasion they spent time alone together was after they'd finished high school. Ten years ago. They were shocked by this. They'd never heard about Ray, but then again, most of what Bennie heard about Martha was what Littlefield told him, and even if Littlefield had heard about the existence of a boyfriend, he probably chose to ignore it.

When Martha started telling stories about Ray, she leaned back in the rocking chair, staring at the fire. Her voice was even and clear. She began with the afternoon Ray invited her to go four-wheeling in the sandpits; they'd seen each other at a town softball game and he'd heard about her off-road driving skills, so he figured it was a safe bet she'd want to go four-wheeling. She did. It was late July and the pits were empty. They rode around for a while, making long, sweeping runs down the steeps. She was sitting on the back of his Polaris Trail Boss and he had asked her to wear a helmet (he only had one for the two of them). At first she wanted to be the one driving, but after a while she realized she liked sitting on the back; it was a cloudy day but the clouds were in large white puffy stands and the air was warm. They rode out of the pits to a trail in the woods behind Jackman Pond, deep lush green woods where the canopy was high above them, pine trees and moss and not too many rocks. They found a flat spot where Ray unloaded his backpack. Martha had tried not to show any surprise when he took out a blanket and a small black radio and a six-pack of High Life, but it was okay, she didn't think it was creepy that he had a plan for them, and even though she wouldn't have chosen to lie on a blanket with him in the woods on what was, really, their first date, she ended up enjoying herself, staring up at the pine branches, listening to the low sounds of the radio and occasionally a partridge flushing from the thicket. For a while, the bugs weren't even that bad. They kissed, and then they fell asleep until the black flies came, at dusk. He gave her a lift home.

They started meeting up at night, regularly. She would sneak into his house after Ray's uncle had gone to sleep. They were nineteen.

A few years later during a stretch when they saw each other only here and there—he would go to Montana and Idaho for months at a time to fight fires—he landed back in Tavis Falls for the winter and found a job plowing the town roads. She worked nights at the Black Harpoon in Harris and was trying to get an associate's degree at USM, too, so she didn't see much of him; it seemed to snow every night, and Ray was often asleep when Martha got back from the Harpoon. She had wondered about talking to him, trying to tell him she wanted to see him more often. One night she came over to his place and he was soaking in the bath; he'd just finished five hours of plowing and was reading a comic book—*The Thing*—and when she came into the bathroom she started telling him she was thinking about taking a break in her classwork, she wasn't sure why she was getting the degree in the first place, and it would mean they'd have more time to spend together, and he continued to read the comic book. She said, "Are you listening to me?" and he said, "Yes," but he kept reading the comic and she said, "It doesn't seem like it," and he repeated her words verbatim. She was angry, but when he put the comic down, he looked at her, frank and clear-eyed. She remembered that look. He had never told her he wanted to be with her forever, never told her they would get married eventually; he had said he loved her, once, but it was when they'd been drunk in an aluminum bass boat on Jackman Pond. When he looked up at her from the tub, he handed her the comic book and said, "Will you throw me that towel?" He stood up out of the water and said, "I'm quitting the plowing job, if that's what you're asking about." He never told her why, but she knew he'd wanted for things to work out between them.

But still, occasionally, months would pass and they wouldn't see each other—Ray would have a job that would take him out of state, or up to New Brunswick, and sometimes he would leave without telling Martha. He would call her once he was settled in whatever town he was working, from a pay phone, and this was never the ideal arrangement, but they both seemed to know it was the way it had to be, at least for now. Martha had never really had another boyfriend, despite all the attention she got from Littlefield and others, so having Ray gone for months at a time, with uncertainty about his return, had become what she expected.

Martha stopped talking for a little while. Helen and Bennie were still lying on their backs, their heads propped up on a pillow, watching the logs burning in the fireplace through the long line of empty beer bottles. Bennie waited for Gwen to chime in again, to fill the silence, asking another question—but then Martha continued.

She told them that when her grandmother died, Ray had just gotten back from a job in Canada and she'd taken him to see her grandfather. He lived on Route 46 just past Dixon Corners in Harris, in a tiny house where he and his wife had lived for fifty-eight years. Martha was nervous, because her grandfather—she called him Pop—was usually grumpy, and though she'd always been close to him, she'd never introduced him to a boyfriend. Martha had seen Pop at the funeral; she'd hugged him, but they hadn't spoken much. After knocking they came inside and took off their snowy boots (he never came to the door) and they heard him bellow from the other room, "Put your goddamn boots back on." So they came into the living room with their boots on, tracking snow in, and he was sitting in his La-Z-Boy, smoking a small black pipe with cherry-flavored tobacco. He looked at Ray—looked him up and down, twice—before saying, "Is that the Perkins boy?"

"No, Pop, this is Ray," Martha had said. "I told you I was bringing him."

"That Perkins boy is a fool," he said.

"This is Ray LaBrecque," she said.

"Hi, Pop," said Ray.

Pop said nothing. Then he said, "He talks like the Perkins boy, too."

"Eno Perkins? I know him. That's not me," said Ray.

Pop exhaled a long plume of smoke. Again, there was a pause before he said, "You play football?"

"No, I don't," he said.

"Not like the Perkins boy," said Pop.

"I played hockey," said Ray.

"Never really cared much for that game," said Pop. He rested the pipe on the arm of the La-Z-Boy. "All that for a little piece of black rubber." He waved his arms dismissively. "Slapping it around. Seems kind of foolish. But they like it, the kids who play it; I guess they do. You might be one of them. You and the rest of the LaBrecques. French Canadian, right?"

"Ray was the best on the team," said Martha.

"Is that what he told you?" asked Pop.

"He was the best until he broke his leg, Pop," she said, knowing he'd appreciate an orthopedic war story. "They had to put screws in."

"Screws? My hip was bad, and then they sawed the bone down and reattached it. I've got some screws in there myself," he said.

"How's that working out for you?" asked Ray.

"Good," said Pop, and Martha was surprised he'd given an earnest answer.

The house was clean, but the table in the kitchen was covered with a huge pile of dirty plates and brown paper shopping bags. "Looks better around here," she said.

"Your mother has been sending a cleaning girl over," he said. "Waste of money. I told her if she touched my table or anything on it I was going to beat her silly."

"You didn't say that," said Martha.

"Might as well have," he said. "She got the idea. She's been doing a good job. Still, it's a waste."

"It's pretty different without Gram around," said Martha.

Pop knocked the spent tobacco into his hand, then dumped it into a coffee can beside his chair. He put the empty pipe back in his mouth. "You're right," he said.

If Ray had asked if he could help out in any way, with shoveling or splitting wood or chipping the ice off the eaves, Pop would have rejected his offer. Instead, Ray started visiting regularly, especially on the weekends when he wasn't working but Martha had double shifts at the Harpoon, and he didn't help out in any way, he just stopped in and took some abuse from Pop, occasionally firing an insult back—or at least that's how he described the visits to Martha. Martha suspected they ended up watching television together, Ray on the couch in the corner, Pop in his chair, refusing to use the remote control, getting up to change the channel only when absolutely necessary, not letting Ray change it for him.

It had been that way for the last few years. When he was around, he was part of her family. When he was gone, he was far away.

In the months before he left to fish on the coast, though, Ray had started talking indirectly about their future together, a topic Martha avoided. Ray had said, "I'm going to be eighty-five and toothless and you'll still be telling me to chew my food slowly." He'd also said, "I think Ray would be a good name for a kid, but we'd have to come up with a nickname." And when they'd passed the town cemetery on their way to go bowling in East Stockton: "If they ask you, let me be cremated. I don't want to rot in the ground."

No one was making eye contact; Bennie was staring at the wall, and Helen was looking up toward the black windows. In the silence they all heard Ronald, who was curled up at the foot of the purple couch, exhale loudly through his nose, a dog sigh. Bennie couldn't feel his own body, only the palm of his hand, where Helen's fingers rested. Gwen looked asleep; her eyes were closed, but he knew she was listening. She said, "Tell us more."

Martha told them about a day she'd had with Ray in the fall; they'd met up in the afternoon when neither of them had anything to do. Martha was looking after her neighbor's dog, Cleo, and they decided to take her out behind the house, across the fields toward the power lines, to see if they could make their way through the woods to her cousin's property by the west branch of the Hollis River. It was October, but there was still a little warmth in the air, and the ground was solid and the wind smelled like beech leaves. Martha told them that crossing a few of the fields they held hands, but most of the time they were just walking side by side. Her legs felt strong and limber; she felt as though she could have walked across the state. Cleo was finding the swamps along the way, dashing through the thickets, popping up in unexpected places. And all along, Ray was keeping up, though she knew it was her job to navigate. She knew the acres behind her house, she'd walked to the West Branch as a kid maybe ten years earlier. They hadn't checked the time before they left, but as they came down off the hill, the woods were thicker and they were losing daylight. They were no longer in the part of Tavis Falls where you could walk from field to field; the woods they passed through were old. She could tell Ray wanted to keep a good pace, but she also felt he trusted her judgment and wasn't worried. They picked up a deer trail and followed it for a while, and when they stopped at a granite boulder beside a dense stand of pine trees, she stood, thinking, and when she started walking at a new angle, following a dried-up creek, Ray asked her if she was sure she knew where she was headed, and she said no, but he followed her.

It was nearly dark when they heard water. At the first sounds, they stopped walking, held hands, and listened, and it was hard to tell how far away the roaring was, but they headed toward it. After ten minutes more of walking down into the valley they listened again, and the sound was the same, so Martha wondered if the sound was just wind in the trees, and she knew Ray was thinking the same thing, so she said it aloud, and he said, no, I think we're close, but she could tell he was unsure. After another ten minutes the sound was louder, and then it was right in front of them, glinting rapids in the darkness, the wind still surprisingly warm, the moon giving them just enough light to see the rocks along the edge. They needed to cross the river, so they took off their clothes quickly and stepped into the cold water, Cleo right behind them. Ray held Martha's hand at first but the water in the middle of the West Branch was deep enough for them not to touch bottom, so he let go and held their clothes above his head. As they swam, the currents pulled them downstream but they made it across. After getting dressed, they still had a few miles to walk but she could see a stone wall that she suspected was at the edge of the McCollough farm. It could have been any stone wall, of course, but she sensed they were close.

It wasn't a miracle that they'd made it through the dense woods in the dark, following the deer trail and the dried-up creek and the West Branch itself and the stone wall, but it felt great to be with him then, that whole afternoon and evening, safe.

Whenever Martha stopped talking, they were all quiet. Gwen was not only silent but perfectly still, with her hands in her lap and her legs stretched out to the end of the couch. After Martha finished the story about her trip across the West Branch, Bennie took Helen's hand and squeezed it. That's when Gwen said, "I've never had a good boyfriend."

This felt like an odd thing to say—Ray was probably dead—but somehow Gwen could pull it off. She and Martha were old friends.

There was a knock at the door. Bennie got up. On the front steps, Sergeant Lynne Pettigrew was knocking the snow off her boots; her cruiser was parked in the driveway, still running.

"Sorry to bother you, Bennie. I know it's late. I'm wondering if your brother is here."

"He's not, Lynne," he said.

"You should know, Bennie—we need to talk with him." When she stepped through the doorway, her glasses fogged.

"I haven't even seen him for a few days." He wondered if by saying this he had already revealed too much. He even wondered, momentarily, if Lynne Pettigrew might be a good person to confide in. Maybe she could help his brother. She seemed reasonable, in her sharply pressed uniform. He could picture her talking to her hockey team before a big game. But all he said was "I don't usually keep track of his comings and goings."

"We've gotten some new statements," she said. "I spoke with Sherry Callahan at Rosie's pub, who had plenty to say about your brother's visits there. He paid calls on a regular basis to Ms. Martha Doyle—Mr. LaBrecque's girlfriend. This mean anything to you?"

"They're old friends, he and Martha," Bennie said, not wanting to speak too loudly. "That doesn't seem like too much to go on."

"This is an unusual situation, Bennie. I was very interested in what Sherry Callahan had to say. Sergeant Thibideaux was, too. I know you're not in charge of your brother's comings and goings, but if you happen to see him, please let him know that we'd like to talk with him. We've made inquiries elsewhere." She looked down at her spiral notebook. "We haven't yet spoken to anyone who's seen him in the last few days. You know of anyone I might contact concerning his whereabouts?"

"Why didn't you come here first?"

"Sergeant Thibideaux has been coming around. He said no one appeared to be home."

"Who have you talked to, besides Sherry?"

She glanced down at her notebook. "No one else who helped any."

"Skunk Gould still hasn't seen him?" asked Bennie.

"No, Bennie. Now, who do you think we should be talking to? We're hoping to find your brother before he gets himself in any trouble."

"If anyone would know, it'd be Skunk," he said. He was sure they were looking for Martha, but without being asked directly about her, he decided it was best that he not mention that she was sitting in the rocking chair, about twenty feet away.

She closed her notebook. "Good night, Bennie. We'll be in touch."

As soon as he shut the door behind her, he felt ashamed. Why hadn't he said anything else? Lynne Pettigrew could help. He wasn't sure that he wanted the cops to find Littlefield before he did, but Lynne Pettigrew was someone he could talk honestly with, wasn't she? She would understand that if something had gone wrong, Littlefield hadn't done it intentionally.

When he returned to the living room, Bennie could tell Martha had stopped telling stories; they were all waiting to hear why Lynne Pettigrew had come to the house.

"They're looking for my brother," said Bennie. "I guess that's not a surprise."

No one responded. Bennie expected Martha to say something, but even she kept quiet.

They went to bed a few minutes later—Martha said she was exhausted. Gwen gave her the purple couch to sleep on and moved down to the rug by the fire. She could have braved the mouse smell and gone up to her own room, but Bennie guessed that she didn't want to leave Martha alone.

From the bedroom Helen and Bennie could hear the clink of empty beer bottles—someone was dismantling the line and bringing them to the kitchen.

Before they climbed into bed, again Bennie thought that if Littlefield had really taken off, he would have left a note. Helen stood in the doorway as Bennie searched his room; he moved the bureau and his trunk and hiked the end of his bed far off the ground, thinking that maybe Littlefield had written it on a small piece of paper and it had slipped underneath. Finally, he tore through all his clothes, unloading the drawers of his bureau, jamming his hands into pocket after pocket, spilling shirts and pants onto the floor. Helen stood back. Where the fuck was he? Bennie could imagine his brother sneaking into the room in the middle of the night, taking money from his wallet and leaving a note underneath the bowl of coins on his bedside table or in the front pocket of his jeans. It had to be there somewhere. He pulled out all of the drawers, rifling through the pants and shirts, anything with a pocket. He found nothing. How could Littlefield have done this? Nothing anywhere—no sign of him. Bennie wanted to bellow like Coach would have, but he just sat at the end of his bed, out of breath, surrounded by clothes. Helen started to calmly refold a pair of pants.

"Go to sleep," he said. "I'll do this."

"Screw you," she said, continuing to fold. They spent the next fifteen minutes putting the clothes back in the bureau.

Some time after they'd fallen asleep, he heard Gwen cry out—a yelp of fear—which he recognized immediately, even in his disoriented state of semisleep, as one of the sounds she made when she was having a nightmare. Afterward he heard Martha consoling her, and then all was quiet again. As he tried to go back to sleep, he thought about when Coach was alive and they all lived in the Manse together: Bennie would wake up in the middle of the night often, not only because of Gwen's nightmare yelps but also because he would have these large, windy thoughts about dying. He would think about the Pharaohs, how long they'd been dead, and he thought about the people who would be living on earth in thousands of years, and what he, Bennie Littlefield, would mean to them. Coach would welcome him into their bedroom at any hour of the night and let Bennie sleep beside him, and in the morning Bennie would try to sneak out before his parents woke up.

He thought, too, about the bundle of raccoons he and Littlefield had left in the snow. Littlefield had assured him they were fine.

After Gwen's yelp—as Bennie was trying to fall asleep again—Helen started talking about Martha, and while he did his best to listen to her, in the midst of one of her questions he fell back asleep again. This annoyed Helen, of course; she nudged him and he felt guilty. She shoved his shoulder. "Bennie, Bennie," she said. "Please. Let's talk." She pulled in close and her T-shirt was hot against his skin. He could tell from the moonlight coming through the window that her eyes were open, shockingly wide, and this startled him.

"Jesus," he said.

"Are you awake?" she asked.

"Okay, okay. Start talking. I'm listening," he said. He closed his exhausted eyes again.

"Martha is strong as hell. I mean, Ray is dead . . . and she's telling us these stories."

"You're right," he said, and it was true: Martha was tough. He tried to imagine what he would do if Helen was missing. He wrapped his arms around her.

"Hey, Bennie?" she said.

"Yeah?"

"I think I know what happened." The sound of these words spread over him like hot, slick liquid. It wasn't just because he was half asleep; there was something about how she kcpt waking him up that both annoyed him and made him ready to believe anything she said.

"You do?"

"I've been thinking all along that Littlefield did something horrible," she whispered. "But I don't think he did. He just wanted to scare Ray, and when he fell—there were lots of places to fall—Littlefield couldn't carry him out, because of the storm."

This seemed plausible, and it was certainly one of the scenarios that they'd all been turning over in their minds. As much as he wanted to, he just couldn't believe it. Littlefield was strong. He would have found a way to get LaBrecque out of the woods.

She whispered, "We'll all get through this."

Bennie wasn't sure this was true. "I hope so."

She said, "You know, Bennie . . . there's something else I wanted to tell you." He could feel that her warm hands were shaking gently. "I love you, too."

He felt a tug of resistance—*she couldn't be serious*—but when she wrapped her arms around him, he felt her warmth, and he tried to ignore his doubts. He wondered if this was how it would always be, if he could really rely on her. He felt her chest rise and fall against his. He wouldn't ever know what she was really thinking; he just had to believe her.

It was Helen who fell asleep, then—she began to snore, a light, pleasant purr—and while he considered waking her up with a nudge, he decided against it.

He dozed off and on for the next few hours. Clouds covered the moon and his room was now completely black. Then the rain came, faint against the shingles, then louder, hammering down, slapping the aluminum gutters. He couldn't sleep. He realized that even though his leg continued to itch beneath the cast, somehow the leg muscles felt stronger. He crawled out of bed. He hopped quietly to the living room.

"Gwennie," he whispered into the darkness.

"Hmmm," she said.

"Will you help me cut open my cast?"

He knew the doctor wanted it on for at least a few more weeks, but he figured if he was careful, it would be good for the leg to finally get some air. She pulled herself out from under the blanket beside the fire. She plodded into the kitchen and turned on the overhead fluorescent light. Bennie sat on the counter and was able to saw a seam with a steak knife from the top of the cast while Gwen—through tired, nearly closed eyes—started working on the bottom. It took a while, and Bennie couldn't reach down below his calf on either side, so Gwen finished the job, all the way down to his foot. She only got through to the skin with the steak knife in a few places, and Bennie was impatient enough that the cuts were barely noticeable. When Gwen cracked the cast open, Bennie's leg was white and thin and he pounced, eager to scratch it, but the skin felt weak and raw. He'd been dreaming of this moment since leaving the hospital, but once the leg met the world again, it didn't itch at all. His knee ached. His limp was pronounced as they headed back to his bedroom, his arm around Gwen's shoulder. Bennie thanked Gwen for the help, and she whispered, "Couldn't this have waited until tomorrow?"

Bennie was lying on his back, wide awake, when Julian called. It was dawn. Not wanting to wake the whole house up, he started jogging to the kitchen to pick up the phone, but his knee ached too much, so he slowed to a walk. He picked up on the fourth ring, hoping it was Littlefield.

Julian was quiet on the other end. "Dude, you've got to help me."

"What is it?"

"Oh, man. I fucked up. I really fucked up. I'm so sorry, man."

"Breathe, Julian. What's going on? What happened?"

"Oh, it's a fucking mess now," he said, between breaths. "But I'm taking care of it. I just want you to know I'm sorry." Then the line was quiet again.

"Julian? What's going on?"

"I need you to do me a favor," he said.

Bennie waited for him to continue.

"I need you to meet me out the Masungun Road."

"Now?"

"I need you to help me with something."

"Julian, if you want me to help you, you need to calm down and tell me what the fuck's going on."

"It's been raining all night. The snow's melting. I need you to help me," he said.

"Dude, you sound like a crazy person. What the fuck is going on?"

"I know where the motorcycle is," he said. "LaBrecque's bike. I know where it is."

"What? I don't understand."

"You don't need to, not right now. I can't explain it. Just meet me at the snowfields."

20

The feeling of cold feet in wet sneakers was the feeling of summer biathlon. After the snow melted, their season continued, and it always involved wet sneakers. Running through the woods. Rifles on their little backs. Gwen's long, skinny legs in front of him, Littlefield's splashing footfalls behind him. Coach would be waiting by the targets, giving his kids instructions. They'd be setting up, lying down on the wet forest floor. He told them to rest their guns on their bones, not their muscles. He told them to keep a rhythm with their breathing. Shoot on the exhale, every other exhale. Squeeze *through* the trigger. Don't hold your breath. Don't wait for your heartbeat to settle; that just fucks up your eyes.

They had three targets—one for each of them—and one long loop. In training, they'd arrive at the targets at the same time. Gwen had learned to be consistent with the rifle, Littlefield was a natural, and Bennie was often a deadeye but he sometimes got the shakes. Coach insisted they not pay attention to the shooters next to them, which made sense; in training, it was when Bennie heard Littlefield clang the targets that his hands would begin to shake. Not too much by normal standards, but enough to upset his aim so that he couldn't depend on the rhythm of his breath.

Coach wasn't hard on them. He just wanted them to love it. He'd say: "You three are all better than I ever was. You three are champions."

Sometimes during training, if Littlefield had a hot hand, he'd clean his own five targets quickly—BANG, BANG, BANG, BANG, BANG—and then he'd clean Gwen and Bennie's targets, too, before they'd even set up to shoot. This usually happened at the end of a training session, and Coach always shouted his disapproval—"Let them shoot their own targets, William!"—but Bennie knew his father was secretly pleased.

When Coach died, Littlefield was working beside him—they were building a shed for the lawn mower. He'd left Coach in the yard to run inside and call Eleanor, but the switchboard at school was closed. He called 911, and after he reported to the emergency operator what had happened, he called Coach's friend Bull Williamson, who worked for the Musquacook Fire Department. Bull was just down the road. Coach was already dead by the time Bull arrived at the house. He waited with Littlefield for Eleanor to get home. Gwen and Bennie were at camp. Littlefield was sixteen.

Littlefield had never said to his brother, or to anyone else, "I feel guilty" or "I feel regret" about any issue, any quandary, any event in his life. Bennie never found out what had happened, exactly, on the day of Coach's death. It wasn't something the family ever talked about. "They were building a shed together" was the story everyone knew. It was a father-and-son project.

Bennie guessed, though, that Littlefield held on to the memories he had from that day. The startled look in Coach's eyes. Maybe he'd dropped a T-square, or a tape measure, or a hammer, and it struck the plywood flooring with a loud bang. Maybe Coach gripped Littlefield's shoulder for balance. Once Coach was on his back in the shed, maybe Littlefield had pounded on his chest, or tried to breathe air into his lungs, while the dog stood in the grass at the doorway, barking.

Everyone else in the house was able to sleep through the heavy rain. When Bennie stepped outside in the early-morning light, the tree trunks nearest the house were dark brown, greasy with water, and there were wide, glossy puddles in the yard. Some overcast days in Maine aren't gray—they're a sickly pale yellow, muted and hollow. Rivers of snowmelt ran down the slope toward the creek in the woods.

As he headed out the Masungun Road toward the snowfields, it was difficult to think above the sound of the rain on the car's roof and the full-speed wipers. The rain fell in wide swaths, pummeling the snow. His breath steamed the windows.

Julian had sounded like a kid who'd fallen on the playground—not only hurt, but confused. It made him wonder how well he knew his friend, and if Julian had ever let his guard down in front of him before.

After parking the Skylark behind Julian's Silverado in the same spot they always parked when they went to the quarry—on the shoulder of the road nearest the corner of the old stone wall—he walked in the melting snowpack along the shoulder toward Julian, who was crouching in the ditch, well down off the road. The telephone poles were shiny with rain. Rivers of water and sand and salt funneled off the shoulder into the ditch. In the woods and fields beside the quarry, briars poked up through the glazed sheet of snow. From his perch on the shoulder, Bennie watched as Julian used a pitchfork to probe the deep slush. He walked a step, jabbed the pitchfork into the snow, pulled it out, then walked another step. In the dim morning light, Julian had already shoveled out the chrome handlebars of the motorcycle, and half of the rest of its twisted body, which was sunk deep in the skeletal briars. He was using the pitchfork to search the surrounding area.

"How'd you find that?" asked Bennie.

"Get down here and help me," said Julian.

"Did you just find it last night?"

"Look, the light's coming up. This road will be busy soon. You've got to help me."

Rain pelted the hood of Bennie's jacket. "Tell me now."

"At least come down off the road."

When Bennie scrambled into the ditch, his knee felt weak but overall his legs felt okay. Julian tossed him a windshield scraper. "Start digging around that back tire."

"I'm not doing shit until you talk to me," said Bennie.

Julian continued to jab the snow with the pitchfork. "I've got to keep looking. We don't have much time."

" 'We'?"

"Will you start digging out that fucking bike?" he shouted.

"You're looking for LaBrecque?"

"Yeah," he said.

"Don't you think someone would have found him here by now?"

"That bike's been here a few weeks and no one's seen it," Julian said. "And no one's been using a pitchfork to find the body."

Bennie dropped the windshield scraper and started walking toward Julian, sinking to his knees in the slushy snow. When he got to him, he grabbed the pitchfork. "Jesus, will you stop that? Talk to me."

"We need to get out of view. Go back down in the ditch," said Julian. They scrambled back toward the motorcycle and crouched beside it. "Listen. I'm not proud of what happened. I was drunk. Too drunk.

The thing is, what I never told you was, LaBrecque—he got out of the woods. Your brother was chasing him, but he got out of the woods." He looked down at his soaked boots. "All I know is, he got all the way out of the woods, to the road, and he got back on his motorcycle. He must have just been trying to get out of the storm—to save himself."

"How do you know this?"

"Because I got out of the woods, too. A while before he did. I didn't know where anyone was. I was lost. I finally found my truck parked on the shoulder and I headed back to the bar. That's where we were all supposed to meet, right? I stayed there for almost an hour. Then I heard you'd landed in the hospital—someone had just brought you in—so I drove back out the Masungun Road, toward the Adventist. No one else was on the road. No one else was crazy enough, I guess. But just as I came around the bend, right up that way"—he pointed back toward town—"the kid was just pulling out onto the road. When I came up on him, he was clear in the middle of the road. I had no time to turn the wheel."

"Holy shit," said Bennie. "You're telling me the truth?"

"I'm telling you the truth, man. I tried to find him in the woods, but I couldn't. I found his bike in the ditch. I looked for him, but the storm was so bad then, I couldn't see anything."

"You left?"

"What else could I do?"

Bennie barreled into Julian with his shoulder down, knocking him to the bottom of the ditch, where he landed on top of him. He pinned his arms down with ease; Julian wasn't resisting. Bennie said, "They're after Littlefield. You know that."

Julian's face was red and wet with rain. "I thought I had some time. I know I fucked up. I thought I had some time to think this over, before the snow melted."

Bennie stood up and walked back to the Skylark, not looking behind him as he drove away, leaving Julian on his own to look for the body. He felt alone in the quiet car; his mind reeled. He kept seeing his friend's panicked face, and the way he stabbed the snow with the pitchfork. It wasn't until he arrived back at the Manse that he realized he was still shivering from the cold rain.

He assumed everyone would still be asleep when he got back, but he heard Gwen call from the living room when he was pulling his jacket off in the kitchen. "There's a message from Mom on the machine. She must have left it last night," she said.

"I can't talk to her now," said Bennie.

"She's coming down today, remember?"

"I need to talk with you and Martha and Helen first."

He brewed a full pot of coffee. Soon the four of them were reassembled by the fire. His voice didn't waver when he looked across the room at Martha and told her that Ray had been hit by a truck that night—by Julian's truck—and that Julian had never reported it. He said Julian had looked for Ray but he hadn't found him. He probably hadn't looked for him for very long, though. It was the middle of the night, the middle of the storm, and Julian had been scared about what he'd done.

"There's a chance he's still alive, then," said Martha.

"No," said Bennie. "He died in the crash. I saw the bike, Martha. Julian never found him. He must have been thrown into the woods."

"We still don't know," said Martha, staring back at Bennie. Then it looked as though all of the muscles in her body relaxed; she exhaled, lay back against the couch cushions, and began to cry.

Helen got up off the rug and sat beside Martha, putting a hand on her shoulder, and Gwen stood up from the rocking chair and went to the couch, too, holding Martha's hand as she cried.

"Is Julian insane?" asked Gwen. "How could he do this? How could he keep this from us?"

"He's a criminal," said Helen.

Bennie said, "He was scared. He didn't know what to do."

"That doesn't excuse anything," said Gwen, and Bennie knew, of course, that she was right.

21

Nixon had wanted to be alone when she died; she must have known it was time, so she went down the hill to the creek and curled up in a patch of grass beside the water. It was August of 1994; major league baseball players were striking, and would continue to strike through the fall and into the winter. The World Series was canceled for the first time in ninety years.

They couldn't play Man Versus Animal, so Bennie asked Littlefield if he'd be willing to go on a short camping trip. Littlefield agreed. They picked a weekend in early November. They were hoping to drive up to Baxter State Park, but when the weekend arrived it was thirty degrees. They decided to drive south. Littlefield was in charge of finding a campsite, but he didn't know southern New England very well. They brought a road atlas and hoped for the best. Bennie said he'd heard good things about Cape Cod. They left Maine in the early afternoon and hit heavy traffic in Boston. The skies were clear and the air was warmer than it had been in Maine. By the time they reached the South Shore, they decided to start looking for a camping spot—in the dark, they weren't sure it was worth driving an extra hour to get to the Cape. The road atlas suggested they'd find camping in Plymouth, but when they got off the exit, they found a campsite that had closed in October, so they pulled into an empty parking lot and pitched their two-man tent in the back of Littlefield's pickup. They played gin rummy for an hour, drinking whiskey, before turning off their flashlights.

In the morning, they unzipped the tent to see that they were parked near the gates to the Pilgrim Nuclear Generating Station. They drove over the Bourne Bridge and onto Cape Cod. They found an empty beach where they could sit and look at the ocean, but the wind was strong and cold, so after Littlefield smoked a cigarette, they got back in the truck and started driving north.

"It's not quite the same as camping in Maine," said Bennie.

"We didn't find the right spot. That's my fault," said Littlefield.

"Maybe Cape Cod wasn't the best place for us to go in November."

"Maybe not," said Littlefield.

They drove for a while, listening to sports radio. This time there was no traffic in Boston; they breezed past downtown, over the Tobin Bridge, and up Route 1. Bennie felt heartsick. "This sucks. Sorry the camping trip didn't work out too well."

"Remember that time we went out to Green's Island?" Littlefield asked. "That fishing trip? That was good."

"Yeah," said Bennie.

"Seems like it was easier to do that kind of shit back then."

"I'm not sure why," said Bennie.

Littlefield shrugged. "Things change."

Bennie knew that even though they could spend a night together playing cards, they weren't friends anymore. Littlefield didn't respect the choices he'd made—trying to go to college but quitting, trying to live in New York but leaving after only one winter, trying to make the Olympic team but never really sticking to his plan. He knew Littlefield had similar failures, but somehow the brothers never found a way to relate their experiences. They didn't seem to understand each other, and being born of the same parents only made things worse. Bennie wondered if there'd be another change, later in life, that would bring them closer together.

When they arrived back at the Manse, Littlefield parked the truck and said, "Not one of our better trips."

"Nope," said Bennie.

"It's always good to get off the island once in a while, though."

"I guess so," said Bennie. He wanted to say more. He wanted to sit in the truck with his brother for a few more hours, even though they'd barely spoken when they'd been on the road. He wanted to say *I know how you're feeling,* even though he couldn't be completely sure that he did. He wanted to say something, anything. But the moment came and went; Littlefield clicked his door open, the dome light came on, and the cold air from outside rushed in.

There wasn't much else to do at the Manse that morning other than to cook bacon and answer the phone. Between the calls, Bennie noticed how quiet it was in the house, with Helen and Gwen and Martha sitting in the living room, shocked, waiting for the next call. These calls came in a seemingly endless string:

1. Eleanor Littlefield, still hoping to talk to either Gwen or Bennie (they let the machine take the message).
2. Hud Kenneally, in a nasally hysterical voice, wanting to speak with Helen. Julian hadn't shown up for the lunch shift. Hud

had left messages at Julian's house and had now worked seven consecutive shifts as the head cook and reported he was losing his mind. Helen picked up the phone at the end of his message and asked him to do his best. She couldn't come in.

3. Eleanor Littlefield, sighing, hanging up.
4. Lynne Pettigrew. As soon as she started to leave a message, Bennie grabbed the phone.

"I thought you should know," she said. "Julian Fischer came to the station an hour ago. This isn't normal procedure, but seeing as our families have known each other for so long, I wanted you to know that his statement suggests that your brother will probably be taken off our list. We'll be holding Mr. Fischer until we learn more. But I wanted to let you know. If you happen to see your brother, you could tell him that while we'd still like to talk to him, his interview is currently a low priority."

"Have you found the body?"

"I'm afraid I can't discuss that right now. We're still in the process of assessing the scene. The rain is making it difficult."

"Thanks for calling, Lynne."

"It's an ongoing investigation, of course."

"Of course."

"Thank you for your cooperation," she said.

After hanging up the phone, he held the receiver and let the charge of emotion flood his chest. He appreciated the formality she used to tell him this news, but at its core, the news was ugly. Julian had turned himself in after trying to keep the secret, and asking Bennie to keep the secret, too.

The phone rang again while Bennie held the receiver. It was his mom. "Sweet Jesus," she said. "Why don't you kids pick up the phone?"

"I just did," he said.

She said, "How are you feeling, Benjamin? How's your leg?"

"I feel okay, Mom."

"That's good, sweetie. I've been trying to reach you because I might not come down tonight after all."

He exhaled, relieved to hear this. "No?"

"Well, I was just unpacking my bathing suit and I was putting together a small bag to come down to the island for a few nights when William arrived. He's out back now, smoking. Has he been smoking a lot recently?" Then she started whispering. "Anyway, I'm surprised he's here. It's very nice to have him visit, but I couldn't believe it when he knocked on the door."

"Yes," said Bennie, trying to sound calm.

"I don't know if he's ever come to visit me without you or Gwennie," she whispered. He could tell she was extremely pleased.

"Mom, can you get him for me? Can you put him on?"

"Of course," she said. "After you speak with him, I need to know what to bring you for dinner." She put the phone down. When he heard the rattle of the phone on the counter, he steeled himself. But it was his mother who came back on.

"Benjamin? William says he'll call you later. He's too tired right now. He's going to take a nap and he'll call you later."

"Please tell him I need to speak to him, Mom. I need to speak to him right now."

"Hold your horses," she said. She would get flustered sometimes when she had to mediate a disagreement within the family. She put the phone down again, and this time he didn't hear any talking. A few minutes later she came back to the phone. "He says he can't talk right now. I'm sorry, Benjamin. I tried. As your humble servant I am happy to pass along a message."

"Will you tell him, please, that Lynne Pettigrew and Vin Thibideaux made a mistake," he said. "They don't need to talk to him."

"The police? For heaven's sake, Benjamin! What on earth for?"

"Parking tickets, Mom. Please tell him they made a mistake."

"You're not telling me the truth, Benjamin."

"Just do me this favor, please, Mom."

"Oh, glory. You and Gwen treat me like a child."

"What are you going to tell him?"

"That Lynne Pettigrew and Vin Thibideaux made a mistake."

"Thank you, Mom."

"What can I bring you for dinner tomorrow?" she asked.

"Don't worry about it. We'll be fine. We'll cook for you."

"How about steak?" she asked. "A special treat. Steak and new potatoes and green beans."

"Okay, Mom. That'd be great."

When he hung up the phone, he was sure Eleanor would be asking too many questions of Littlefield about the parking tickets. The message would be botched. It would be no real error on his mother's part, but her curiosity would annoy Littlefield, and he wouldn't call Bennie for clarification. Bennie needed to drive up to Clover Lake and deliver the message himself.

He told the women in the living room—they were still on the purple couch—that Littlefield was in Clover Lake. Gwen and Helen offered to come with him, but he figured it would be better for them to stay with Martha, so he told them he wanted to go alone.

On the drive up Route 26, the road was dark in the rain, but he kept a steady pace. He knew Littlefield wouldn't be staying at Eleanor's house for long. As he passed through Mechanic Falls and Oxford, he turned it over and over in his mind, not knowing how Littlefield could possibly feel guilty about LaBrecque's death if he hadn't been involved.

He pulled up to the house and could see his mother peering through the porch window. She came onto the front steps wearing a purple raincoat, hood up, white sweatpants, and sandals. Without her glasses, she squinted to see who it was. When Bennie rolled down the window, she said, "Oh, my goodness!" Her face was tan beneath the hood of the jacket.

"Did you give him the message?" asked Bennie.

"For Pete's sake. I told him your ridiculous message, of course I did. Come inside," she said.

He told Eleanor he needed to speak to Littlefield in private. He went to the guest room and found Littlefield lying in the middle of the king-size bed. The blinds were closed and he was smoking in the dark room.

"Thanks for taking my phone call," said Bennie.

"I'm taking a nap," he said.

"Why are you here?"

"I'm napping," he said.

"Put the cigarette out," said Bennie.

"Please?"

"Put the cigarette out, please," said Bennie.

He stubbed it out in a coffee cup on the bedside table.

Bennie sat on the edge of the bed. "You didn't leave me a note."

"Nope," said Littlefield. "I was planning on calling you. Or writing you—you know, after things were settled."

"Julian just turned himself in. He hit LaBrecque with his truck. He killed LaBrecque."

Littlefield shook his head, disgusted. "That's wrong."

"How do you know?" Bennie asked. "I saw his fucking motorcycle, Littlefield. I saw it in the ditch."

"That must have been where he parked it."

"It was mangled."

"Maybe he parked it on the shoulder and someone knocked it in the ditch."

"Julian was driving on the Masungun and hit LaBrecque. He saw him right in the middle of the road before he hit him. He couldn't stop."

"Fuck you," said Littlefield.

"What do you mean?"

"Fuck you. That's not what happened."

Bennie jumped on top of his brother, trying to pin his arms down, but Littlefield slipped out from under him and got to his feet on the other side of the bed. Bennie lunged at him again, grabbing him around the waist, tackling him to the plush carpet. They rolled once, and Littlefield landed on top. "You're a psycho," said Littlefield.

"Listen to me. Julian has no reason to lie about this."

"What happened to your cast?" He held Bennie firmly against the carpet, his forearm pinning Bennie's neck.

"Gwen helped me take it off," said Bennie. They hadn't wrestled like this since they were teenagers. Littlefield was still much stronger. Bennie used his free hand to reach up and grab the front of Littlefield's plaid shirt.

"Don't rip it," said Littlefield.

Bennie pulled as hard as he could. It ripped somewhere in the back, and two of the front buttons popped.

"Christ!" Littlefield released Bennie's neck. Bennie squirmed out from under him and jumped on his back, putting him in a headlock.

Bennie said, "Julian just turned himself in. Why else would he do that?"

"I have no idea," said Littlefield. He pried Bennie's arm from his neck, shook his brother off. They both landed on the carpet. There was a knock at the door.

"Are you two okay in there?" their mother asked.

"Fine," said Littlefield.

"Has someone been smoking?" she asked.

"Yes," Littlefield said. "I'll open the windows."

They remained kneeling on the carpet, facing each other, out of breath. "Look, Bennie. I'm about to leave. It's not about telling you what happened. That's not going to help any. It's done."

"It's not done. You're not listening to me. Julian hit LaBrecque with his truck. That's what happened. I saw the bike."

"Yeah? Well, I saw the body. Did you see the body? No. I saw the fucking body, Bennie. What do you think of that?" Littlefield whispered, fiercely.

"Where?"

"Out by the corner of the stone wall. I didn't find him that night, but I went back at dawn, after the snow lightened up, and I found him. Stiff as a fucking board."

"You did?" In all of his imaginings of that night, Bennie was never able to picture LaBrecque's face, but as soon as Littlefield said this—*stiff as a board*—Bennie could picture LaBrecque's placid expression, his icy eyebrows, with Littlefield stooped over him, digging him out. Bennie imagined his own hands doing the same work, brushing aside the snow, seeing the face.

Littlefield took out his pack of Winstons, shook one out, and lit it. He blew smoke out the corner of his mouth, a long breath. "I ran after him, Bennie—just like I told you. He kept running and running. It was hard to tell what direction we were going in. Sometimes I would see something I recognized, like the edge of the quarry or the stone wall, but most of the time I was just following his tracks."

"I couldn't see a damn thing that night," said Bennie.

"It seemed like I could see the next two or three tracks in front of me—that was all."

"You couldn't hear him?"

"Hell no."

"But you knew he was running?"

"I wasn't thinking about what he was doing. I was just trying to catch up with him, but it was like he knew where he was going. I wanted to win the game. That's what I was thinking about—winning. Finishing the job. That snow was fucking awful—you know how it was. I kept my head down and followed the trail he was making—I couldn't hear him, but I'm sure he was getting tired, Bennie. I had to have been catching up to him. That's all I was thinking about. I was like, *He's got to be tired.* And I came right up to the edge of the quarry and I could have run right down onto the rocks, but his gun was lying there in the snow, on the edge."

Bennie thought about how he would have reacted if he'd seen a paint gun lying in the snow. "You didn't see him then?"

"There were no tracks. It was steep. I knew right then that things had gotten bad. I knew I'd fucked up by chasing him so hard, all the way out there. He ditched his gun."

"Right there at the edge? Did he drop it?"

"I have no fucking clue, Bennie. If I hadn't seen it there, I would have probably tumbled right down into the rockfall myself. I left my gun next to his and I went down in there looking for him. I was trying to hold on to the rocks, but my hands were numb in my gloves, so it took me a while. And it was dark—too dark to see much of anything. I'm not even sure why I went down there—I knew he was fucked—I should have left right then, as soon as I saw his gun. But I went down, and I couldn't find him. I looked everywhere. I had a light with me, but I couldn't see much in the snow. I was thinking I might even hear him, but I didn't. Shit. I couldn't even see the rocks anymore. I stayed there for a while, but then I took off."

"So when did you find him?" he said.

Littlefield shook his head, looking down. "Early the next morning."

"Not in the quarry."

"No. He might have fallen off the edge, but if he did, he climbed out. I found him out by the corner of the stone wall."

"That's right near the road. Don't you see? You thought it was your fault, but it wasn't."

"I chased him until he couldn't get out of the woods, Bennie."

"He made it out of the woods. He made it to his motorcycle, and just as he was getting back on the road, Julian hit him."

This time, Littlefield didn't say anything. He looked back at Bennie, squarely. He shook a cigarette from his pack and lit it.

Bennie said, again, "You've done nothing wrong."

"I can't talk with you about this."

"Why not, asshole? Why can't you talk to me? Who can you talk to if you can't talk to me?"

"You're acting like a crazy person," said Littlefield.

"Yeah? What if I am? Why didn't you ever tell me any of this?"

"You wouldn't have understood," said Littlefield.

"I'm your brother."

"That doesn't matter."

"What matters, then?"

"The things I've done," said Littlefield.

"You didn't kill LaBrecque."

"Maybe not. It doesn't matter now, does it." He held his head in his hands.

"Will you talk to me about this, Littlefield?"

Littlefield took his hands away from his face and looked up. His eyes were red and wet with tears. "We're different, Bennie. You and I are different. I can't hold it together. I really thought something would happen between me and Martha. I'm a fucking idiot. Is that what you want to hear?"

"That's a start," said Bennie.

"Here's what I want, Bennie. I want you to trust me. I can't talk it through with you. I want you to trust me that I need to leave. I need to get the fuck out of Maine, okay?"

Bennie had never heard his brother ask for something like this. He answered him quickly. "Okay."

"I also need to know that if I stand up, you're not going to tackle me again."

"Okay," said Bennie.

Littlefield looked down and took another drag from his cigarette. "You're pretty sure about Julian hitting LaBrecque with the truck?"

"I'm positive."

Littlefield shook his head. "I am so fucked."

When they stood up, Bennie took a small step forward and put his arms around his brother. Littlefield hugged him back. "Jesus," he said. "I didn't ask you to hug me."

Bennie squeezed, hard, and Littlefield held on tightly, too.

"Don't leave, Littlefield," he said. "I really don't want you to go. I think things could change here, for both of us. Things could get better."

"You've got to trust me, Ben. You really do this time." He picked up his backpack and slung it over his shoulder. "I've had a good visit with Mom. Real good. When I leave, I want you to explain it however you feel is right. I can't say goodbye to her."

He was crying, still, and Bennie was, too. Littlefield walked past him to the back door. "I appreciate what you're doing, Bennie. Trust me, though. I've got to leave."

The door shut. Bennie stayed inside and watched his brother walk out to the Chevette. Littlefield started the engine, turned on the lights, and drove away.

Bennie walked through the house to find his mother.

"Did William leave?" she asked.

Bennie told her he had—he said Littlefield had been in love with a girl but it hadn't worked out, and that he was probably going to spend some time away from the island. He told her Littlefield might try to get a fresh start somewhere else, and he needed to do it on his own.

She shook her head. "I don't understand. You should have seen him, Benjamin," she said. "He was being very nice to me. Very loving. If he was leaving, he would have told me." When she looked at Bennie, though, he could see that she knew he had left and wouldn't be coming back any time soon.

22

Even after spending a long string of winters in Maine, it's difficult to stop thinking spring might come early. They didn't get a lot of sun that year, but the temperatures started rising, the streams and rivers flooded, everything was brown and sandy and dead, and then all at once—they thought it was a false start—the world was green.

Bennie was working the weekend shift for Handelmann, who'd left early on Friday. In the warm months Handelmann motored regularly in the aluminum boat to Quohog Island, the two-acre crag he owned, to camp for the weekend. Because of this, Bennie worked extra hours at the shelter, which was at its best in early summer, when everyone adopts. The dogs were spending more time in the outside pen and less time bothering the cats. The indoor cages weren't getting used, so they didn't need to be washed.

The last Friday in June, Handelmann put Bennie in charge of the four o'clock appointments. He sped through them, giving a few shots, doling out heartworm meds, and only one dog, a miniature schnauzer, needed to have his anal glands expressed. Bennie was hoping to have the doors locked at five sharp. He'd told Helen to meet him then, so that they'd have time to pick up food and bring it to Singer's Cove for an early-evening picnic. They still tried to walk out to the water there every afternoon. His leg was feeling stronger than ever, so he only noticed the break when the weather was changing. The walks, and the time he spent with Helen, were helping him heal.

By early May, Gwen and Jamie Swensen had started dating, and by June it seemed Gwen was falling for him. Bennie had been worried at first—he liked Swensen okay, but with Gwen? She said he had a good heart, and he wasn't nearly as much of a drunk as he'd seemed on St. Patrick's Day. They liked to fish together. He had his own boat, a little wooden skiff his grandfather had built. She found a subletter, postponed her plans to return to Brooklyn for another few months, and was waiting to hear back from auditions at Portland Stage Company.

Martha went back to her shifts at Rosie's. She'd found her own apartment in Westbrook. She still spent plenty of time with them on the island, though, and she came up whenever she had a night off. A week after Littlefield left, she'd gotten a letter from him. She showed it to Bennie and Gwen. All he said was that he was going to be missing his regular Tuesday-night visits to Rosie's. "I'm sorry for your loss," he wrote. He said he had more he wanted to tell her, and that he'd write again soon. As of early May, she hadn't gotten another letter.

In Handelmann's office, Bennie sent out the latest round of bills. He did a final check on the overnight animals, though he knew he'd be on duty again early in the morning, so there wasn't much to worry about. The Australian shepherd mutt who'd been brought in at noon after being hit by a sand truck was hooked up to an IV, with fluids and a narcotic skin patch, and even though she'd lost a front leg in the accident, she was sleeping peacefully. With Handelmann gone for the weekend, Bennie wanted to catch up with the pile in the crematorium shack so he wouldn't have to go in there on Saturday or Sunday, when he was the only one on duty.

At five minutes before the hour, he walked out back and was surprised how high the sun was in the sky. It was warm and bright and the grass between the main building and the crematorium shack needed mowing. He'd started the fire an hour earlier, and when he stepped inside he knew right away it was hot enough. All he had left was a Great Dane. He tried putting him in lengthwise, knowing that a dog of his size would normally fit, but he felt one of his legs catch on the metal seam near the back door, so he pulled him partway out—the dog had already started to burn, of course, so he shoved him back in. Bennie scampered to the rear of the kiln to fix the snag. He opened the smaller door in back to find that the dog was caught up in the usual place, the metal seam, so he used a poker to free its legs. Just as he was pulling the poker out of the fire, he spotted two small cylindrical lengths of metal beside the seam, hidden from view when looking into the oven from the front. He scraped them out of the kiln and onto the floor, and saw that they were charred metal screws. When he looked at them on the ground, it was no less shocking to see them, and his first thought was that they seemed like they could have been part of a story Coach might have told: the screws that had once helped repair the leg of a hockey star from Tavis Falls were now blackened by fire in a pet crematorium on Meadow Island.

The kiln was closed, but he stayed near the back side of it, looking down at the screws as they cooled there on the ground. They were a horrifying and very real piece of his brother's life, his actual experience. He picked the screws up off the ground. They were warm, without burning his palm, and they were black with soot and the grooves were caked with resin. When he closed his hand around them, they were hotter than he thought, and sharp.

Helen was punctual, as always. Within a few minutes he heard her calling his name outside the door.

"Just a minute. I'm almost done," he said.

He waited to catch his breath. Littlefield had been all alone, through everything: going back to the woods beside the road, bringing the body out, getting it to the kiln. He had made this decision on his own. He had assumed he was guilty, and that he needed to take care of what he'd done—all of this he had done on his own. And now he was gone, living someplace new, among strangers.

Bennie walked back around the kiln to the door. When he saw Helen, he opened his hand and showed her what he'd found.

23

When Bennie knocked on Vin's door in June, in the early evening, there was still plenty of light outside, and Elizabeth, Vin's wife, came to greet him. She was a tired and sour-looking woman; Coach had said on a few different occasions that she'd been pretty in high school, like a Scandinavian model, with round cheeks and long blond hair, but whenever Bennie saw her she looked like she hadn't been sleeping. She called for Vin, who was watching TV with their granddaughter Sadie, and he called back to her, inviting Bennie in. When he walked into their living room, Vin was stretched out on the couch; Sadie was lying on her stomach on the tan carpet, propped up by her elbows.

Elizabeth yawned, switched off the TV, and offered Bennie a beer. He asked for a cup of water and sat with them for fifteen minutes, long enough to finish his glass; they listened to Sadie tell them about the robot she and her classmates were making at school. It was made of cardboard but could tell fortunes. Vin didn't say a word to Bennie; they just listened to Sadie's story, and when she was finished Elizabeth offered Bennie more water, but he wasn't thirsty, and they sat there for a moment after Sadie skipped into the other room to get some of the drawings she was working on. Vin wasn't being his normal, boisterous self—he was unruffled and quiet. Before Sadie got back he stood up and gestured for Bennie to come outside with him. Bennie knew he was a smoker, but when they stepped into his yard, past the empty doghouse, Vin didn't take out his cigarettes.

It was one of those warm, perfect, fresh-smelling early summer evenings, and they stepped down to the lawn, in the blue shadows. "Fucking Benjamin," he said. "Benjamin Littlefield."

"I'll tell you why I'm here," said Bennie. He felt himself shaking. "I want you to apologize for going after my brother."

Vin shook his head. He hit Bennie in the stomach, which bent him over. Then Vin kicked him—a quick punt to the groin.

He fell down into the grass.

"Stand up," Vin said.

Bennie knew it was going to take him a while to satisfy this request. With his cheek in the grass, he wheezed, "What's your problem?"

"I never got you back for that stunt in the bar," said Vin. "Okay. Now we're even. Now I can apologize to you. It's true. I was wrong about your brother."

After catching his breath, Bennie tried to climb to his feet, and as he stumbled Vin grabbed his arm, pulled him up, and led him to the edge of his back porch. They sat for a few minutes—Vin took out his cigarettes, lit one for himself, then handed Bennie the pack and his lighter. While they smoked, Vin told Bennie that he knew Littlefield was prone to trouble but he'd always thought he was a decent person, regardless. "Why'd he leave?" Vin asked.

"I can't believe you just kicked me in the balls."

"He must have needed a change in scenery," said Vin. "You and I could probably use that, too."

"What, are we buddies now?" asked Bennie.

"Let me give you some advice, Bennie. Marry that girl. Helen. She seems like a good one for you. Marry her and start having kids. That's the best thing I ever did."

They tossed the butts toward Vin's hibachi. When they stood up, Bennie's balls were still aching. Vin led him through the house to the front door. As he started the Skylark, he looked back at the house, and through the window in the door he saw Vin's granddaughter Sadie raise her hand in a wave. He waved back.

He drove slowly, noticing the cool touch of the steering wheel and the grip of the tires on the road, not thinking about the pain in his balls too much, trying to mind the yellow lines but also looking up at the new light green leaves in uncountable bunches in the boughs that hung above the road, the dust in the young blackberry thicket, and, as he came down into the hollow by Esker Cove, the tails of fog moving between islands outside his passenger-side window.

It was mostly a clear night, and warm, and the only fog he could see was in thin wisps at the outer edge of the harbor. He pulled over, parked on the shoulder, and stepped out into the warm evening, leaning against the Skylark, taking in the full ocean view from the mouth of the cove. Out by Watson Point, within minutes thicker fog rolled in, making trees and rocks and water disappear. He'd seen this many times, of course, but mostly he'd been out in the harbor in a boat when it happened: the fog appearing silently, almost instantly, so that one minute you'd spy the sharp-angled rocks on the far shore and the next minute mist had swept across your bow like kettle steam. All you can manage to see, then, are your own hands sorting through the anchor box in search of a chart.

He would see his brother again. Two years later. He'd get a phone call on a Sunday afternoon, and Littlefield would be in Vancouver. He'd tell Bennie how his life still had its challenges—Bennie would hear traffic in the background and know Littlefield was calling from a pay phone—but he would also say he was glad to be experiencing a different part of the world for a while. He would tell Bennie he'd met a girl he wanted to introduce to Mom. He would tell Bennie he was coming back, to check in with the family, to meet Gwen's new husband, and Bennie and Helen's daughter. It would take him another year to actually make good on these plans, but he would.

As Bennie watched the fog, he wondered if someone he knew might drive down into the hollow and be curious about what he was looking at. But no cars passed. Everyone was home, eating dinner, and he was glad to have the view to himself. It felt good to survey the fog from a distance—to see it erase island after island from a place where he had his bearings. He was eager to get home to see Helen, but he waited long enough to watch the fog roll all the way through—revealing trees and rocks and sky as quickly as it had hidden them.

Acknowledgments

I am deeply indebted to the generosity of the Mrs. Giles Whiting Foundation and Deerfield Academy's Wallace Wilson Fellows Program. Thank you also, B Love, Jeff Harrison, Leslie Falk, Alison Kerr Miller, Suzanne Strempek Shea, Monica Wood, Dan Abbott, Kai Bicknell, Jaed Coffin, and Mark Scandling. Thank you, Herb Taylor, for letting me use your living room in Spar Cove as an office, and for not kicking me out after I let the pipes freeze. Thank you, Theo Emery, Alix Ohlin, Kate Sullivan, Aaron McCollough, Curtis Sittenfeld, Eric Jones, Howard Rosenfield, Matthew Vollmer, and Amy Hassinger, for reading early drafts. Thank you to my brothers, Sam, Seth, Jake, and Jeff, and my sisters, Jesse,

Kim, and Heather. Thank you to my intrepid and talented agent, David McCormick, and my editor, the patient, savvy, and kind Laura Ford. Thank you, Suegra, David Riley, and Linda Robinson. Thank you for your inspiration, Tom Robinson, for checking up on me. Thank you to my parents, Sam Robinson and Mimo Riley, for the love and guidance you provided. And thank you, CC and Maisie, always.

ABOUT THE AUTHOR

LEWIS ROBINSON is the author of *Officer Friendly and Other Stories,* winner of the PEN/Oakland–Josephine Miles Award. A graduate of Middlebury College and the Iowa Writers' Workshop, he has also received a Whiting Writers' Award. He now teaches in the Stonecoast MFA program at the University of Southern Maine and coaches middle-school basketball in Portland, Maine, where he lives with his wife and daughter. Visit his website at lewisrobinson.com.